THE ACCIDENTAL FAMILIAR

DAKOTA CASSIDY

COPYRIGHT

ACKNOWLEDGMENTS

Darling readers,

As I'm wont to do, in this particular addition to The Accidentals, I've taken some liberties with witches and their folklore. I've tweaked and toyed with some hard and fast rules, and created others to suit my own devilish desires in order to put my stamp on this world. So if you note things that appear a bit outlandish and absolutely implausible, you'll know you're in the middle of an Accidental!

And it goes without saying my BFF, Renee George, isn't just the most supportive, awesome friend a girl can have, she's also super-plotter and a great writer to boot. I'd still be lost somewhere back on book three of The Accidentals without her brainstorming. Love you much, friend!

Last, but never least, thank you for your continued, amazingly awesome support of The Accidentals! You've consistently shown the girls your love by emailing me, posting reviews, sharing your concerns (mostly about Nina and the loss of her vampirism. LOL! I'm sorry. I made it right —swear!), asking whether Carl, Darnell, and Arch will ever get their own stories, and I'm so grateful to find you all so invested in this monster I've created.

Much love always,
  Dakota XXOO

THE ACCIDENTAL FAMILIAR

BY DAKOTA CASSIDY

CHAPTER 1

"*Y*ou're talking. Like *talking-talking*, as in your mouth is moving and words are coming out. Words, I might add, that make total sense."

"Totally fucked-up, right?"

Poppy McGuillicuddy snorted. *So totally.* "*How* is it even possible that you're talking to me?"

"You have three choices."

She gulped in the chilled autumn air, inhaling the scent of damp fur and the lingering stench of cheap booze before she sat up straighter and looked the talking cat in the eye (*the talking cat*).

"Okay, give me my choices. I'm listening."

The tiny, round black cat began to pace the length of the brick garden wall they'd sat upon when Poppy had demanded she needed air after their "accident".

The cat stretched, arching its rippling spine, the blue-black of its fur shimmering under the street lamp at the end of the driveway. "First, I just have to make mention. Cooler than coolio costume. Big KISS fan here."

Poppy preened, fluffing her Afro wig and puffing out her

1

chest to accent the shirt she wore, nude in color with glued-on patches of cotton balls she'd dyed black to mimic copious amounts of chest hair.

"Thanks. I worked extra hard on the star over my eye. Rock and roll hootchie-koo."

"It totally shows. I'd know you were Paul Stanley if I was blind. Kudos for not going with the obvious choice, too."

She flapped a hand at the cat and smiled at how clever she'd felt when she'd put this crazy costume together. "Gene's so overdone. Plus, there's the tongue thing, you know? I'm just not qualified. Anyway, where were we?"

"Choices," the cat repeated.

"Right."

"So let me lay this out for you in list form. You sure you're ready?"

"Probably not, but I feel like choices are probably moot."

The feline dipped its shiny, dark head. "No truer words. So here it is in a nutshell. Option one: you can hear me talking to you because you're fuckin' nuts. Two: you're on drugs or have been drugged, which wouldn't surprise me with that crowd of bananapants stoners in there at that lame excuse for a Halloween party. Three: I'm really talking to you."

Poppy looked off toward her best friend's house, sitting just behind the garden wall, and shivered. "I don't like any of those categories, Alex. Can I have another?"

"*Jeopardy* doesn't work that way, Poppy, and you know it," the cat scolded. "Alex Trebek would be so insulted."

She gaped at the cat. "How do you know my name?"

The cat scoffed, sitting up straight and affecting a jaunty pose. "Well, it went something like this: 'Yo, yo, yo, girlz and booooyz! This is Poppy M to the C to the Guill-i-cudd-E in da house, spinnin' you some oldies but goodies tonight! Who all remembers this mad-ass hit by the Spin Doooctooooors?' So see? It wasn't like you kept your name some big secret."

Right. Her Run DMC impression. She'd been DJ-ing at her old friend Mel's party before all this had gone down. And what had gone down during that party was nutters. Everything was nutters.

So she said as much to the cat as she rubbed her hands together to keep them warm. "This is insane."

"Or maybe *you* are," the feline offered, dry with sarcasm, sitting back on its haunches and eyeballing her with those wide green orbs.

Poppy cocked her head, remembering the cat's words. "Insanity… That was one of the choices you laid out, right?"

"Yep. Because sometimes if you're crazy, it goes hand and hand with delusions. Maybe I'm just a delusion you've cooked up in your nutbag head."

Right. Maybe this was all a delusion. She wasn't prone to them that she knew of, but how would you know you were having delusions if you were delusional?

She looked down at her phone and the number the cat had told her to call when it realized something was terribly out of whack and talked her into coming outside to handle their little indiscretion with less Blink-182 and Rick James blaring in their ears.

Poppy picked up her phone, letting her feline companion hear the endless drone of ringing on the other end. "I don't think anyone's going to pick up. Maybe I dialed the wrong—"

"This is Nina Blackman-Statleon of OOPS, for all your dramatic, life-altering emergency paranormal needs. Recently PA- and ratchety-ass, bag-o'-old-crusty-Paranormal-Council-bones approved as a legitimate source for the stickier paranormal events in your life. So, do tell. How can I help your pathetic, whiny soul today?"

Before Poppy was able to ask what all this talk about crisis and crusty-bones approved business was about, someone cut off the woman on the other end of the line.

"Nina!" a woman with a melodic voice chastised in the background. "Stop that! That could be a real client on the other end in dire need!"

"What, Fakey-Locks? Like they're not pathetic when they're all needy and clingy? Please. You asked me to answer the phones tonight, and that's what I'm doin'. Just shut your over-glossed lips and let me handle this."

Poppy waivered, rethinking the cat's nutball suggestion to ring up this hotline called OOPS, one alleging it offered help when you were in paranormal crisis.

But the cat had told her to call this number as if the number itself were a lifeline to God. The *talking* cat said this was who to call—nay, it had insisted these were the people to bring into this so-called mess.

"Well speak, for catnip's sake!" the persistent feline urged, nudging her elbow with its peculiarly round head. "We don't have all stinkin' night. We need to get this shit straightened out before Familiar Central sends someone in. It won't look good if we dawdle. You don't want to look bad in front of your new superiors, do you, Spin Doctor?"

"Poppy!" she blurted out her name, because for some reason it seemed important she be known as something more than the DJ. "My name is Poppy. DJ-ing is just something I do on the side for a little extra cash," she stated with as much clarity as one could muster when having a conversation with a house pet.

"It'll be Shit On A Stick if you don't get crackin'." The cat's tail swished in an agitated semi-circle over the surface of the bricks again. "Now talk!" it hissed.

"Hellooo? You've got twenty GD seconds before I use my internal GPS and hunt your ass down for crank calling me," the woman named Nina groused. "I'm gonna start counting now. One..."

Poppy closed her eyes and took a shaky, deep breath of the cold night air, trying to sort through the bits and pieces about familiars and superiors and focus on the fact that this person on the other end of the line was supposed to help her.

With a trembling hand, Poppy finally held the phone up to her ear. "Um, hello?" she whispered into the phone, attempting a calm tone.

No one was going to retell this horror story someday and call Poppy McGuillicuddy a chicken-shit. Not on your life. When witnesses retold this harrowing tale, it would always be prefaced by how brave she'd been.

"I *said,* how the eff can I help you?" the voice belonging to Nina, the OOPS operator, growled.

Okay, so forget valor. Shit, shit, shit. This was a mistake. A big mistake.

But the cat, the damn *talking* cat, nudged Poppy again and shouted over the screech of Run DMC still blaring from inside her best friend's house, "Tell that crabby-AF, pale-faced beast of the female persuasion it's her friggin' reluctant-as-hell familiar calling!"

She looked down at the tiny cat with the round head and eyes the color and shape of green marbles and bit the inside of her cheek to keep from screaming.

In and out, Poppy. Breathe in and out. Don't panic.

"Yo?" Nina prodded, still growling and quite clearly annoyed.

Finally composed, she waded into the conversation pool carefully, because the person on the other end of the phone sounded like everything would be much less explosive if you spoke delicately.

"Your talking cat said I should call you at this number. Did I mention your cat talks? Like, it actually talks. Can I ask you something before we shift into high gear and get to the root of my phone call to you?"

There was a long sigh and then the cantankerous woman said, "You get one question. After that, I get annoyed as all hell, and if you don't like me now—which, based on my past history with first impressions, I'm guessin' you're not a fucking fan yet—then you sure as shit won't like me when I'm aggravated."

Poppy swallowed, smoothing the leggings she wore as part of her Paul Stanley costume over her knees. "Just *one* question? That's all I get? That seems wholly unfair. This is a crisis hotline, isn't it?"

"Is that how you want to spend your one question—in negotiations?"

She blinked and came to her senses almost instantly. "No! Sorry. Okay. My one question. Why does your cat talk, lady? Why am I sitting here, outside what was supposed to be a fun, easy DJ-ing gig for some extra vacation money at my best friend's Halloween Party turned waking nightmare, with a talking cat?"

"Put the GD *talking* cat on the phone, Cupcake," Nina's husky voice demanded.

Poppy paused with a frown and considered how exactly to do that. "Like, hold the phone to its ear? Are you serious?"

"Is the cat talking to you, Princess?" Nina snarled.

Poppy squirmed on the uncomfortable garden wall of bricks she'd perched herself on after this series of unfortunate events had all gone down. "Well, yeah..."

"Then is it a stretch it would talk to me, too, Kumquat? *Now put the cat on the GD phone!*"

Poppy pulled her cell from her ear and held it up to the cat, putting the phone on speaker. "She wants to talk to you. As in you, the cat. The *talking* cat."

There was just no way around this. This was really

happening. Or it *felt* like it was really happening. Maybe someone had dropped acid in her drink? A roofie? No. She'd be passed out if she'd been roofied. Right?

Besides, she was always careful about where she set her water. Even at a party hosted by a friend, she took precautions, because that's just how Poppy McGuillicuddy rolled. Cautiously.

The cat blinked its overly large, utterly mesmerizing eyes and cocked its head, leaning closer to the phone. "That you, Pale One?"

"That you, Catastrophe?"

"It's Calamity, you ridiculously, unfairly gorgeous waste of a great ass. We got some shit. Some deep, dark, murky shit going on here."

"Like?"

Poppy heard the tension in this woman Nina's voice. She sounded really mad. It almost sounded as if she were the parent and the talking cat was her toddler.

"Calamity? Answer the flippin' question!" the woman roared in such a forceful way, even the leaves on the trees shook.

The cat, possibly named Calamity—Poppy couldn't be sure because the woman on the other end of the phone had used two adjectives when addressing said cat—rasped a sigh of full-on exasperation.

"Don't get your fangs twisted, Blood Lover Lite. Just get here and bring the ditzy blonde with all that lip gloss and hair bleach. Oh, and the nice one who sneaks me the real tuna, not that crap in the can packed in water."

"Wanda. That's Wanda, and if she's sneaking you tuna, I'm going to kick her perfectly mannered ass. What have I told you about tuna, Calamity? *What?*"

Calamity The Talking Cat lifted her chin. "Oh, blah, blah, blah. Tuna is too rich for my touchy tummy. Blah, blah, blah.

Makes me puke all over the carpet in the castle. Blah, blah, blah. You hate cleaning up the chunky effin' puke. Blah, blah, blah."

"Exactly. Now, tell me what's going on, C, or I'm gonna make you wear those stupid sweaters with the glitter on them from the Martha Stewart Collection at PetSmart every day for a GD week."

Calamity rocked back on her hind paws and gasped in outraged horror. "You wouldn't! Fuck, those are ugly, you monster."

"Sooo would," the husky voice crooned with a tone screaming devilish glee. "I'd damn well grin from ear to ear while I did that shit, too. Now what's going on? Spit it the fuck out *now*."

Calamity rolled to her back, inching along the bricks to scratch her spine, her response rather cavalier, considering the magnitude of the alleged incident. "So there was an accident at a party I'm at, and as a byproduct of this accident, something happened. Not a big deal, really. Nothing I can't handle."

"*What accident*, Calamity? And why the fuck are you crashing parties? What did I tell you about that shit?"

"As I recall," Calamity drawled. "You said no *wedding* crashing. There was nothing about party crashing in general."

"Don't you mince motherfluffin' words with me, Calamity! Now knock it the shit off and—"

There was a muffled sound, as though someone was trying to wrestle the phone from Nina, and then a much sweeter, far more affable voice came on the line. "Calamity, honey? It's Marty. You know the one. The blonde with all the lipstick and hair bleach? Talk to Auntie Marty, Precious, and tell me what happened so we can help. Maybe it's not such an emergency after all."

"That's Marty. Super nice, fashionista, not very brainy. A werewolf, by the way," Calamity whispered as though no one but Poppy could hear. Clearing her throat, the cat continued. "So here's the prob in a nutshell. I think. Nothing for certain here, mind you, but I think I turned the party DJ into one of my own."

"A cat?"

"No, Marty—a familiar. I think I turned the DJ into a familiar."

"You think?" Auntie Marty repeated, her tone still almost as sweet with only a hint of an angry tremor.

There was more rustling and another muffled, "Give me the damn phone, Ass Sniffer," before the mean one named Nina was back on the line. "Location!" she bellowed, making Poppy wince. "Now, Calamity!"

As Calamity The Talking Cat rattled off the location, Poppy looked at the inside of her wrist and ran a finger over the raised picture now on her flesh, growing more dazed and confused by the second.

Sure, there was a half moon tattoo-ish looking thing with a sprinkle of stars across the center of it in a place she had no recollection of ever getting a tattoo. In fact, she didn't have any tattoos at all. Her mother would kill her if she got a tattoo, but this was what had convinced the cat, er, Calamity, that she was now a familiar.

Whatever one of those was. She vaguely remembered watching *Charmed* as a teenager and the mention of familiars, but that had been a long time ago, and the definition of one and their place in the witch world were both very vague.

Holding her wrist up, she inspected the mark in question under the light of the streetlamps. Maybe it was one of those temporary tattoos, and this was all a joke? Licking her finger, Poppy scrubbed it over her skin, but the half moon remained clear as day.

All right. So this wasn't some kind of joke.

"What in the fresh hell are you doing?" Calamity asked, dancing over the garden wall, swatting at dust particles.

"Trying to figure out if this is all some elaborate prank played on me by my BFF."

"You mean the skinny one dressed up like Kanye West, guzzling that cheap bottle of Boones Farm like it was her last night on earth while she rocked back and forth pressed up to the guy dressed like Kim Kardashian, who was at least ten years younger than her and stoned half out of his gourd?"

Poppy smiled briefly. Her pal Mel had never graduated college-level drinking. Even at thirty-four, she was still boozing it up like she was twenty. In fact, she was still dating like she was twenty.

She sighed in resignation. "Yeah, that's her."

Calamity snorted indignantly, the small puff of air turning to a cloud of condensation. "She couldn't even make decent appetizers—Triscuits and Vienna sausages in a can do not a party make. Even a heathen troglodyte would turn their nose up at that crap. That in mind, do you really think someone dressed as Kanye West is capable of pulling off some shit like this?"

Poppy put her arm back at her side and looked directly into the cat's mesmerizing eyes, trying to rationalize—or maybe the better word was minimize—what was currently happening.

"What exactly is *this shit*? I just have a tattoo I don't remember getting. So what? Lot's of people have tattoos they don't remember getting. In fact, half my night-school college class has tattoos they don't remember getting. Big deal."

Calamity cocked her head as though assessing her. "Well, sure. That's true. You could sweep this shit under the carpet with some implausible, farfetched explanation. *But* you're also talking to a cat like Dr. Doolittle's spirit took possession of your body. So there's that. What more proof do you need?"

Poppy winced. "Like you said, maybe I've been drugged?"

Calamity made a clicking noise in the back of her throat. "You won't be able to use that excuse when you wake up tomorrow, and you're in the same boat. Because you'll still be a familiar, and I'll still be talking."

Pulling off the Paul Stanley Afro wig, Poppy ran her hands through her hair and sighed again. "Okay, so if I'm not drugged, and this isn't some version of Punk'd complete with sound effects and live animation, what is *this shit?*"

"This shit is bullshit. That's what this shit is," a familiar voice from the shadows groused.

As if out of nowhere, three women appeared, their hair billowing about their shoulders in the frigid winds of Staten Island, their strides confident, their eyes focused and glimmering in the night. Like some new millennium Charlie's Angels, they strode toward her with confidence, all long legs, beautiful clothing, expensive perfume and glittery jewelry.

Well, except for the dark one. She had long legs and the billowy hair for sure, but she wasn't dressed like she was going to the same party the other two women were. She wore work boots, a thick black hoodie, low-slung black jeans and a big ol' scowl on her utterly perfect, scarily pale face.

"You Poppy?" she demand-asked, coming to stand in front of her, arms crossed over her hoodie-covered chest.

She gulped, looking up into this woman's flashing coal-black eyes. "Will a brutal beating follow if I say yes?"

The blonde woman with loads of swirly hair and clacking jewelry nudged the dark-haired woman in the ribs with a frown. "I'm sorry for how abrupt Nina is. You'll adjust as we move forward. Forget her and focus on me. I'm Marty Flaherty, this ogre is Nina Statleon, and this," she pointed just over her shoulder to the tall chestnut-haired lady with mahogany highlights, "is Wanda Jefferson. We're OOPS, and we're here to help." Then she smiled, dazzlingly white and perfect.

As though the wind had re-inflated her sails, Poppy jumped up, putting a defensive hand in front of her. "Help with *what*? This is all crazy. Look, I don't know what the cat told you or why it even insisted I call you. Forget about the fact that it can speak and has the ability to use a phone. We'll get to that later. Now, I looked at your website online, and it says you help people in paranormal crisis. I don't know if that means you host drug interventions for ghosts—do ghosts become addicts or were they addicts before they died and need ongoing afterlife care? For that matter, what does 'paranormal crisis' even mean and why am I supposedly having one?"

The woman named Nina reached for Poppy's wrist so fast, so freakishly fast, Poppy gasped. "I'm gonna ask you to chill the fuck out, okay? Stop gettin' all jenky with your hands because you don't want to get defensive with the likes o' me. Now breathe, Petunia."

It was almost a relief to have someone give her some direction. Bending at the waist, she let her hands rest on her knees, and her head hang low. "Maybe we should start over and reintroduce ourselves?"

Nina put a hand on the back of her head, keeping her face pointed downward at the driveway. "I said breathe, Rock Star—great costume, by the way. Paul Stanley's no fucking Barry Manilow, but you killed the makeup. Now, get your shit together. While you do that, I'm gonna kick the living crap out of my damn familiar for ignoring my house rules, and then we'll make nice, and I'll explain what we do at OOPS and all that bullshit."

Poppy blinked as the blood rushed to her head in a swoosh of pounding waves. "The cat's yours?"

Nina snorted. "It sure as fuck wasn't my idea, but yeah. She's mine."

"It talks." She realized she kept saying that, but c'mon! Wasn't anyone else as in awe of that fact?

Nina clucked her tongue in admonishment. "Been down this road, Poppy. You're getting repetitive. A sure sign you're playing possum."

She tried to lift her head, but Nina's hand was like a vise grip, forcing her to keep her eyes level with her feet. "Possum?"

"Yeah, it's when everyone says they're fine while they beat their panic down, bottle it the fuck up or whatever so they can give good face, which always leads to total meltdown. It's pathetic and ugly, and usually involves tears and loads of the sympathy I'm working really hard to get better at giving because my therapist says I suck ass at it."

"This is your version of sympathy?"

"This is me *working* on being sympathetic. Don't fuck up my flow."

"So you've done this before? This crisis thing?" If that was true, that almost made her feel better. Almost. Though, she still couldn't quite connect the dots between what had happened back at the house to needing a crisis counselor. Still, she didn't sense these women were dangerous.

In fact, she was very clear about the notion they *weren't* dangerous. Though, why the feeling was so vivid, she couldn't say. She possessed her own kind of intuition for sure, but it was a very average sort of intuition. This? Well, this sort of intuition was different.

Nina's patted the back of her head before her cool fingers clasped her neck. "More times than Marty's got lipsticks. Keep breathing."

"I'm really dizzy," Poppy complained, her spine beginning to ache.

"It's those pants," Nina commented. "Always wondered how Stanley managed to squeeze into 'em without popping the top of his head off.

A soft hand reached down and grabbed Poppy's, pulling her up and holding her firm when she stumbled from lack of blood flow. "Let her up, Nina." The lady named Marty righted Poppy and smiled. "So tell us what happened so we best know how to help you."

Poppy stared at the woman with eyes of cornflower blue and hair in more shades of blonde than she even knew existed, and thought about her request. She wasn't quite sure how this had happened...or if anything had really happened at all.

Marty pressed with a warm smile, "Poppy, honey? How did this happen?"

Words escaped her.

But they didn't escape the cat. It hopped down from the garden wall and wound its long tail around Marty's legs. "Ask me, Bleached One. I know how it happened."

The woman named Wanda bent and scooped the cat up, snuggling her close to her porcelain cheek with a smile. "What kind of mischief have you been into now, Miss Calamity?" she asked, her tone oozing indulgence.

Calamity purred in return, curling into Wanda's arms. "It was an accident, I swear, Wanda."

Nina tweaked the cat's ear, her face stern against the backdrop of the dark night. "Quit coddlin' her like she's some baby, Wanda. She was out way past curfew, which is bullshit. She damn well knows better. And lay off the tuna when I'm not lookin'. It makes her puke."

Wanda flapped an irritated hand at Nina before resuming her cuddle with the cat. "Hush. She's just acting out because you're so hard on her. Now, tell Auntie Wanda what happened here, Calamity, and I promise there'll be some warm milk tonight before bed."

Calamity purred and brushed Wanda's cheek with her paw. "Okay, it went down like this. M to the C to the Guill-i-cudd-E was spinning records at this lame Halloween party—"

"A party you didn't ask fucking permission to go to," Nina growled, her black eyes narrowing as she jammed her hands into her hoodie pockets.

Calamity stopped purring and gave Nina a hard glare. "You don't ask permission to crash a party, Beastmaster. It's not a goddamn crash if you ask for entry. Anyway, I was chillin' to Poppy's beat and I got a little carried away when I broke out my smooth MC Hammer moves. I tripped on a glass of water, knocked it over on the wiring for the speakers, which I'm pretty sure weren't up to code, and *wham*! Almost electrocuted Poppy. So I try to do the right thing by knocking her wee sprite ass out of the way with my magic, but I slipped and fell into her, and then we both fell—"

"Into the puddle of water!" Poppy spat as she retreated from her fog, the entire episode coming together in a clatter of memory. "That's exactly what happened! When the cat jumped on me, she dug her claws into my shoulder, and I tripped and fell into the water where the speaker wires were. See?" She pulled her pleather jacket with the stars she'd bedazzled on herself away from her shoulder, pointing to the scratch marks to show the women.

Marty winced, leaning in closer to inspect her wounds.

Nina swished a hand at Marty, pointing to her purse. "Dig around in your mom bag there and get this kid some Neosporin, Blondie."

But Poppy waved a hand in dismissive fashion. "I swear I saw stars and a big flash of light. Then there was this tingle… like a weird shiver that raced all along my limbs, and then the cat was freaking out and yelling at me to come outside and call you before someone, I can't remember who, came and picked me up—"

"That bitch Cecily from Familiar Central," Calamity interjected with a scoff. "Swear, she can smell a newb from a realm away. She's gonna show up here and demand to take DJ Puts The Needle On The Record back to the realm so she can claim her as her own, and I'll be dipped in cow dung before I'll let that happen."

"*Claim me?*" Poppy squeaked, scanning the dark neighborhood for this woman named Cecily.

Calamity tilted her head so Wanda could scratch her neck. "Yeah. She gets like frequent flier miles for every newb familiar she sucks into her dark void or some shit. If she gets enough miles, she gets to go to some familiar retreat in Baja. Why the fuck should she get all the miles? I did this to ya, I win. That's how it works with all familiars who are found or made—in your case, accidentally made—rather than born into the realm, by the way. If one of us finds you, it's our duty to turn you in. Also, if that crazy hag Cecily gets her hands on you, who knows who the hell you'll end up with. She just doesn't care the way I do, and because this was my fault, the least I can do is try to make sure you get a good witch."

A witch? She was getting a witch? What did that mean? Did it mean a job that paid money? Because she could use a job that paid money. God, could she ever.

Nina jammed her hands into her black hoodie pocket. "So let me get this shiz straight. Basically, you zapped a bitch and transferred some of your mojo to her, and that means she's a familiar now, too? How the hell do you know that for sure?"

Calamity harrumphed at Nina. "All you gotta do is look at her wrist. She does have *The Mark*, Keeper of My Cage. It's just like the one on the underside of my paw. We all have 'em."

Poppy immediately began to back away, but she held up her wrist so they could all see the half-moon shape, which, as was becoming increasingly clear, apparently represented her status as a familiar.

"Hol-ee shitballs," Nina muttered. "And you're sure this means she's like you? I thought familiars were all animals?"

"That's because you don't listen when I'm trying to school your sorry ass, Half-Breed!" Calamity exclaimed in a tone screaming exasperation. "Familiars come in all sorts of shapes and sizes these days. Animals are the least likely suspects for prying human eyes, but there are plenty of uprights to be had nowadays. You'd know that if you'd just become a little more involved in the community, you dolt!"

Nina snarled, reaching for Calamity, but Wanda took a step back to avoid her.

Suddenly, Poppy couldn't take it anymore. Scooping up her Paul Stanley wig from the brick wall, she shook it at the group as though it would ward off impending danger.

"What does *like her* mean?" she shouted. Everything was moving at the speed of light while she was still stuck on the fact that a cat could talk.

Calamity sighed in what sounded like resignation, as though Poppy should know exactly what she was talking about. "It means we gotta get you to Familiar Central so you can get in the good line to get a nice witch. You do *not* want to wait for them to assign you somebody or you'll end up like I did, with a leftover with anger management issues. That's how I landed this crazy half-breed, scowling-at-everything-that-moves bitch on monster truck wheels." Calamity lifted her jaw in Nina's direction.

"A leftover..." Poppy muttered, but that didn't slow Calamity's tirade even a little.

"Now, I admit, I was lazy as fuck, and I should've gotten my shit together a lot sooner than I did when my old witch died. I lollygagged, hung out, threw back a bunch of brewskies, watched a lot of shitty reality TV and in general took a break from all the hocus-pocus crap. My old witch was a handful. But who knew I'd end up with the bottom of the barrel just because I was on sabbatical? And to add insult to injury, I ended up with an ogre who's half *vampire*. Like I know a friggin' thing about vampires. But there was no talking the head honcho out of this match made in the inner circle of Hell. So here I am—stuck with a psychotic, nay, violent, half-vampire/half-witch. *Forever.*"

Nina eyeballed Calamity, and to say she wasn't exactly pleased was likely an understatement. But oddly, her next words were far more levelheaded than Poppy would have expected, even though her fists were tightly clenched at her sides and her teeth could quite possibly crack from the pressure of grinding them.

"We're working through some shit. Boundaries, rules, crap like that."

"Yeah," the cat scoffed, curling into Wanda's protective hold. "Boundaries and crap. That's what we're working through. I hope that helps you sleep at night. Oh, wait. You don't sleep at night, do you, Blood Sucker?"

Marty grabbed one of Poppy's hands and held it to her chest, her warm, smooth skin soothing Poppy, lulling her into a sense of security. Probably a false sense of one, but still a comfort. "To say Calamity was a surprise is an understatement. She and Nina are in the adjustment phase of their relationship—still working out the kinks, you know?"

"You mean the phase where she doesn't fucking do what she's told?" Nina asked.

Calamity crawled to Wanda's shoulder and perched herself there. If cats could give dirty looks, she was shooting daggers at Nina. "I'll say this one more time, Pale Face. I am your *guide*, your helper, your GD advisor to the magical realm. Not your slave in perpetuity. Got that, you colossal PITA? You can't tell me what to do. I'm a hundred and fifty years old, not ten!"

Wanda chuckled and scratched Calamity under the chin, burying her face in the cat's neck. "You tell her, Snookiepuss."

Nina openly gaped at Wanda, her flawless face a tight mask of anger. "What the fuck is wrong with you, Wanda? Why the hell are you taking her side? Stop gettin' in the middle of our shit, for Christ's sake! If she didn't behave like a motherfluffin' kid, I wouldn't treat her like one! I've been chasin' after this toddler on steroids since she got here, putting out fire after fucking fire just as she lights another damn match. Now mind your damn P's and Q's!"

Marty popped her glossed lips and clapped her hands, a cheerfully forced smile on her face. "Ladies! Knock it off!" she shouted then squared her shoulders and smoothed her faux fur vest over her waistline. "We have no time to spare while the two of you argue over how Nina parents her unruly familiar. We have a job to do. Let's do it before this Cecily shows up and steals Calamity's thunder or Poppy ends up with an ogre like Nina for the rest of her days. Now, what do we do next, Calamity?"

Calamity hopped from Wanda's shoulder to the ground and stretched. "It's a doozy of a ride. You sure you're up for it?"

As Poppy listened to Calamity's explanation and watched the drama between the women unfold, she remained quiet, dealing with this new feeling she had. This new *certainty* was maybe a better word.

She knew, without a shadow of a doubt, what these women spoke was the truth. There was no second-guessing, no quibbling. She instinctually knew the cat really could talk. Nina really was half-vampire, half-witch, and Poppy really did have to get to this place called Familiar Central.

She didn't quite understand this innate sense of the truth; she wasn't even sure how she was keeping from freaking out about the fact that Nina was a vampire-witch.

Maybe that would come later? For now, she had to take care of this. There was a pressing urgency in her gut that said she needed to trust her instincts.

"Does this familiar thing pay?"

"Like in money?" Calamity asked, cocking her round head.

She needed money. It wasn't likely Mel was going to pay her now after she'd obliterated her sound system. To make everything worse, she was surely on the verge of being booted from her apartment if she didn't come up with three months' rent by next week.

Old Mr. Rush, her landlord, was an understanding guy, a great guy, in fact. But he couldn't live on nothing any more than she could. And that's what she'd been paid for spending almost four months on the road in a show that had such low attendance, the audiences were all but taking naps.

Nothing.

That son of a bitch Randall Cranston had run off with what little profit they'd made, leaving her and the rest of the cast high and dry.

She hated leaving her apartment and all the incredible people who'd been her neighbors for almost five years now, but she'd come to the realization her choices were growing slimmer by the day.

She'd even considered going back to her parents in Cincinnati. While she loved them, she didn't necessarily want to live with them and their paneled walls and meals with a *Wheel of Fortune/Jeopardy!* double whammy anymore.

So this was a possible answer to all her financial problems.

Besides, she'd done crazier things for cash.

Finally, she said, "Well, yeah, I mean in money. I have to eat."

"Not in money, no. But it does include room and board. Er, mostly…"

Calamity's vague answer went by the wayside, almost unheard after the words "room and board." Looking down at the cat, Poppy nodded with total calm. "I'm ready."

For the first time since she'd met her, Nina grinned as she scanned Poppy's face, her glimmering eyes searching. "Holy fuck. You're serious?"

She was. She didn't know why she was, but she was. "I am. Let's go."

Nina gazed down at Calamity and pointed a long finger at her. "Then let's get it on before she comes down off her high o' crazy and changes her mind."

"Did you bring your wand?" she asked Nina, stretching a paw forward.

Nina made a face, the hard lines of her jaw tightening. "No, I didn't bring my fucking wand. That shit is like holding a hand grenade. I never know whether I'm going to blow crap up or turn it into a friggin' animated ice sculpture. I'm not good enough at it yet to carry it around full time. Christ, it was much easier just being a vampire. All I had to do was flash my fangs and shit got done."

Calamity clucked her tongue. "What have I told you about your wand, you beast? Ya gotta keep it with you at all damn times. It's like leaving an organ behind."

"I don't have any organs."

"Okay, it's like leaving your sunscreen behind. Crucially important. I've only told you that a bafrillion times, Nina. You do know you just made this shit much harder?"

Poppy blinked. Nina had a wand? "Why does that make shit harder?" she asked.

Calamity snorted. "Hold one minute, and I'll show you…"

CHAPTER 2

"*I* think I'm broke," Poppy moaned as she hoisted herself up from the hard-tiled floor they'd been dumped on, looking down in disgust at her leggings, which now had a jagged tear in them. A stray cotton ball from the chest hair she'd made for her costume fell to the ground in a sad plop, and her wig was a tangled mess on the floor.

Shit. Hal's House of Howl was never going to take this costume back now.

But that was okay because a place to sleep was in the offing. Room and board, baby.

Calamity hopped around in front of her with a scoff. "You can thank the vampire for that. It's a bumpy enough ride to the realm even *with* the wand. But using the wand's like flying first class. When we just use straight-up magic, you're in the cheap seats."

"I said I forgot, okay? Jesus, get off my jock, would you?" Nina groused as she rose on her long limbs from the pristine white floor and rolled her head on her neck.

Now Calamity did a little dance and taunted, "Is that how

you're supposed to use your words, Vampire? Doc Malone would be ashamed."

Poppy worked her way up the wall using her palms as she took in the long, sterile hallway leading to a wide white door. Bending at the waist, she scooped up her fallen wig. "Who's Doc Malone?"

"Our witch therapist. She's helping me to cope with this damn boil on my ass," Nina snarled, flashing her teeth.

Calamity hissed right back at Nina. "Oh, shut your pie hole. It's the other way around. If not for Doc Malone, I'd have zapped your supermodel butt to Mars by now."

Wanda had somehow managed to remain infuriatingly upright during their journey, wherein one minute they'd been standing in her friend's driveway, then the next, squeezed like sausages from a casing into this hallway. "Come to Auntie Wanda, Calamity," she cooed, patting her knee.

Nina's beautiful face scrunched up in confusion. "Wanda? What the shit? Stop babying her while she laps this attention up like milk."

And then Wanda made a face at Nina, rolling her eyes as she smoothed stray strands of her hair back in place and her posture took on the look of royalty. "Hush, you animal! How many times have I told you, you'll catch more flies with honey than vinegar? Why must you always be so hard on her? She's just a little thing who's been thrust into our world without consent. She needs love and attention, not berating."

Nina narrowed her eyes at Wanda. "Fuck your vinegar, and yeah, she's so little and lost she managed to turn someone into a familiar. She might be little on the outside, but her inside is big on trouble. Quit coddling the out-of-control cat or I'm gonna whip up a spell and turn you into a damn mannequin in the girdle aisle at Macy's."

Calamity swirled in and out of Wanda's ankles, clearly pleased she had such a devout ally. "Don't worry, Wanda. She can't even turn water into a Capri Sun. No way she can turn you into a mannequin. I'll protect you."

Wanda giggled, reaching down and stroking Calamity's back.

Nina's outraged expression as she circled the pair made Poppy press herself to the hallway wall, clinging to her wig.

"I said knock it the fuck off, Wanda, or—"

The clack of Marty's heeled boots as she finally rose jarred Poppy, and made both Nina and Wanda turn their heads in her direction. "I can't even believe it's me saying this, but if the two of you don't quit with the arguing over Calamity like she's some kind of ribeye in the height of a zombie apocalypse, I'll put you both through a wall. Got me? Wanda, I don't know what's happening with you these days, but you're doing everything you possibly can to provoke Nina, and I've about had it right up to the tip of my bleached-blonde roots! Since when am *I* the one who has to mediate? Does anyone see the absurdity in this?"

When no one answered Marty with anything other than pursed lips and angry eyes, she continued, her gaze fixed on Wanda. "Last I checked, it was *your* job, sister, but lately, you've been all wrapped up in devilishly poking Nina, using Calamity as your stick."

And still, they all remained freakishly quiet.

But Marty wasn't done. Then she strolled toward Nina, her hair swishing about her shoulders, her index finger in motion. "And you, Wicked Half-Witch of The East—cut it the hell out! You'd better find some kind of common ground with Calamity and find it soon because she's here forever, or I'm going to put *you* in the ground. Clear?"

Neither woman said anything, but they didn't have to. Their flashing eyes and tense body language said it all. Something was happening between them all. And it wasn't just a spat. It was more like a shift in dynamic, a change in the terrain of their friendship. Poppy was sure of it.

Now Marty squatted down beside Calamity and cupped her jaw, her blue eyes intense. "Pussycat? You're enjoying playing both ends against the middle. Under normal circumstances, because it makes me giggle my ass off to see Nina so riled, I'd enjoy this almost as much as I enjoy an eyeshadow that doesn't crease. But this becomes a real thorn in my side when we have a client who needs our help. So cut it out, since, as I recall, big bad werewolves love to chase little kitties cuz little kitties are mmm-mmm-good—especially ones full up like fat sausages with magic. *Capisce?*"

Calamity blinked, shifting from paw to paw, her tone subdued now. "Got it."

Marty stood and brushed her thighs off then smiled. "Now that we're clear, tell us where we go from here, Calamity. Poppy is waiting."

And she *was* waiting. Watching and waiting as these women argued, trying to understand the dynamic between them all, yet instinctively knowing they each had a deep, abiding loyalty to one another.

And that was freaking her out. How could she possibly know how deep their roots went?

Yet, she did. She'd gamble her life on it.

"Okay, so let me just give you a couple of helpful tips before we get inside," Calamity said, forcing her to focus on the task at hand.

Reaching into her jacket, Poppy pulled out an elastic band, scrunching her hair into one hand and wrapping the band around it with the other. This felt like a hair up problem.

Tightening her ponytail, she plopped her wig back on her

skull and squared her shoulders. "Okay. Tips. Hit me. I'm ready."

Calamity began to walk the long hallway to a door at the end of the white walls, her tail swishing back and forth. "Never leave the line. For the love of Jesus and all that's good, *never* leave the line. I don't care if you're on fire and your head's about to pop off your tiny shoulders. Do *not* leave the line."

Poppy trudged behind the cat, wishing she'd changed back into her street clothes before doing something as important as being inducted into the Familiar Hall of Fame. Surely that called for something more appropriate than a Paul Stanley costume.

"Why can't I leave the line?"

"Because one wrong move and you could end up like me. With someone like her."

"*Shut up, Calamity*," Nina warned with tight words, the clomp of her feet heavy against the tile.

But Poppy scoffed. "You don't really feel that way about Nina, and you know it."

Aw, hell. Had that just popped out of her mouth? Why would she say something like that at such a tentative time in their newly minted relationship? Furthermore, how could she even know a personal detail like that?

She didn't know these people from a hole in the wall, and suddenly she was the authority on their deepest feelings? The guru of deep-seated emotions?

Calamity stopped in her tracks and swiveled her head. "What do you know from shit about how I feel?"

Poppy stopped, too, nervously twisting a curl in her wig between her fingers, worried she'd offended Calamity. "I...I don't know. I just *know*...I mean guessed. I'm a good guesser." But that wasn't entirely true. This wasn't some guess. She knew. Like bone-deep knew Calamity loved yanking Nina's chain.

They clashed because she and the vampire were so alike. Yet, she also respected her, and coming to terms with that was part of Calamity's trouble. Calamity didn't want to care —or maybe *invest* was a better word—in a relationship with another witch after losing the last one. It hurt.

But Calamity was having none of it. "Oh, fuck that noise. Forget I asked."

"Fine. Forgotten. Now, what else do I need to know?" Poppy asked as they came to a halt outside a heavy rectangular door.

But Calamity didn't have time to answer before the door swung open and chaos ensued.

POPPY YAWNED as she waited in the line titled First Time Familiars with Calamity and the women of OOPS. The moment the door in that hallway had popped open, and the masses of people and all varieties of the animal kingdom milling about had filled her vision, she'd somehow taken it all in stride.

She'd eyed the long lines with black signs above them and white lettering that read Familiar Renewal and Change of Familiar Address as though they were perfectly normal. It didn't seem like such a big deal that the armadillo two spots back and one line over was shooting the breeze with the zebra in the next row.

She'd viewed the never-ending chain of glass windows with peepholes and the most colorful people animatedly working behind them like they were a row of those protected windows in a bodega, and she was just here to grab a bag of chips on the way to her next shitty job.

Here she was in a strange *realm*, as Calamity had called it, with even stranger people, waiting to find out who she'd end up spending forever with as their magical guide without an inkling about what a familiar was or what their place in this weird society was, and she was feeling completely unaffected.

Not numb, per se, just unaffected. And since she'd gotten past the talking cat thing, the vampire/werewolf with these women thing made sense.

Though in a moment of complete honesty, she had to admit, she'd run the words *room and board* in a continual loop inside her head in order to assure herself this wasn't as crazy as she was supposed to think it was.

"This is worse than any DMV I've ever been to." Running a hand over her temple, she massaged it with her fingertips. "What's the dang hold up?"

"It's a Friday night."

She looked down at Calamity, who sat on her haunches, her wide eyes only occasionally blinking. "A popular night for turning unsuspecting victims into familiars, I gather?"

"I apologized, didn't I?"

Poppy cocked an eyebrow. "No. I don't think you did."

"Fine. Sorry. Hashtag regrets."

"Accepted. So talk to me about room and board. Is it the kind of room and board you get when you live in the basement of your employer's house? Or the carriage-house kind? Do I get time off? Sick days? Health insurance? Are snacks included?"

Nina nudged her shoulder, looking down at her with those intense coal-black eyes. "Okay. What's the rub? Why aren't you crying and carrying on? Why the hell aren't you freaked the eff out after everything we told you about us? After what we showed you? I'm a vampire, for Christ's sake.

You know—bloodsucking, night-loving, fang-flashing *vampire?*"

Poppy shrugged, fanning herself. God, it was hot in Familiar Central. As they waited in this line as long as a checkout at Walmart with only one register open, Nina, Marty and, intermittently, Wanda, had explained how they'd come to be OOPS, what their paranormal standings were, and even some of the cases they'd been involved with.

She knew she should be frightened. She knew she should refute the very idea one iota of this was real. She knew these events should leave her questioning her sanity for even considering what they'd told her was true. She knew her calm acceptance of was likely frightening to an outsider looking in.

But she couldn't. Like, literally couldn't deny the validity of their tales. Not even when Nina went the extra mile and flashed her fangs or earlier when Marty shifted in the Ladies' Room for Familiars.

She'd watched it all with as much unflinching disinterest as she was watching what was unfolding in front of her right now. As if it were every day you saw someone's flesh and bones virtually morph in a public bathroom.

In fact, the only thing she'd added to that scene straight out of *American Horror Story* was her distress that some poor soul was going to have to sweep up all the hair Marty had shed.

"Poppy? What gives?" Nina prodded, tapping the toe of her work boot as though she almost hoped she'd collapse and tremble at her feet in fear.

But she just shrugged and sighed. "Yeah. I get what it means. I heard every word. I heard about Carl and Darnell. I get the comparisons to *Sean of The Dead*, *Teen Wolf*, and so on. I've watched them. I already told you I get it. How many ways can I say that before you believe me?"

In fact, the longer they stood in line, the more rooted this certainty became. Yeah, so you're a vampire. Whoopee.

Nina shook her head, her gloriously silky dark hair shifting over her shoulders. "So you get that your life's now changed forever, right? You get that you can't go back to doing whateverthehell you did for a living, that you can't tell your family and friends about this? That you're a walking, talking episode of *Supernatural*?"

Why was Nina so determined to drill this point home? They'd each taken a turn at reminding her how different her life was now, moving forward.

Finally, Poppy asked, "Is crying what you want to see? Because you know you don't like tears, Nina."

Nina popped her lips, cracking her knuckles. "How the eff do you know what I do or don't like?"

Poppy blinked, astonished she'd said those words out loud. Yeah. How the eff did she know?

Licking her lips, she winced when she answered, "I don't *know*. I just do. Tears make you uncomfortable. Compliments more so." Eek, had she said that, too?

Nina frowned, glaring down at her.

She'd definitely said that. *Bad, Poppy.*

Nina poked her, jabbing a finger between the muscles connecting her collarbone and shoulder. "What are you, fucking psychic, Madam McGuillicuddy?"

"Next!" an authoritative voice behind the glass windows yelled.

Calamity bumped her calves with a swish of her hip. "Shit. That's us. Now remember what I said, P. Shut up and let me do the talking. You do not want to end up with one of those ratchety-ass, last-century mothereffers who still think *Salem's Lot* is a documentary."

Okay, so if she wasn't feeling terribly freaked out before now—not even about discovering vampires and werewolves were real—her frame of mind had definitely changed. She was on the precipice of being assigned her witch, someone she had to help. It wasn't the paranormal part that had her freaked out, or the immortality Calamity spoke of either.

It was the part about guiding someone using her advice as their narrative. It was bananapants.

How could Poppy McGuillicuddy, the girl secretly voted least likely to succeed, possibly guide anyone anywhere?

Her life had already been a flippin' mess before she'd left for the road. She lived in a tiny studio apartment—one she barely held on to each month doing odd jobs, like DJ-ing parties for instance. And if not for the people in her building, people she loved, and their kindness, she'd have likely starved to death by now.

She'd failed miserably at becoming the next Broadway sensation a long time ago and now only got gigs in the chorus if she was lucky, because, by industry standards, she was an old hag—even if she could still do a split at the ripe old age of thirty-four.

She had twelve dollars in her checking account. Two in her pocket. And she'd had to ask for more from her buddy as part of her DJ-ing fee in order to catch public transportation home after the party.

She had no career, no purpose, no solid plan for the future beyond next week when she had to figure out a way to cough up her rent. So the question was, did familiars collect paychecks? Have 401ks? Bennies? She couldn't live on air. She barely did now.

But the biggest question of all? How was she expected to help someone else when she had enough trouble helping herself? It wasn't like she was decision maker extraordinaire. She was considering doing this familiar thing for room and board after a vampire/witch, a werewolf, a talking cat and a half-vampire, half-werewolf had told her it would all be okay.

That struck more fear in her heart than any vampire could.

Room and board, Poppy...

Marty tapped Poppy on the back with a warm smile, startling her from her mantra and pointed forward with a perfectly painted crimson nail to where there was a gap in the line. "Poppy, honey? I hate to nag, but let's move this along. I have a mani/pedi tomorrow at ten sharp, and I don't want to wake with ugly bags under my eyes."

Jarring her from her downward spiral, and with a refusal to give in to all this whining Nina complained about, she blindly moved forward, stepping around a small crowd of people who'd begun to bleed into their line.

Someone from behind gave her a sharp nudge to her shoulder blade. "Go, already, would ya!"

Reaching forward to prevent crashing into the person who'd somehow magically appeared in front of her, she instead smashed right into her, smacking her head against the reed-thin woman's back as she pitched forward.

The beautiful redhead righted herself and hissed her displeasure, her hazel eyes flashing an angry message at Poppy. "Watch where you're going, you imbecile!"

"Oh, pipe down, for Christ's sake!" Nina growled in the woman's face, flashing her fangs. "It was an accident. Now move along before I give you something to really get hot about."

Without another word, the vampire grabbed Poppy's hand in her steely grip and pulled her around the much taller woman, planting her at the window of First Time Familiars. "Now. Go get your witch and make it snappy."

As Poppy stood before the glass window and a stout woman with cat eyeglasses and hair resembling one of those poofy, spouting fountains at the Bellagio, she took a deep breath, the wheezy tremble of it making her wince.

She didn't pay attention to the commotion behind her or the sound of Wanda snapping, "Behave like a lady, for heaven's sake!" to someone.

Instead, Poppy looked straight ahead through the peephole into the glass and directly into her future's fate.

CHAPTER 3

"*I* told you not to leave the line, didn't I?" Calamity asked, nudging her platform boot.

Straightening her wig, Poppy scowled down at Calamity. "I didn't leave the line. I tripped and moved up because Nina threatened the redhead with violence. There's a difference. One is a willful act, the other is an *accident*. You know about those, right?"

"And now look," the cat said, deadpan.

Okay, so her new assignment wasn't the ideal of ideal.

The woman behind the glass tapped it, recapturing her attention. "Paul Stanley, right? Rock and roll kootchie koo!"

"Yeah." Poppy rolled her eyes and made the universal sign for rock and roll, still reeling from her new assignment. "KISS forever," she offered woodenly, the grease paint on her face beginning to smother her skin.

Gladys, according to her nametag, and the woman in charge of assigning familiars to their charges nodded her approval from behind the window. "Well done on the chest hair. Very creative."

"Thanks, now where were we?"

"Your warlock," Gladys ever so kindly reminded while she all but tapped her toe.

Again, Poppy attempted to hide her surprise, because no one but her seemed to think a male assignment was out of the ordinary. "He comes with room and board, right?"

"They all do, honey. Some roomier and board-ier than others."

"But a *warlock*? That's a guy witch." Guy witches had familiars? Was that common? This was nothing like *Sabrina, The Teenage Witch.*

Her warlock's name was Ricardo—or Rick, as he preferred to be called—Delassantos, and he lived just outside of NYC in a fully refurbished warehouse—which, according to Calamity, was a sweet start to a familiar/warlock relationship—even if he was a man. Digs were very important, as outlined by Calamity and her stories about some of her more quirky living quarters as a familiar.

Rick, along with his partner, was a property developer/entrepreneur, self-made and worth millions, which was also good if you listened to Calamity and again, despite the fact that he was a man. A rich warlock meant no scrounging for cash to buy your supper by performing cheap magic tricks in the subway.

All that aside, she couldn't wrap her head around the idea that she was supposed to advise a *man*. Oh, this poor soul Ricardo/Rick was in for some good times.

Gladys tapped the sill of the window in front of her and pointed, using her festively painted orange-and-black fingernail. "You got a problem with a warlock? Because you can always go over to the line to your left and ask for a refund. The Wish I Were Anywhere But Here line. See it?"

She did, and it was pretty dang short. Which spoke volumes on behalf of familiar customer service.

"Aw, hell no you won't!" Calamity whisper-yelled as she

paced the ledge of the window. "You don't wanna know what happens to complainers in the realm. You get a reputation for being difficult. Why do you think I haven't asked for a refund for the blood-lover here? Because if nothing else, at least she mentally resides in *this* century. Like I told you before, no way was I gonna end up with one of those old-ass mothereffers who live in a drafty castle with no Wi-Fi or even electricity while I snuggle up to a herd of sheep on a moor in No Mans Land."

Marty snaked her head around Poppy's shoulder and clucked her tongue. "Gosh, I'm hungry. I feel like a snack, Calamity. How do you feel about being my snack?" she asked, her words dripping with menacing sarcasm. "Last chance to shut that yap of yours before I pick your flesh from my teeth with your tiny bones."

Calamity's fur rippled, but her tone was instantly contrite. "Okay, fine. Sorry. I'm just saying, bad shit happens when you complain. Now take your lumps and like it, newb."

Gladys blinked, her blue-frosted eyes wide, her lips pursed into a thin line as she waited for an answer. "So?"

Poppy gulped, shifting her stance. "Nope, Gladys. Not a one. I'm here to do whatever I'm supposed to do. You'll never hear Poppy McGuillicuddy complain."

Gladys thrust some paper through the small peephole and pursed her thin lips. "Then sign there and initial here and then I'll need a blood sample."

Twisting the length of her ponytail, she grew more agitated. "Sign? What am I signing?"

"Your life away, of course." Gladys gave her a "duh, stupid" look, as though she were the one who was half-baked for thinking she was doing anything else but.

Her eyes flew open wide, her legs growing limp. *"My life?"*

Gladys sighed, her plump shoulders, encased in a sweat-shirt with a shiny bedazzled purple pumpkin, rose and fell in clear disgust. "This says you'll serve your warlock until one of you goes to the great beyond. It's all very standard. Didn't the familiar who inducted you tell you that?"

Poppy looked to Calamity, who nodded. "Oh, yeah. I forgot to tell you. This is a lifetime gig. When you sign on, you sign on for life."

All that certainty she'd been lobbing around like so much confetti evaporated into thin air and panic began to set in. "Life?" she squeaked. That was crazy. How could she promise a lifetime to someone she didn't even know? Didn't you only do that when you got married?

But Gladys was having none of it, as indicated by her scowl. "Look, Ms. McGuillicuddy, if you have a problem, there's a line for it, but you're holding up this one, and I won't have my efficiency rating slip because of you. Now either sign or move the heck along."

Wow. Harsh. "What happens if I don't sign?" She had to ask. She wasn't just going to sign her life away without at least some details.

"You go to *the Bad Place*," Calamity whispered, her tone bespeaking unknown horrors.

"The Bad Place? You mean to tell me your people punish me for not agreeing to lifelong servitude with a man I don't even know because I won't sign my life away? What kinda third-world country are you running in this realm?"

There was a collective gasp just before the enormous room, milling with people, went silent. Everyone stopped and stared at the newb with the big mouth and the fake hair on her chest.

But the biggest gasp of all came from Calamity, who she'd obviously offended. The feline let out a low growl, hunching her back. "I've never been so insulted in my damn life! We're not servants, you uneducated, ill-informed human! We're respected, and in some cultures revered! There are statues made of us. Days set aside in some cultures to celebrate us! We're advisors. Life coaches. Magical guides, and we keep the balance of the realm so the temptation to use magic isn't used for evil, Ignoramus!"

Oh.

Suddenly, it all became clear. It wasn't just Calamity's rant or the ugly stares of her fellow newbs, it was that certainty returning, full on, deep in her gut. She had to do this. She was meant to do this.

Grabbing the pen without another thought, she scribbled her name with flourish.

And just like that, it was done.

THE IMPACT of their fall was buffered only by the fact that they hit a pile of garbage, the stench clinging to her nose as the whoosh of air they created when they landed rose upward.

Poppy lay there for a moment, staring up at the multitude of stars in the inky black of night, trying to catch her breath as she rubbed her arm in the spot Gladys had taken her blood sample.

She held it up and examined the crook of her elbow under the half moon. "Wow. Gladys is a harsh opponent when it comes to a needle."

Marty sat up, jackknifing to a sitting position, a piece of stray paper stuck to one of the swirly curls of her hair. "Where the heck are we?" she groaned, hopping upward and holding a hand of assistance out to Poppy, who took it with a matching groan.

"At Poppy's new gig," Calamity offered, circling the group as they each began to rise to their feet.

"Already?" Poppy squeaked, looking around to assess

38

her surroundings. They'd landed in front of what looked like an abandoned warehouse on an all but deserted street, the tall gray and red brick structure with window after tall, dirty window looming upward in the cold night. The very air of the building was gloomy and dark, making her shiver. "So they just dump you here in a pile of trash? No directions? No getting-to-know-your-warlock pre-introductions? Just tag, you're it—go be a familiar, Grasshopper?"

Nina cracked her knuckles, staring down at Calamity, the backdrop of the dark night making her pale skin almost glow. "So are we done here?"

Alarm skittered along Poppy's spine, making her blood go cold. They were just going to leave her? Forever? What happened to all those stories about friends for life and ride or die?

She had no one. It wasn't like she could call her mother and say, "Hey, Ma. I need your advice. Due to a crazy-as-fuck accident, I'm now a familiar. I have magic, Ma! But I also have a man I'm supposed to partner up with. A man I guide through life forever. Can you believe I actually had to sign a paper that said I'd do this forever? So…got any advice?"

Her mother would pass out in her corned beef and cabbage. These women and this talking cat were all she had, and she wasn't letting them go so easily.

"Done?" she squawked. "Wait. You're all just going to leave me here as though I were some unwanted newborn you're dropping off on the steps of a church?"

Nina snorted, jamming her hands into her hoodie. "Dramatic analogy, but yeah, if you wanna look at it like that. We got ya to the realm, didn't we? You got your assignment. You're not in a state of total fucked-up. There were no tears. No denial. You seem okay with your new lot in life, which, I gotta say, I admire because shit doesn't usually go down like this. You're a badder bitch than most. So what the fuck do you need us for?"

Poppy looked up at Nina, an overwhelming sense of fear washing over her in a swell of desperation. She gripped the vampire's slender hand, pulling her cool digits to her chest as she blinked away those tears Nina talked about. "I don't know!" she yelped while the unfamiliar emotion clawed at her from the inside out, but as she caught the alarmed gazes in the other women's eyes, she quieted her tone. "I don't know. I just do. I really just do…"

And that was true. She knew it.

But why did she know?

Surprisingly, Nina didn't pull away. Instead, she gripped Poppy's fingers tighter, steadying her rising panic. Nina's next words didn't betray her gruff demeanor, but she somehow knew the woman wouldn't abandon her. "Fine, Chicken-shit. We'll stay."

"Of course we will," Marty reassured, rubbing Poppy's arm with her hand. "We never abandon ship no matter how steady the captain seems. Not until we're sure you're safe and sound."

Wanda nodded her consent, too, planting her hands on her hips. "Ditto. So where are we, Calamity, and how do we help make this transition for Poppy smoother?"

With the swish of her tail and a wisp of confetti-like sparkle, a stack of papers the size of *War and Peace* appeared before crashing onto the pile of garbage with a puff of the stench of rotten sardines and stale cigarette butts.

Calamity hopped on top of it and began to pace. "Finally. Now we can really get down to business."

"What is that?" Poppy asked, sure she'd regret it the moment the words left her big mouth.

"It's your warlock's life story—all neatly logged by time and date with every single life event, important or otherwise, grades, achievements, involvements, relationships, etcetera, all documented for your reading pleasure."

Scratching her forehead, she grated a sigh. "I can't even focus long enough to read a pamphlet on birth control, how am I supposed to read all of that?"

"In order to learn all of your warlock's quirks, to really know what makes him tick, you need to do your research. So we've made things easy for you and consolidated everything into this handy tome. It's less intimidating than it looks."

Poppy eyed her skeptically, narrowing her gaze. "So you're telling me you read a stack of papers like this on Nina before you became her familiar?"

"Don't be a moron, newb. This is the half-breed we're talking about. It was like a paragraph long. You want the CliffsNotes? Never mind. I'll give them to you anyway. It read like this: Subject, Nina Statleon. Has big mouth. Thrives on threats and confrontation. Has really big mouth. The end."

"Fuck you, Calamity," Nina crowed, making Poppy snort a giggle.

"What the hell are you all doing out here?" a low, raspy voice with just the slightest hint of a Spanish accent asked.

All of the women whipped around in sync, their eyes peering into the darkness. Startled by the voice, Poppy fell into Wanda, who patted her on the back and righted her, easing the trembling of her knees.

"More to the point, who the fuck are *you* and why are you sticking your nose in our business?" Nina asked, approaching the stranger as though she were approaching enemy lines.

The man's features were hidden in the shadows of the dull streetlamp, but his size was clear. Tall and well muscled, every stitch of clothing he wore clung to his bulk like a second skin, enhancing his thick thighs and ripped arms.

The moment Nina's stance became menacing was the

moment he held up his hand and, without a word, froze her right in place. The wind that had whistled like white noise in the background suddenly stopped, as did the leaves rushing against the sidewalk in a crinkle of rustling fall goodness.

No one appeared all that surprised that Nina was instantly immobilized. So she tried to roll with her peers and behave as though a simple hand gesture freezing someone in their tracks was no big deal, but on the inside, Poppy McGuillicuddy was terrified speechless.

She'd considered lots of things while they'd waited in line at Familiar Central. Like, spells and voodoo and all manner of *Bewitched*. She'd tried to recall all the shows and books she'd ever seen or read dealing with witches and magic, but nothing quite compared to actually seeing it happen.

"I said, *who* are you?" the stranger demanded, moving around Nina's unmoving form and closer to the group, his body language rigid and tense.

"Oh, knock it the hell off with the fancy freezing spells, ya big galoot! Stop showing off and unfreeze the pain in my ass before I turn you into the prize cow at the 4-H fair," Calamity ordered, rising on her hind legs.

The man eyed them all, his icy stare enough to make Poppy visibly cringe, but Wanda kept her hands firmly planted on her shoulders in support and squeezed. "We're here. We won't let him hurt you," she whispered, and somehow, that made everything okay—even with a freezing spell.

"Do I know you?" he asked as he moved forward, eating up the sidewalk with long, purposeful strides.

As his features become more defined, her eyes went wider. The man responsible for freezing poor Nina in place was an absolute hottie. Like, brick shithouse hot, hot, hot.

The dark turtleneck and thick down vest he wore accented his even darker features. Eyes the color of a moonless night, evenly spaced and fringed heavily with thick dark lashes, assessed them all. Prominent cheekbones with a razor's edge and a hard, square jaw enhanced his full-ish lips and bracketed his long straight nose.

His skin was smooth and medium-toned with nary a blemish, putting his age at roughly thirty-five, if Poppy were to guess.

When he asked again, "Do I know you?" the hard edge to his tone said he'd known trouble before, and he was prepared to handle any that crossed his path.

"Ish," Calamity responded with a calm Poppy definitely wasn't feeling as she dropped back to her haunches and padded toward him on soft kitty feet. "Are you who I think you are?"

"*Who* do you think I am and why are you rooting around in my garbage?" he asked, locking gazes with Poppy.

His glare made her stand taller, even though she was only five feet and one-half inch, if you didn't count her six-inch platforms. Why he'd chosen her out of the pack of women to shoot his hateful stares at took her by surprise. But she squared her shoulders anyway and glared right back.

She probably looked like an idiot doing it in her torn Paul Stanley leggings, afro wig, and big clunky platform boots, but whatever. Nobody intimidated Poppy McGuillicuddy. She might be tiny, but she was damn well mighty.

Calamity sniffed the air around this delicious, if not possibly dangerous man and made a clucking noise in the back of her throat. "Yep. I think he's our guy, girls."

"Ooo, lucky Poppy!" Marty chirped, patting her on the back in approval. "Nice coup, kiddo."

Planting his hands on lean hips encased in tighter-than-tight jeans, his eyebrow rose. Just one, but it was a perfectly groomed, raven-tipped one. "Your guy?"

"Oh, stop playing coy with us, Mr. Smexy," Calamity cooed, winding her tail around his ankle and purring a thick, sultry sound in the back of her throat. "You know why we're here."

His lips thinned when he crossed his arms over his burly chest. "Explain yourself."

Calamity reached upward with her front paws, planting them on his knees and stretching as she tilted her head to look up at him. "I'm here to hand-deliver your new familiar, Sexy Pants. Make sure when the powers that be send out that survey, you remember to mention how timely I was. It counts for points toward a new travel tote. If you give me a five-star rating, it'll push me right over the top, and that tote'll be mine in no time flat."

"Ahh," he muttered, driving a wide hand through his thick, dark hair with a raspy sigh. "I should have known. You're from Familiar Central."

"Yep," Calamity declared, dropping down and dancing about on all four of her dainty paws. "So show us where to go so we can get settled and then we'll all sit down and have a nice little getting-to-know-you session. Also, if you have some tuna handy, I'd appreciate the shit out of a bowl—packed in water only, please. This has been one of the longest nights of my fekkin' life. Do you have any idea how exhausting it is to induct a familiar? Especially a newb. Jesus and a popsicle. It's more paperwork than leasing a damn car."

Marty scooped up Calamity and tucked her under her arm, sticking her other hand out to the stranger. "Introductions are in order. I'm Marty Flaherty. The bully you froze on the spot—thank you for that, by the way—is Nina Statleon. Behind me is Wanda Jefferson, and the woman clinging to Wanda as though she were the last pint of Häagen-Dazs on earth is Poppy McGuillicuddy, your new familiar."

He lifted his square chin with a dimple in it and nodded with a curt bob of his dark head. "I know who she is. Now take her and your friend here and go the hell away. I've already told Familiar Central I'm good. So, if you'll excuse me, ladies, have a good night."

And with that, he was gone.

As in, took his gorgeous self and disappeared into the ether, leaving behind only the scent of ozone and sardines.

Well, that was a fine how-do-ya-do.

CHAPTER 4

*P*oppy looked at the women, stunned, her fingers twining together to find her palms cold and clammy. "So was that what we, in my human circle, call the big dis? I think we'd better go back to Familiar Central and get in the line labeled Rejected By A Total Douche Witch, because if there's one thing he doesn't want, I'd say a familiar is on the top of the list."

Calamity rasped a sigh, moving in and out of Nina's still unmoving form. "Sometimes they're reluctant. Case in point, my half-breed. She hated my guts at first."

"And this thing you guys are in the throes of right now is called what? Mad-like? Because I'm afraid to know what hated your guts meant," Poppy wondered out loud, shifting from foot to foot.

"We're in the throes of making shit work because we have no choice *but* to make things work. I refer back to my Scottish castle hell as a point of reference. I'd rather be with these loony-toon bitches in all their perfume and mascara than with some old, crusty dude who doesn't wear any underwear beneath his musty robes."

Sure, that scenario sounded crappy, but how much crappier could it be than being hated by a hot guy with a shitty attitude—for life?

"But did the sheep like you?"

"Well, yeah. We got along pretty well. They have amazingly soft fur, too. Nothing like hunkering down with them on a cold winter's night."

"I think I'll take getting along with a herd of sheep who at least let me snuggle with them as opposed to hating my guts." Pausing, she looked at the women and asked, "Everybody who thinks Poppy should get a new witch, raise your hand." She lifted hers high above her head.

"No! Did you hear me when I told you what happens when you complain?" Calamity asked, the warning tone in her voice clear.

Poppy nodded, backing away from the group. "Yep. You said I go to the Bad Place. I don't know what the Bad Place is like, or even what they do in the Bad Place, but I'm willing to bet there's a sense of solidarity in the Bad Place because we'd all be rejects together as a big group. I'm willing to take the risk. I'm not willing to have some guy behave like an asshole to me because he doesn't want a familiar. And I don't care how hot he is."

"And he was definitely hot. And that accent? Phew, *mi corazón,*" Wanda murmured, her hand at her throat, her cheeks flushed, and it wasn't from the chilly air.

"Yeah," Marty agreed, fanning herself. "Sooo hot."

Poppy nodded as she backed even farther away, stepping off the curb. "Now that Crankypants's objectification is out of the way, I don't care if he's Benedict Cumberbatch and Idris Elba's love child. I'm out. Let's go cement my seat in the Bad Place."

"Stop!" Calamity yowled. "Don't you move, Poppy McGuillicuddy!"

Poppy's feet instantly rooted to the spot. When she tried to lift her platform boots, it was in vain. "Calamity, knock it off with the hocus-pocus and let me go!" She bent at the waist, reaching forward to attempt to lift her feet, only to watch her shadow on the pavement resemble something out of the *Matrix*.

"I'm not letting you go, Poppy!" Calamity yelled back. "Not until you agree you're going to suck it up, march your tiny ass to Mr. Sexy-Smexy's door, demand entry, and force him to bend to your will. He needs you, and it's your job!"

Then something occurred to her, something in this whirlwind of crazy she hadn't even stopped to take into consideration, and it hit her like a ton of bricks.

Everyone kept telling her what *she* had to do, but where was Calamity's accountability in all this?

Dropping her hands to her hips, she narrowed her eyes at the cat. "Says who? I didn't ask for this job. I wasn't born a familiar. I didn't inherit this title like you and the rest of your kind. You did this to me, Calamity. *You!* I was minding my own business, doing what I do, until you showed up at a party you weren't even supposed to be at, if you listen to your keeper Nina. Then you have the balls to tell me I have to sign my life away to a guy who's clearly a douchecanoe when I was given no choice in the matter to begin with! I wonder what would happen if Familiar Central knew about that? What do you suppose they'd say?"

"You're panicking," Calamity said with quiet calm, her wide eyes blinking.

Maybe she was. Maybe all that stoic bravery she'd been feeling earlier had evaporated like one's adrenaline after realizing, sure, you'd climbed the side of the mountain, but now you were dangling mid-air while you clung to a flimsy limb.

Wanda and Marty came to stand behind Calamity, but

Poppy held up her hand to stop them from interfering. She was sure they meant well but now was not the time.

"Who *wouldn't* panic when they're being asked to give up their entire life to cater to a man who obviously doesn't want to be catered to?" she asked on a screech.

"Because you had a life before this, Poppy McGuillicuddy? Please," Calamity spat. "I used my magic to dig around a little into your past. Is working temp jobs as Bo-Bo the clown at kids' parties and getting paid per pound to shovel dog poop while you mourn the fact that you're still not Broadway's next Kristin Chenoweth really a life? You're just livin' the dream, aren't you?"

Okay, so she hadn't found what she was meant to do just yet.

At thirty-four.

She'd been sure she was destined for Broadway when she'd moved to New York at nineteen. Fifteen years later, her destiny was murky and ill-defined. But scraping by the way she did had taught her to be scrappy and, above all, creative.

Though, nowhere in all the pounds of poop she'd shoveled, or the stupid cheeseburgers she'd slung had she been expected to give up everything.

But poop, though. You shovel poop for cash, Poppy... What do you go back to if you don't do this? An upset landlord who's been nothing but kind and patient with you, overdue rent on an apartment you can no longer afford, and a worn-out pooper scooper. That's what.

Calamity hopped up on a nearby garbage can, her sleek body glistening under the star-studded night. "You have the chance to have purpose here, Poppy. A reason to get up in the morning—to make a difference. A community who'll welcome you with open arms and make you one of them."

Still, she resisted. "But I have a community now. They live

49

in my apartment building as we speak." She loved the blend of seniors and empty-nesters in her building.

"But you can't afford to live there anymore, Poppy," Calamity reminded her.

She couldn't afford to live under a bridge, and she'd only be taking advantage of her landlord's kind nature if she tried talking him into letting her stay.

Calamity was right.

"How can helping a millionaire, who doesn't want to be helped, make a difference?"

"Oh, you'd be surprised. Mo' money, mo' problems and all."

That made the hair on her arms rise and internal alarm bells ring. A brief flash of suspicion made her ask, "Do you know something I don't know?"

But Calamity clucked her tongue. "I know nothing, Jon Snow. I only know you've wandered aimlessly through your twenties and thirties long enough. It's time to get you some roots."

"And what happens if I go back to Familiar Central and tell them you did this to me and I want out. Do you get in trouble?"

"Yep. But I'm not talking you out of that because I'm worried about punishment. Just ask me about the year 2006 after I crashed Tom and Katie's wedding. I can take a hit. I'm talking you out of this because I think you're in for something great if you'll just give it a chance, Poppy McGuillicuddy."

Her gut instincts had discovered a lot of things tonight, and one of them was that Calamity had no ill intentions, not a malicious bone in her tiny body. She was inherently a good soul at her core, if not mouthy just like her vampire-witch Nina.

"How do you know?"

"Call it instinct."

"You just want the frequent flyer miles so you can go to Baja and scoop Cecily," Poppy teased, her shoulders relaxing a little.

"There's that, too. Also, something of note. I can't turn you back into a human, Poppy. I made a mistake. I'll own the shit out of that if you want to go back and speak to the powers that be, but it won't change the fact that you now have magical properties. They won't let you loose with them in your possession, which is why I told you they'd send you to the Bad Place. Because anyone with magic not employed and not being used toward the greater good has to be harnessed. There are plenty of jobs available that don't entail saddling your ass to someone, too. The problem is, you're not qualified for any of them."

Somehow, that made total sense, rather like keeping a pin in a grenade. And she said as much. "That makes sense, I guess," she murmured.

"So, are we a go?" Calamity asked, her wide eyes scanning Poppy. "Because if not, I have a butt I need to warm up for the reaming I'm gonna take straight up my backend. No pressure, though."

Poppy sighed and looked to Wanda and Marty for advice, but Marty shook her head. "This is your choice to make, Poppy. If you decide to go back to Familiar Central, we'll support that decision one hundred. No one's going to make you do something you don't want to do."

Wanda nodded her head, making a basket of her hands in front of her, her sympathetic eyes capturing Poppy's. "What Marty said. No one wants you to do anything you don't want to do, Poppy. And we're definitely here for you either way."

There was that damn gut feeling again, pushing its way past her fears and insecurities. It said do this.

Roomandboardroomandboard.

Soothing herself with the notion she could always go visit her old neighbors, Poppy let her head fall back on her shoulders, following with a raspy sigh before nodding. "Okay, fine. Let's go get a warlock. But I'm warning you, if he's an asshole, I can be an asshole right back. Like a *big* asshole. Wait…" She paused and bit her lip. "That sounded wrong."

Marty and Wanda chuckled as they gathered 'round her and gave her a quick hug. "Calamity—undo this whatever so we can get our girl to her man and she can begin this new journey."

Calamity circled Marty's feet with a sigh, hitching her jaw at Frozen Nina. "Do I have to undo Nina, too? Look at all the peace and frickin' quiet since Mr. Hot Pants walloped her with his mojo. You gotta admit, it's kinda nice…"

"Do I have to make you my lunch?" Marty attempted a stern gaze, but it was clear she was fighting a smile.

"Fine, but you know I'm right," Calamity chirped, dancing around Nina and swishing her tail. A burst of color shot forth from the slender length, whooshing around Nina, making a cloud of purple dust.

Seconds later, Nina was back, stronger than ever. Instantly, she was in action, moving forward, her head swiveling from side to side. "Where the fuck did the bastard go?"

Calamity sighed in irritation before skipping toward the alleyway next to Ricardo Delassantos's house. "Never you mind, Half-Breed. Forget that and come with me. We have shit to do!"

* * *

"ROOM AND BOARD. ROOM AND BOARD," Poppy muttered as they knocked on Ricardo's door, decorated in orange and purple lights for Halloween, while he continued to ignore their knocking.

"What the hell are you babbling about?" Nina asked, leaning against the side of the building.

Poppy rolled her eyes. "I'm just keeping myself motivated. Forget it and answer me this. Why is Douchecanoe ignoring us? The lights are on, and it's not like we can't hear him," she yelled into the night for Ricardo's benefit.

Nina popped her lips and shrugged. "Dunno, but if he keeps fucking playing like we're not here, I'm going to knock down this door and beat his ass to within an inch of his life with the damn arm I rip from his ripply body."

Poppy looked up at Nina, biting the inside of her cheek as she attempted to hide her sheer terror. "Is it my job as his familiar to protect him from you?"

"Your first priority is always your warlock, no matter how dangerous," Calamity provided in a helpful tone.

Poppy gulped with a wince of fear and then she banged that much harder on the door. "Hey in there, Jerkface! Stop being such a shithead and open the damn door. It's freezing out here! Do you want to wake up to a frozen familiar in Popsicle-still-life on your doorstep tomorrow?"

Calamity tsked her with a noise from the back of her throat. "Nice way to inspire a bond between the two of you."

"You can't bond with someone who doesn't want to bond, Calamity." She paused a moment and took a deep breath. Surely he couldn't be this childish. So she banged again. "If you don't open this door, I'm going to scream!"

But the door didn't budge.

And she'd had just about enough. This day had gone on for at least an eternity. She was tired, her makeup was beginning to crack, her feet were numb from her stupid platform shoes and her ridiculous Afro wig was tangled into a big knot from her fingers worrying the plastic threads to death.

Her eyes were grainy, her nose was runny and cold, and she was suffering from realm lag, a condition Calamity told her would leave her feeling edgy and raw. The edgy part was an understatement, and while patience wasn't exactly her biggest virtue, even Jesus himself couldn't withstand this kind of blatant disregard.

So she kept her promise and screamed for all she was worth. Banging on the door one more time, she flung herself against it and began a dramatic plight. "Stop! Help! Someone help me! He's hurting me! You're hurting me! Stranger danger! Someone help! Call 9-1-1! *Helllppppp!*"

Just as she wound up, the red steel door on the side of the warehouse swung open, knocking her back into Nina.

Ricardo stuck his gorgeous head out and tilted it to the right as though they were all crazy. "Why are you yelling?" he asked, pulling a pair of earplugs from his ears.

She also noted Mr. Warlock was naked from the waist up. Her eyes warred with her brain as she fought not to gaze, wide-eyed and starry, at his smooth olive skin and the line of dark hair, running from his belly button into his tight jeans.

Her eyes narrowed as she scoffed at him, fighting the chatter of her teeth. "We've been banging on the door for at least ten minutes! What the hell were you doing in there?"

"Break-dancing. Duh." Then he grinned, all heart pounding and delicious.

Poppy was in no mood for anything, least of all his sarcasm. She held up a hand and narrowed her eyes. "If you make one sound of protest about letting us in and I end up in the Bad Place because you're a big fat dick, I'll punch you in the face. Got that? Now move out of my way!"

With that, she stomped inside his big, fancy, refurbished warehouse, her legs wobbling as she went, so much so, she had to loop her arm through Wanda's to keep from collapsing.

But as she entered the space, Poppy caught her breath. Wow. Was this what it was like to be rich?

Her eyes didn't know where to look first—to the black industrial pipes lining the walls used as sort of statement art, or the smooth gray-and-red kitchen cabinets and shiny steel countertops. The place had hints of Spanish accents in the way of a colorful vase or two and was ultra manly with clean lines, sharp edges.

Just like him.

Her mouth formed an O as she scanned the landscape, the sheer size of the warehouse. In the center of the wide room, a big couch in black leather with plump teal and red pillows called to her, invited her to sit and allow the smooth fabric to envelop her.

Every table, from the coffee table to the nightstand way at the far end of the room, was made out of some sort of recycled plumbing pipe, reclaimed wood and steel. Abstract pictures in black and silver frames hung on the walls in groups of three; their splashes of orange, red and variations of that same teal on his pillows all but bellowed his love of strong decor statements.

His bed, the one where he rested his perfect head, was as masculine as he was. The black wrought iron and thick tree limbs that made up the headboard, an odd combination in theory, somehow worked in reality. Pillows in solid shades of gray, blue and a burnt umber, stacked one in front of the other, sat on a fluffy comforter in geometric patterns of the same colors.

Poppy blinked, but Nina was the one who made the first comment. She held up her fist to Ricardo, who'd sauntered over to and back from a tall armoire to grab a T-shirt. "Dude. Rad fucking place."

He grinned again and amicably bumped her fist with his. "Thanks. You are?"

"A vampire. A vampire who will eat your face off if you ever damn well freeze me again, and if you don't start cooperating so I can go home to my kids and my husband before the end of GD eternity. Nice to meet ya."

Ricardo made an adorable pouty face. "That's sort of rash, don't you think? But in case my name hasn't already been thrown around, I'm Ricardo Delassantos, and I'm a warlock who'll zap you to the outer galaxy if you four and your cat don't go away." To back up that statement, he smiled that infuriatingly handsome smile again.

Calamity hopped up on the counter and sat back on her haunches. "Now, now, Pretty Boy. Don't be like that. Every warlock needs a familiar. It's the law. It's how we keep each other in check. You know it and I know it. Stop fighting the tide, brother."

"So why don't you tell me exactly why I need this particular familiar." He stared right through her, burning holes in her face with his glare.

With this new position of familiar, Poppy felt like some earthy, sage answer was in order, something that would make her sound like she knew what the hell she was doing.

"The universe tends to unfold as it should."

Pulling the shirt over his head, Ricardo rolled his eyes. "From the infamous *Harold and Kumar Go To White Castle*. Hardly original, Sage One."

"Look, I'm new at this, okay? I don't know a single thing about being a familiar other than I'm supposed to dole out advice and protect you. So there. Have some advice. I interpret those words to mean, the universe put me here with cranky you for a reason. I'm doubting the universe's sanity right now because you're kind of a butthead. But there it is. Take it or leave it."

His dark eyebrow rose in crystal clear condescension. "And I'm supposed to just say 'let's do this' to someone who quotes *Harold and Kumar* and dresses like Paul Stanley? Nice boots, by the way." He pointed a lean finger at her beloved platforms.

Now Poppy rolled her eyes, tapping her fingers on the steel countertop. "Good guess! And don't hide behind pretension. You knew who Harold and Kumar were, buddy. And I don't always dress like this. I was at a Halloween party when this all went down. So lay off the judgey Paul Stanley shaming and let's get this sorted out."

Rolling his tongue inside his lean cheek, Ricardo's jaw tensed and clenched, the strong muscles ticking out a rhythm. "I said I didn't want a familiar. I don't know how much clearer I can be."

Roomandboardroomandboard, Poppy.

Lifting her shoulders in a sigh, Poppy clucked her tongue and decided it was sink-or-swim time. If she was supposed to be his guide, she had to show him how stupid he was for turning her away. That she was an asset to him. Or at least make him believe she was—even if she didn't believe it herself.

So she put her acting hat on, the one she wore to all her Broadway auditions, and stared him right in his gorgeous eyes. "I guess that's your tough shit then. Because I'm not going anywhere. So suck it."

Taking a step back, he glared at them—but mostly he glared at Poppy. "I said, I don't want nor do I need a familiar. Now get out of my house!" he shouted, lifting his wide hand.

And that was when Poppy lifted her hand, too. She wasn't sure why she did it. In that flash of a moment, she knew it wasn't because she was afraid Ricardo would strike her. Not at all. Yet, she felt as though she needed to prevent something, and throwing up her hand was her best defense.

Turned out, she blew something up instead.

Whoops.

CHAPTER 5

*A*s the black and silver industrial hanging lights over the island countertop sparked and sputtered before exploding and crashing to the ground, Nina was the first to yell, "Incoming!" diving for Poppy in an effort to protect her from the spray of electricity.

Instead of connecting with Poppy, the vampire crashed into Ricardo, who'd surprisingly taken a lunge to knock her out of the way, too, spewing a string of expletives in Spanish. As the two smashed into each other, they fell to the floor with grunts, tangled limbs and some pretty foul language.

Nina was the first to squirm her way out of their clench, giving Ricardo a shove before she rose and shrugged off their fall.

"Holy house afire!" Calamity howled when the dust had settled, hopping from the floor where she'd saved her hide from injury and back up to the countertop where the fallen lights crackled and spat. "*You* did that, Poppy!"

She blinked, looking up at the lights and then back to the counter. "Did what?"

Though, she wasn't sure her question rang true. She knew

she'd done *something*. She felt the tingle, the slither of electricity shooting from her hand. She'd shuddered as it had coursed through her body in a split-second of heat and sizzle.

"You connected your magic to Mr. Smexy's and created an explosion! Holy corn fritters!"

As Ricardo rose, too, grappling with untangling himself from Poppy's platforms Marty brushed some Sheetrock from Nina's hair and Wanda instantly began brushing the chunks of debris and metal into a neat pile.

"Explain, Calamity," Marty demanded, ignoring Nina's dismissive hands shooing her away. "How does one connect magic and what does that mean in the long run?"

"Don't you feel it, Rickster? Don't lie and say you don't, either. You smell it, too, don't you?" Calamity gave the air a purposeful sniff. "You're a warlock, and while you have magic, it's weaker than a witch's, but still capable enough to do party tricks like freezing Nina in her tracks, whisking someone away, etcetera. Except when you mix it with someone else's. That's when shit gets real! When Poppy held up her hand to stop you from shipping us off to parts unknown—"

"Siberia," Rick interrupted, his eyes intense, his posture rigid. "I was thinking the wilds of Siberia."

"Yeah, yeah," Calamity dismissed, stalking to where he stood with his lean hip pressed against the counter and his bulky arms crossed over his chest. "But you know what I say is true. You felt it. I saw the look on your face just before the lights blew up. When your magic connected with Poppy's, it was total bazinga!"

Scrunching her eyes shut, she did it partially to block out Ricardo's near perfect Photoshopped body, but also because she'd developed quite a headache. "So let me get this straight. I have magic, too?"

How had magic of her own come into this deal? She didn't want magic. She couldn't even be trusted to renew her driver's license, how could she be trusted with something as dangerous as magic?

"You do!" Calamity all but screeched. "I had no idea it would be this powerful just yet, but your magic plus Crabby Patty's magic equals uber magic. Which means you two are better together than apart. If it were ever needed—like, say we had an uprising in the realm—you guys would be like Murtaugh and Riggs together. Like Tommy Lee Jones and Will Smith in *Men In Black*! Hell, you might even rival Thelma and Louise!"

Uprising? Was that a common occurrence in the realm? She didn't want any part of uprisings. She was just here for the room and board.

"What if I told you I don't want uber magic?" Rick asked, strolling to a pantry, where he pulled a dustpan and broom out.

Calamity paced the length of the counter, hopping gracefully over the crushed lights. "Don't be a stupidhead. Everyone wants uber magic, Ricky baby."

If Ricky baby's jaw could clench any tighter, his perfect, shiny white teeth would crack. "I'm not everyone. I don't know if Familiar Central told you, but I like blending with humans in the human world. My clients are human. With an exception or two, most of my employees are human. I live in a primarily human world. I don't use my magic often, which could be why it was so strong just then, and that's all there is to it."

"The. Hell!" Calamity barked, the hair on her spine rising. "I felt the vibe, buddy. It was much more than storing up your magic points and you know it."

Rick shook his head. "That doesn't change the fact that I don't want a familiar. I don't need a familiar any more than I need a hemorrhoid," he spat, pushing the broom into the pile on the floor with an agitated sweep of its bristles.

You know, she'd had enough damn rejection for one night. She was like a total of four hours into this familiar thing and already she'd been dumped. Which meant, unless good old Gladys had another available witch or warlock on hand, she had to go to the Bad Place.

Sure, she'd been all mouth and threats earlier when she'd said she'd rather go to the Bad Place than be stuck for an eternity with Ricky baby. But she'd been hasty. The Bad Place was called the Bad Place for a reason.

With that realization, she squared her shoulders, yanking her itchy wig off and throwing it down on the ground like some bizarre gauntlet. "You know what, Ricardo—"

"I can't wait till you tell me what—er, what's your name again? Peppy?" he interrupted, his eyes narrowing, his words swimming in sarcasm.

She stomped toward him, her calves aching more in her platform boots than even when she'd been in the chorus of *Guys and Dolls,* and she'd had to wear three-inch heels.

Her breathing became ragged as desperation and fear began to set in. If she was going to the Bad Place, she wasn't going without an all-out brawl.

"It's Poppy. Poppy McGuillicuddy. M to the C to the Guill-i-cudd-E, and you'd damn well better get used to saying my name because I'm not going anywhere, buddy. If I don't hook up with you and your shitty attitude, I end up in the Bad Place. I'm sure that's just fine for somebody like you, who has millions of dollars to grease the palms of whoever's in charge of your kooky world in order to prevent you from doing things you don't want to do. *But I do not.* In fact, I'm damn well broke, and there will be absolutely no icing my hard luck cake by shipping me off to the Bad Place. Now, shut up and suck it up until you, with all your big, big brains and piles of money, can find me something better. Got that, *Ricky baby?*"

All motion ceased, including Rick's sweeping. Each of the women's mouths fell open. Except, of course, Nina's. She slapped Poppy on the back in approval, jolting her forward with the force of the gesture. "Way to get your own, kiddo. I remain fucking impressed."

Heaving a breath, Poppy moved in closer to Ricardo. Likely a mistake because he smelled like sheer heaven, but whatever.

Zeroing in on his face, her nostrils flared. "Now, where's my room and where do you keep the coffee in this shiny steel cage—because I need it in the morning. And I swear to God, if I hear one more protest from you, Ricardo Delassantos, I'm going to wrap my fingers around your neck and choke you out!"

"Ooo, violence as a vehicle to make a point. Jesus Christ, I like you, Poppy M to the C to the Guill-i-cudd-E," Nina crowed, wrapping an arm around her neck and ruffling the top of her head with her knuckles.

Rick set the broom against the fridge and put his hands on his hips and shook his head in disgust. *"Madre mia.* The Bad Place, huh? They still threaten with that? Clearly, it's effective."

But Poppy was in no mood to dick with him. "My room, please. *Now,*" she snarled, wiping the bead of spit lodged at the corner of her mouth.

Grabbing a set of keys from a hook hanging inside the pantry door, he lobbed them to her. "Out back—there's an adjoining shed. It's all yours."

"A shed?" Marty gasped. "No, no, no. This isn't how you treat one of yours. Poppy's not living in a shed."

Wanda backed up that statement by pulling Poppy close to her side, her lips turning thin. *"A shed?* Oh, no sir," she said with deadly calm. "There'll be no treating our girl here like she's the hired help. In fact, is this how you treat the hired help? It's appalling, dehumanizing—and I won't stand for it!"

Nina bobbed her head, gripping Poppy's shoulder. "Yeah. I'm with Blondie. No fucking way I'm leaving the feisty kid here in some GD shitass shed. It's cold, she's been through enough, and you're an asshole. In case you wondered."

Wagging his index finger, Rick ignored their protests and made his way to the far window at the other end of the warehouse, pointing to the inky-black backyard. "It's not what you think." As they followed him, he flipped on a floodlight, casting a bright glare over the "shed."

Everyone, even Poppy, gasped at once as they all huddled together and looked out the window.

Calamity scurried to a plaid armchair and jumped up on the back of the cushiony surface. "Whaaat? What's happening?"

But then she quieted, too, but only after she sighed an, "Ahhh."

Rick was right. It wasn't what they'd thought when he'd said shed. This was no shed as in garden shed-shed. This was a damn Victorian palace in miniature form. From the adorable white gingerbread trim above the doors and along the tiny white porch with spindled railings, to the barn-red siding and square, crosshatched windows, it was precious.

The mini house sat amidst mums in every color, in pots of all shades, sizes and shapes, and also sprouting from the ground, presenting a veritable sea of orange, burgundy, yellow and dark pink. There were bushes in all the deep hues of fall, popping up between the blossoming flowers, their leaves beginning to turn with the onset of fall.

A white stone path to the front door was lined with white lantern lights, swinging in the cold breeze, completing a picturesque setting she'd only ever dared dream.

"That's mine?" Poppy finally managed to squeak.

"Until I can *grease a palm* or two, yeah," he said, his tone almost teasing. "Everything you need is there. Towels, fresh linens, food, coffee, a big cushy bed. So, if you ladies don't mind, and if we're done with asshole orientation for the day, it's late. Maybe you could go settle in, and we'll touch base tomorrow morning."

Which meant get the hell out.

Fine. She could do that. She needed a shower and a stiff drink. But she'd settle for a shower and a hot cup of cocoa. Jingling the keys under his nose, Poppy nodded. "Ladies, let's go check out my new, probably not-forever home."

Turning on her heel, she began to make her way across the wide room, planning to make a big exit like she'd just dropped the mic. But as was her MO, and maybe one of the reasons she wasn't Broadway's biggest hit, she stumbled in her platforms and tripped over Rick's big, clunky shoes that sat by the door.

His laughter as she yanked the door open rankled right down to the tips of her cold, numb toes.

* * *

SON OF A BITCH.

Pacing the length of his kitchen floor, Rick, kicked at the dust left by the gaping hole in his ceiling with an angry foot.

He did not want a new damn familiar.

He'd had a familiar. That lifelong friend, that trusted confidant, that almost-like-a-father-to-him familiar.

The familiar who had up and left him. Literally abandoned him a year ago, leaving everything he owned behind.

Everything that was, in fact, all still in what they'd both once jokingly called the very shed he'd sent Poppy and the group of women to settle into. But who needed everything when you could buy *more* everything? If what Rick suspected was true, Yash didn't need his things from the shed.

The shed was a sore spot for him now. Yash had turned that shed into his solace. His sanctuary, a place he could seek respite when the weight of a being familiar and the world became too much. And then he'd jumped ship after twenty-five years.

No explanation. No note. No phone call. No whispers from the other side about his whereabouts. Yash had just been gone, and he'd left Rick frantic and worried sick.

But that wasn't all he'd left Rick with. He'd also left his business in ashes. Well, almost. Somehow, Yash had siphoned millions from his development company. Rick had found the proof on a thumb drive in the shed. All just out there for anyone to find.

Likely, he'd used his magic to find the passwords he'd needed, conjured a spell dripping with greed, and then he'd stolen away like some thief in the night. But what bothered Rick the most was the fact that Yash hadn't taken any pains to hide his deception. Not a one.

Yash was one of the smartest men Rick knew, and he'd desperately wanted to believe the theory his partner and longtime friend, Avis Mackland, spouted as a way to explain Yash's one-eighty, which was that something had happened and his familiar had experienced an event so horrible, he couldn't share. Avid had said time and again he didn't believe Yash was a crook. Yet, it was a theory Rick still couldn't swallow.

Stealing those millions of dollars had nothing to do with some crisis Yash had encountered in his life—something he couldn't tell anyone else—no matter how strong a case Avis pleaded in his favor.

Thankfully, all their assets weren't wrapped up in the development company he shared with Avis, and they'd managed to save their asses with their own personal capital, but it'd been one rough year.

One they were finally digging themselves out from. The black hole they'd been in had a light at the end of the tunnel, and due to Avis's business savvy and numerous connections, they were once more seeing a profit. But it was small and still in the process.

But goddammit, Yash had really ripped them a new asshole. It hadn't only been the two of them who'd suffered, but their employees, their employees' families.

And he still didn't understand it. There'd never been a single sign Yash was even a little shady, let alone capable of stealing millions from him. In fact, he'd spent a lot of Rick's childhood poo-pooing money as the root of all evil, and, instead, taught him the ways of kindness and about the simple joys drawn from the earth and sky.

When he'd surprised Yash with the shed, he'd at first been too humble to accept it because it had cost more than the earth, as his familiar had put it.

And that total betrayal of life lessons damn well still smarted. So no way was he exposing himself and all his regained assets to a new familiar just so he could end up screwed over again.

Not even if she *was* cute. And Poppy M to the C to the Guill-i-cudd-E was definitely cute.

It was harder to tell *how* cute she was with all that KISS makeup on, but when she'd yanked her wig off and thrown it down on the floor, and her chocolate-colored hair had spilled down over her shoulders to the middle of her back like some wave of silk, he'd decided she was as cute as he'd first feared when they'd met outside his place.

She had a great ass, too, and he hated himself for noticing that. While she was pretty petite to his six-three, her limbs were long and slender, and her torso, tucked into that hysterical shirt with all the chest hair, was swan-like.

Even in those ridiculous platform boots, she'd literally floated across his house with measured, soft steps, her thigh muscles flexing as she walked. Her eyes were almond shaped, a deep misty blue, fringed with thick lashes, and they'd flashed all sorts of levels of emotions while she'd given him hell.

He wouldn't deny he liked her mouth, either, cute as a bow-shaped button when she'd spewed profanities and ordered him around. He wondered if her lips were as soft as her skin.

When Poppy pushed past him, storming her way into his house, her hand had brushed his chest, leaving behind a warm tingle of awareness he was not about to let get any further into his head.

He didn't know if familiars getting involved with their assignments was off-limits, but he wasn't about to find out.

What he *was* about to do was call up Familiar Central and bitch some poor soul out. How Poppy didn't know there was no such thing as "greasing a palm" in the white witch world confused him. She should know the rules of the realm at her age.

Which made him wonder how old she was.

And then he shook his head, staring off into the backyard where the lights from the shed shone bright. It didn't matter.

Either way, a couple of bucks as a bribe would never change anyone's mind in the realm. It didn't work like that. When you were assigned a familiar, the powers that be considered it your destiny. No exchange of money could change that.

But if money wasn't the answer, he'd find another one, because no way was he getting saddled with a smart-mouthed, platform-boot-wearing familiar.

No matter how damn cute.

He'd given his complete trust once before—he'd have given his own life in exchange for Yash's.

He was never going to invest in someone that deeply again.

Not ever.

* * *

"DAMN, GIRL. LOOK AT YOU!" Calamity squealed. "Jesus, you hit the mothereffin' warlock jackpot, Poppy! Do you have any idea how fortunate you are to get this kind of gig first time around? It's like someone in the universe didn't expect you to pay your dues like the rest of us."

"Pay my dues?" Poppy asked, her mouth still agape.

"Yeah. Usually a first timer gets some old witch or warlock from back in the day. You know, warts, gnarled fingers, a smoker's cough, Merlin-wannabes galore, at least two centuries old. It's a test of your tenacity, your gumption. Most of us have at least one in our past. But not only did you get a sweet piece of ass, you got a *rich* sweet piece of ass with a place that's all yours. Shit, dude, you don't know the half of how you lucked out."

Okay, so even she had to admit the "shed" was pretty great—every inch of it was magnificent. The overstuffed white couch, the pearl and oyster-white colored pillows lining it, the white brick fireplace, the barn wood and wrought iron coffee table, the old sky-blue milk jugs in variegated heights, housing stems of willow trees placed strategically in a brick-faced arched cutout in the wall.

The compact kitchen, with its gleaming antique white cabinets and polished onyx-and-white-veined granite counters. The bleached white wood floors throughout the entire space. The strange, shimmering rocks in various muted colors placed all around the tiny abode.

The bedroom and its white, puffy comforter with a lavender and gray floral coverlet, a connecting bathroom with an oval tub, and more gauzy shower curtain material flowing to the floor than a production of Cinderella.

Yeah. Yeah. Yeah. The tiny house was great. But the master of the tiny house was a dick. How was she supposed to live with a dick for the rest of her eternity?

Dragging a finger over one of the pale green rocks sitting on a round end table, Poppy shivered. "Calamity? I have a question. What happens if you're not compatible with your warlock? Like, maybe I won't go to the Bad Place if we just cite incompatibility, right? It has to have happened."

The feline strode across the hearth of the fireplace, finally settling in a corner. "Oh, it's happened, but it's never ended up good. We make it work no matter what. If you can't make it work, what kind of peacemaker and advisor are you?"

So much for that idea. "God, that's so extreme. Why is everything so damn black and white? It's either suck it or go to the Bad Place. Shut up or go to the Bad Place."

Wanda grabbed her hand, redirecting her attention, pulling Poppy to her side, the warmth of her skin heating up her cold fingers. "Let's not think about the Bad Place. Let's instead focus on this amazing little house. It's beautiful, don't you think?"

Poppy nodded with a long sigh. "It's the nicest place I've ever lived since I left home." Even though it didn't hold any of her most treasured things, it was still beautiful.

Wanda peered into her eyes. "But?"

"But I think it's obvious, don't you?"

"You mean Ricardo's reluctance about your arrival?"

She snorted. "I'm sorry, did you say his all-out hatred of

my arrival?" He wanted a familiar as much as Poppy wanted a root canal.

Wanda giggled, rubbing Poppy's hand with reassuring strokes. "Oh, honey, he's just in shock. He'll get past it."

"You think?" If he tried to trade her in, she was toast.

"I dunno," Nina said from her place on the couch, where she'd sunk into a corner, tucking a pillow behind her head and latching her fingers behind her dark nest of hair. "I'm with the kid on this. He's kind of a dick. I was this close to ripping his head off his damn shoulders for being such a dick."

Wanda's lips thinned, her eyes narrowing in Nina's direction. "You're always this close to ripping someone's head off their shoulders. Maybe he just needs to sleep on it, Nina. We *did* just show up and blindside him. Don't be such a Negative Nellie, for the love of Pete. We're here to support, not tear down."

Nina flicked her fingers in the air. "Just because you put a positive spin on it doesn't make it the fucking reality, Pollyanna."

Nina's realism rankled her. Under normal circumstances, she'd look this problem straight in the eye and agree. She was, after all, pretty used to rejection after at least a thousand auditions in her pursuit to become a star on Broadway. But with Nina's skepticism, she realized she needed this more than she was comfortable admitting.

Marty came out of the kitchen holding a cup of cocoa, steam from the rich chocolate rising from the thick white mug. She waved it under Poppy's nose and smiled warmly. "I say we ignore Nina like we always do and we *all* sleep on it. Now drink this and grab a shower, and then it's lights out. Everything's clearer after a good night's sleep. Okay?"

Taking the cocoa, she let Marty lead her into the tiny, glossy kitchen, through the bedroom and to the connecting bathroom. Flipping the taps of the shower to warm the water, she sat Poppy on the toilet seat and grabbed some fluffy white towels.

A thought occurred to Poppy then, one that terrified her.

She couldn't do this alone.

Not yet, anyway. She didn't know how to do any of this. The very thought made her literally tremble.

Grabbing Marty's arm, she looked up into her beautiful eyes, so warm and kind. "Will you guys come back tomorrow?"

Marty grabbed her chin and squeezed with a grin. "We'll do better than that. We'll stay here with you. When you wake up, we'll be right out there. Don't worry, honey. You're not alone. Not until you're ready. Promise. Okay?"

Shuddering a breath, she nodded as the steam in the bathroom rose, soothing her frazzled nerves. "Thank you," she whispered in relief.

Whoever these people were, wherever they'd come from, Poppy was grateful. She'd been alone in New York a long time, and she'd never needed anyone. She'd never asked for help from her parents when she was flat-ass broke. She'd never resorted to bank loans or credit cards. She'd managed her fears alone because no one was going to see Poppy McGuillicuddy scared witless.

She'd left home with something to prove to her parents, who'd wanted her to go to college and get a degree, and even if she hadn't fulfilled her dreams, she'd gotten by. She knew she'd disappointed them; each year wrought a visit during which they ended up leaving after giving her a long lecture about how dismal her future was destined to turn out if she didn't get a "real" job.

And she let them leave with a smile on her face and words filled with dogged determination, each year that passed becoming more defensively determined than ever to convince them she was going to break out.

But they'd been right. She was thirty-four. She wasn't a Broadway star. She had no insurance. No 401K. And still, she'd refused to face the truth.

But this one time, this one time when her fears wouldn't be pacified by her fierce independence, she was grateful to not have to put on a brave front.

Tomorrow would be much better.

She was counting on it.

Hear that, universe? I'm talkin' to you!

CHAPTER 6

*O*h, fine. Tomorrow wasn't any better than the day before.

The only difference being, she no longer had a greasy face full of Paul Stanley makeup and her hair was washed.

The rest of it just sucked.

As morning had dawned, the crisp scent of fall in the air, the sun playing peek-a-boo through gray clouds outlined with purple and deep blue against the backdrop of autumn trees, they'd trudged the small distance to Rick's house.

As promised, the women and Calamity had stayed the night; two of them sprawled on the small couch, with Nina in an armchair. While they'd had a little sleep, they all looked fresh as daisies.

Even Nina—who, according to Calamity, didn't need as much sleep during the day now that she was half witch as she once had when she was full vampire—was as beautiful as she'd been the night before in dim lighting.

She was also just as grumpy because she needed blood—a notion Poppy couldn't linger too long on for fear of freaking out and making herself appear weak.

When Poppy had gasped at the thought, Calamity assured her it was synthetic and easily conjured by a spell. Which made all of this very, very real. She really was in the company of werewolves and vampires and last night was not just a bad dream.

She herself had risen to find her new familiar-in-arms tucked against her side, snuggled up to her hip and purring softly, a soothing sound. As her eyes had opened and she'd adjusted to the streaky gray of a new day, she'd fought the intense need to run back to her apartment and hide under the crocheted blanket her grandmother had sent with her when she'd left for New York all those years ago.

Poppy had been right on the money to want to hide, because Rick was still as reluctant today, if not more so than he'd been last night.

They were all standing around his kitchen island, almost the exact position and setting as last night—well, except for the gaping holes in the ceiling—and he was still singing the same worn-out tune.

Yes, we'll have no familiars today!

Swirling his coffee in his cup, his tanned fingers gripping the mug, Rick shook his freshly showered dark head. "Already told you. I don't need a familiar. Now you can stay in the shed for as long as you like, until I get in touch with Familiar Central and fix this, but that's as far as this goes."

"Dick," Nina muttered under her breath, crossing her arms over her chest. Wanda and Marty glared at him, too, while Calamity hissed, sharing her disapproval by hacking up a hairball in the center of his gleaming kitchen floor.

Somehow, Poppy had expected his attitude would be just a smidge better today than it had been yesterday. That maybe Wanda's advice about a good night's sleep really was all Rick needed to rethink ditching her.

But as he glared at her over his mug of morning coffee, his dark eyes and even darker eyebrows making that frowny face of displeasure, out of the blue, she knew the right thing to do was convince him he needed her. *Make* him like her.

She'd done it dozens of times and managed to wheedle her way into the chorus line of one play or another. She'd done it this last time on the road show from hell with the director from hell who'd stolen the production's money on their last tour.

Why couldn't she do it now? Despite the fact that director after director had told her she couldn't act if the spirit of Meryl Streep possessed her, she'd never listened.

She'd kept right on taking classes, practicing, and taking more classes. She knew a thing or two about improv. If it kept her out of the Bad Place, she was all systems go.

Grabbing the bulk of her hair, Poppy swung it over her shoulder and braided it, then threw it behind her like a gladiator going into battle.

Now that was a good thought. *Pretend you're Russell Crowe, Poppy. Play the part like you've played a million other parts in the mirror of your bathroom. Be the gladiator.*

Hands on hips, she squared her shoulders and affected a confident gaze. "So I have a proposition, Ricardo. Mind if I toss if out to you?"

Shoving his hand in the pocket of his crisp black trousers, he sighed, the rumbly sound emitting from his throat raspy and sexy even in agitation. "Rick. I prefer Rick."

Which totally rhymes with dick... Clearing her throat, Poppy considered her words as she shoved her own hands inside the pockets of her jacket. "Okay, Rick. Listen, what if you just take me on a ride-along? Just a test ride? Maybe I might prove more valuable than you think. You don't know, right? I might not look like it, but maybe I have all the answers right upstairs here in my brain. Maybe I just might be an asset to you. But all I ask, before you complain to HR or whomever it is you tattle to in the realm when you don't like your familiar, is that you at least give me a chance."

He looked at his phone, scrolling through something he made appear incredibly important. "It isn't that I don't like you, Miss McGuillicuddy. I don't know you enough to decide one way or the other. I just don't want or need a familiar."

"That's not what the realm says," Calamity bristled.

But Poppy held up a hand to thwart an argument. "Right. Potato-potahto. Forget the realm's rules and all that nonsense. Are you going to give me a chance or not?"

"Define 'giving you a chance' in terms of time."

Licking her dry lips, Poppy lifted her chin. "Give me ten days. If I haven't proven my worth to you by then, I'll personally hand myself over to the Bad Place, and you won't have to do a thing. I won't fight you on it, and you won't have to deal with the powers that be labeling you difficult—which you totally are. But that's beside the point. If you're going into this determined to ditch me anyway, what do you have to lose but ten days of your time? You prove to HR you at least tried. I leave willingly. This way, there's no muss, no fuss." She swiped her hands together in a gesture of *no fuss*.

But Rick's head popped up as he moved closer to her, the scent of his delicious cologne wafting under her nose. "Ten days?"

His tone suggested she'd asked for forever, but she held her ground. In her mostly broke years in New York, she'd also learned to negotiate all sorts of things from free meals at the various waitressing jobs she'd had in order to have enough money to pay the electric bill or by walking her neighbor's dogs in exchange for subway money.

Planting a hand on his counter, Poppy slapped the shiny steel. "Yep. Ten. Deal?"

Rick frowned, the lines in his forehead deepening. "I'll give you three."

"Aw, c'mon. Walk on the edge a little. Three's not long enough to prove my worth. The universe unfolding takes at least four," she teased, giving him the grin she reserved for the kind of part requiring she be eternally optimistic and sunshiney—the grin that also best showcased her dimples.

Lifting his chin, his eyes lit up. Somebody liked to negotiate. She saw it in the gleam of his eyes.

"Okay, four days."

"Eight," she countered. "Less than ten but more than four. And I'll make you Rose McGuillicuddy's famous corned beef and cabbage as a bonus."

"I'd rather eat goat eyeballs than cabbage."

Her eyes went wide as she fought a gag. "Is that a thing among witches and warlocks?"

He nodded, but Poppy could see he was fighting a grin. "But I do like corned beef. And seven days. One week. That's my final offer. Take it or leave it. And you have to agree to stay out of my hair. Observe only. It's a really busy week— we're closing on a new development deal, and I'm jam-packed with last-minute details."

Relief flooded her veins in a sweet rush. "Deal." She held out her hand, which he promptly ignored as he made his way to the door, grabbing a light jacket from a hook and pushing his bulky arms into the sleeves.

As Rick grabbed the door handle, he pivoted on his heel and asked, "Well? Are you coming?"

Poppy stepped into high gear, slapping a smile on her face. "I'm there. Let's go familiaring."

"Not without us," Nina said, pushing her way past Poppy to get between her and Rick. "If he's gonna be a dick, he's gonna be a dick with us there to have your back."

Rick's chin went rigid. "The deal didn't include the three of you and the cat."

But Nina leered at him, flashing her fangs. "And now it does, *Rick*. Consider that shit amended. Like it or I eat your face off."

"Nina!" Wanda gasped, gripping her friend's arm in admonishment.

But Rick nodded after he'd muttered something unintelligible in Spanish, almost as though he admired the vampire's protective gesture. "Save your incisors for more important things. You're welcome to come along."

With that, he blew out the door and down the small path, heading to a red van labeled ARMD Development Corp in thick white and black lettering.

Ah. This must be how Rick made his money. Developing things. She didn't know much about developers or what he was specifically into developing, and mostly she didn't care. What she *did* care about was hanging on to this gig.

So she climbed into the wide side door and dropped into a seat between Wanda and Marty. Nina took shotgun, her sunglasses firmly on her nose as Marty passed her some sunscreen to cover her pale skin.

As Calamity hopped into her lap and settled against her, Poppy took deep breaths.

She could do this.

She would do this.

* * *

SHE'D BEGUN to nod off while they'd fought early morning traffic, her head falling to Wanda's shoulder, drool forming at the corner of her mouth. The stop they came to was abrupt and sharp, jolting her awake.

Wanda reached for her hand and squeezed it. "Wake up, Sleepyhead. We've arrived somewhere. Though Mr. Strong and Silent hasn't offered us an ounce of information about where," she drawled, her words full of sarcasm.

With a yawn, her eyes opened in increments, the scent of Polish sausage and sauerkraut drifting past her nose. Familiar scents, scents she'd become accustomed to since she'd moved to New York.

And that was when she caught a glimpse of her surroundings and realized she knew exactly where they were.

Why were they parked in front of her apartment building?

The old, faded brick structure, crumbling in some areas, was well worn, but deeply loved by all its residents. The windows, square and unusually tall, sparkled in the gold and gray of the day, each sporting a flower box her landlord's father had insisted on installing and which remained even now, some forty years later.

The garden just beyond the black iron gates and to the left of the double front doors had been lovingly planted and tended on rotation by her and the other residents. She loved the opaque blue gazing ball in the center, especially at this time of year with all the mums in bloom. Spiral bonsais made a small maze that led to a bench, where she often sat with one neighbor or another when she was between jobs.

But that wasn't the best part of this apartment building by a long shot. What had intrigued Poppy from the get-go was the spire peak on the roof. Carved from stone, its swirling pattern and ornate ball topper with some sort of fancy symbols had enchanted her. The building also sported four matching square stones in the lobby with the same design.

The elaborate pieces, clearly made to match the spire, sat on thick pillars, bracketing the front doors and the elevators.

She jokingly rubbed them for good luck every time she left for an audition

The spire undoubtedly looked ridiculously out of place and too grand on such a quaint building, but when she saw it after a long day, it let her know she was home. She'd always meant to ask about how the spire had come to be, but in her quest to become Broadway's hottest ticket, she'd never taken the time.

Rick's deep dark eyes met hers in the rearview mirror. "Ladies, we've arrived. I'll trust you can find something to do. It's going to take me at least an hour here at this site, so maybe grab some breakfast at the diner. They have the best omelets in the city," he coaxed.

"Well, if Rick says they're the best, who are we to fucking question it? Rick knows everything, don't'cha, Rick?" Nina asked sarcastically, punching his upper arm.

If Rick had been nicer to her in the beginning, she'd owe him saint status for not throttling Nina by now. She'd taken outright jabs at him without hesitation since they'd left his house, and the foreseeable future didn't look jab free for him either.

Poppy reached forward and gripped Rick's shoulder, preventing him from climbing from the van. For some odd reason, one she didn't understand at all, but one she knew she needed to trust, she didn't tell him this was where she lived.

Not yet anyway. Though it would be aces to grab some clothes and personal items and find out how to reach her landlord in order to hopefully arrange to make payments on the rent she owed.

"Why are we here again? I mean, I'm just asking in an effort to better understand what you do."

Turning to gaze at her, his eyes less icy than earlier this morning, he said, "I'm doing my job," before sliding out of the van.

On impulse, she climbed over the driver's seat, knocking Nina in the head with her platform boot.

"Watch it!" she yelped, swatting at the heel of her boot.

"Wait!" Marty tugged the length of her hair. "You want us to come with?"

Poppy offered a quick apology to Nina before she shook her head. "I think I need to handle this alone. But stay close?"

"Always," Wanda murmured, tucking her purse under her breasts and looking out at the children playing on the swing set in the park.

Hopping out with a clunk of her boots to the concrete, she ran after Rick to catch up to him, hoping none of her neighbors saw her.

Making a grab for his arm, she tried not to think about the ripple of his muscle beneath her fingertips or the oddly pleasant thrill she got when she touched him.

She managed to thwart him beneath one of the old oak trees bracketing the entryway just outside the black iron gates to her home, noting the gold and burnt orange colors of the leaves made his dark presence even sexier.

God. She had to stop thinking of him as sexy. She was his advisor, not his Sugar Mama.

Taking a deep breath, she fought the appeal of his cologne and the olive tones to his perfect skin. "Tell me about your job. I mean, in an effort to help me show you what a rad familiar I can be. Let's get to know each other. Okay?"

Standing tall, his reluctance clear, he loomed over her, even with her in platform boots. "I told you about my job."

She shook her head as the wind picked up, pushing her hair into her face. "No. You told me your job's title. What does one do when they develop? Develop can mean lots of things. Software, buildings, concepts."

"I buy things and develop them."

She let her shoulders sag and made a pouty face, stuffing her cold hands into her pockets. "Aw, c'mon, Ricky baby. Help a girl out here. That's so vague. Like, for instance, if you asked me what kind of an actress I am, I'd tell you my specialties are improvisational with a little method thrown in. Also, I can dance. Ballet, tap, ballroom, but my true calling is contemporary. Oh! And I sing. Er, mostly karaoke."

Now Rick almost smiled, further making her cheeks warm. "You're an actress? Have I seen you in something?"

"Hah! Not likely. Unless you saw my commercial for Red's Rides Used Cars. It was local. You know, 'Come to Red's and save some bread!' and then because Red turned into a fan, mostly because I was cheap and I'd wear the costume, I did a commercial for his brother Hank's sister dealership, too. Maybe you recognize 'Let Hank fill your tank!' Buy a used car, get a free tank of gas!'"

Her eyes momentarily fell to the ground to hide her shame. She'd been in dire straights at the time, and while most of the acting community would frown upon stooping to a cheesy local commercial, it had paid her rent for four months.

There was nothing cheesy about cash when you didn't have any. Except until you had to reveal to some rich guy what you'd done for a little cash.

But Rick's face was blank. "Can't say I've heard of it. Doesn't mean a thing though. I don't watch much TV. I don't have a lot of extra time."

Poppy shrugged with a self-conscious smile. "Me neither. Mostly because I can't afford a cable bill, but I probably would have hit the fast-forward on my remote even if I did. I was awful. Plus, I wore Daisy Dukes. Anyone with chicken legs like mine should never wear Daisy Dukes."

As the words spilled out of her mouth, she reflected upon how pathetic they made her sound. No. In her almost-mid-thirties, she even didn't own a television. She'd hocked it in order to pay her dry cleaning bill. Sometimes she didn't even have electricity, but she did have heart, and she could still fit into the Daisy Dukes.

Rick's posture loosened a bit as his eyes scanned her legs, still in her Paul Stanley costume, before returning to her face, one eyebrow raised. "Daisy Dukes, huh?"

"Probably one of my more embarrassing moments. So anyway, enough about me and my sad television commercial career. As the warlock, you're the important person in this relationship. This is all about you. So, explain the title developer and why you're at this particular place today. But before you do, what do the initials ARMD on the side of your van mean?"

"First, it's not all about me. In fact, my old—" He shook his head, as though he were clearing cobwebs. "This isn't just about me, Poppy. That makes it sound like I'm some kind of entitled royalty. Which is hardly the case. I was poor once, too, and a familiar-warlock relationship is a team effort. Anyway, the initials are a combination of my name and Avis Mackland. Avis is my partner. You know the story. Old college buddies with a dream."

Her stomach turned just a little. She didn't know a lot about developers, other than they usually bought up properties and turned them into high rises. Which didn't bode well for her little apartment building—a building that had somehow escaped the typical ruin you saw in a place so affordable.

She'd lucked out when an old friend from acting class had nabbed a big part on a soap opera and moved to L.A., offering her lease to Poppy. Back in the day, while she hadn't been rolling in dough, she'd at least managed to make decent enough money to keep the place.

When the friend's lease was up five years ago, her landlord had agreed to rent to Poppy, and it had been a struggle ever since. Still, she'd managed until these last three months.

Trying to calm her fears, Poppy rationalized. Maybe Rick did something different than steal from the working class to make a quick buck. Maybe he was just here to see what he could see. There was no harm in checking out new prospects, right? That's what made the rich richer.

Not that old man Rush would ever sell anyway. This apartment building had been in his family since his father was alive and old man Rush was seventy-two. He loved this place, and so did the residents.

She'd loved it, too. It was one of the cheapest places to live in the city, with a bodega right down at the end of the block that connected to some of the best Chinese food in New York; a park across the street, and her favorite diner right next door to the playground.

Maybe he was just testing the water. "So why are you here today? At this apartment building? Testing the water to see if the guy'll sell?"

"Nope," he responded, but added nothing helpful in the way of information.

Poppy cocked her head though inside she was flooded with relief. "Got a friend here? Girlfriend, maybe?"

Now he smiled, and when he did, it was as though the heavens had opened and rained down their special magic perfectness upon his gorgeous head. "No, again."

God, this was like pulling teeth. "No, you don't have a friend who lives here? Or no, you don't have a girlfriend who lives here—or both?"

As she asked the question, she found she rather wanted to know if he had a girlfriend. How did that work if he was part of a couple? How did she stay out of his personal affairs if she was supposed to advise on his personal affairs?

And something else Poppy discovered. She didn't want him to have a girlfriend

The wrought iron gate separating the sidewalk from the front entry of her building opened just then, and Mr. and Mrs. Paxton and their toothless Chinese Crested dog, Titan, strolled out, arm-in-arm.

They were going for their mid-morning walk together, something they did without fail every day but Sunday, when Mrs. Paxton made a pot roast and Mr. Paxton watched The History Channel.

She quickly turned her back to them, pulling Rick farther under the oak tree. As their bodies briefly brushed together when she stumbled over a tree stump, her heart began to throb. When he righted her, his hand at the small of her back elicited a small gasp of a confused thrill.

Taking a step back to clear her head, Poppy looked up at him. "Okay, enough subterfuge. Why are you here at this specific location today?"

"To check on everyone and make sure they've all received their relocation packages. Despite the fact that you and your friends have dubbed me The Asshole, I'm actually quite good with people."

"Relocation packages?" she repeated woodenly. She hadn't received any relocation package. Of course, she probably wouldn't because she was three months behind in her rent. No one was going to relocate her unless it was to renter's jail. Also, she hadn't opened her mail in at least two months because there was never any good news contained within. Just bills.

"Yep. We offer relocations packages to everyone when we purchase a building. I wouldn't do it any other way."

Poppy thumbed over her shoulder. "You bought this building? This one right behind me with the cute wrought iron fence, awesome spiral thingamajig on the rooftop, and continuing theme of spiral bonsai trees in that little garden to the left?" She'd helped plant those trees…

Now Rick cocked his head, running a hand through his chin-length hair. "Am I speaking another language, Poppy McGuillicuddy? Yes, *this* building."

Alarm bells went off in her head. "And what are you doing with all the people in the building?"

If he wasn't annoyed before, he sure was now. On a grating sigh, his chest heaving with an exaggerated rise and fall of impatience, Rick nodded. "I just told you. Relocating them. Well, except for one. We can't seem to find her. A Lennox Griffith has apparently left this plane, because *I* sure can't locate her. Unless she's the soap opera star I found on Google, which is ridiculous."

Hah! Not so ridiculous.

Shit. Lennox, who's real name was Ethel Leeman, was the friend she'd rented the apartment from. Mr. Rush had probably never changed the name on the apartment because she'd never signed anything official. He'd taken her on her word when she'd said she'd pay her rent.

Shitshitshit!

But wait. How had he gotten the Paxtons to agree to relocate? They'd been here as far back as the fifties, when they'd married. Not even their son, Jeremy, with talk of sunshine, palm trees, and oceanfront retirement homes, had been able to convince them to leave their beloved home.

And Mrs. Bernbaum? No way Mrs. Bernbaum and her latest sixty-five-year-old boy-toy, Rockland—the youngest boy-toy she'd ever had, and at the ripe old age of seventy-four—were agreeing to relocate without a fight.

Rockland had tried to talk Mitzi Bernbaum into looking at something on the Upper East Side, and she'd staunchly refused to budge. This was her home. It was where she'd birthed her children. It was where her beloved Abraham had lived and died.

This was insanity.

Squeezing her temples, she asked one more time, "Are you sure this is the place you're buying? Like a million percent sure?"

"I'm a million and two percent sure. This building is scheduled for demolition on the thirty-first of October."

CHAPTER 7

*W*hoa, whoa and whoa. This wasn't happening.

As she followed Rick into her beloved building, trying to not only decide when the best time was to tell him she lived here, but to ask him what God he'd sacrificed an organ to in order to get her neighbors to agree to relocate, she inhaled with shallow breaths. The checkered black and white floor in the entryway threatened to swallow her up as he crossed it in swift strides and she tried to reorient herself.

There were fifteen units in this apartment building, and he'd managed to talk every single one of them into relocating? Who was he? The reincarnation of Gandhi?

As they proceeded to the elevators, Leona Machowski headed straight for them, a wide smile on her gracefully aging face. "There you are, you handsome Latin devil!" she called, waving a hand to Rick. "*Hola, mi amigo!*"

Poppy, who it appeared had become completely invisible, seeing as Golden Boy Rick had entered the building, slid behind the fake potted palm tree in the lobby, ducking behind it just in time to see Leona virtually beam at Rick, who smiled right back.

In her usual neon-green and black jogging suit, her sneakers whiter than freshly fallen snow, Leona zipped up to Rick and winked flirtatiously, swatting at his shoulder with playfulness.

"*Hola*, Leona. *Como estas?*" he asked, making it clear they'd had prior interaction.

"*Muy bien!*" she shot back, outwardly gushing at her clever use of Spanish.

"Well done, Leona! Your Spanish is really coming along. I'm continually impressed."

"Well, you did inspire me to move to Mexico. The pictures are beautiful, and I love my Spanish teacher at the Y. She's everything you said she'd be and more."

Her move to Mexico? Leona was moving to Mexico? What the fresh hell was going on?

"I just want to check a couple of things with you about my relocation, Rick. Have a minute before you go?"

Rick smiled back just as warmly, his charisma oozing from his pores and dripping all over Leona. "For you, Leona, *mi amiga?* I have decades. Can I swing by when I'm done at Mr. Rush's? That work?"

She giggled, delirious and girlish—giggled like a giddy teenage girl, nodding her freshly dyed ash-blonde head. "I'll be sure and keep the sauerkraut warm. I made kielbasa just for you!"

"You're the best, Leona," Rick offered in return, gravelly and low, before she took off toward the door, almost skipping along the way.

Poppy looked around aghast, her mouth wide open. What the hell was going on? Mr. Rush had gotten offers before— decent, solid, some might say incredibly generous offers—for this building, and he'd turned every single one of them down, and the residents of 54 Littleton Park Square had all nodded their heads in agreement and appreciation for his steadfast loyalty to them. He didn't have to keep the building.

He'd kept it because he loved it—it was his legacy.

Now Mr. Rush and everyone in the building was handing over their beloved homes as though they were giving them to Jesus himself? What kind of relocation package was ARMD offering—a ticket to Utopia?

When the elevator bell dinged, and the coast was clear, Poppy scooted in alongside Rick, fighting the urge to scream her frustration as the musty air of the boxy car settled in her nose.

She was going to have to tell him she lived here eventually—like probably within the next five minutes. But until then, she'd silently rage.

How had he talked them all into this? It couldn't be anything other than some kind of crazy, fast talking persuasion. Had he used his magic to do this?

When the rickety old elevator signaled their arrival—to her floor, no less—their silence had become deafening. As the doors opened with a rumble, he swept his hand in front of him in a gallant gesture. "After you."

Poppy poked her head around the corner and scanned the hallway with its patched but cleanly painted walls. Around this time of day, most everyone was either on their first nap or headed off to run errands. Thankfully, the hallway was deserted.

Stepping out, she stood off to the side and waited for Rick to take the lead. And lead he did, right to her apartment door —number 7E.

Now her throat was threatening to close up and her eyes grew grainy and blurry with her fear. But Rick turned to her and offered a short yet succinct explanation. "Lennox Griffith lives here."

Oh, no she did not either. Hadn't Mr. Rush told him Lennox no longer lived here?

"Didn't the landlord have a way to contact her? Didn't any of the residents know how to find her?"

Poppy, Poppy, Poppy. You're a bad person. What kind of familiar looks right in their warlock's eye and doesn't tell him the truth? But that aside, how was this happening? Everyone knew her in the building. Hadn't he asked any of them who actually lived in 7E?

Hadn't he asked the Paxton's, who, without fail, always brought her a plate of pot roast on Sunday evening so the starving artist wouldn't starve?

Rick smiled, the grin coming off as rather indulgent and sweet, as though the memory of Mr. Rush and his experience with him was a good one.

"Old Mr. Rush isn't exactly the best at keeping records. From what I understand, he mostly hires out the work done on the place, so he doesn't personally check in very often. But just after he agreed to sell, and we had everything in place, papers signed and such, he had a stroke. He's in a nursing home now, but unable to speak. However, he'll be in terrific hands for the rest of his life. I made sure of it...in case you were going to tack on more proof I'm a complete asshole."

But she couldn't decipher most of what was coming out of Rick's beautiful mouth. Instead, Poppy had to lean against the wall to keep from literally falling over. She'd only been gone four months, but it was as though she'd stepped into an alternate dimension.

"And everyone just said yippee skippee to relocating?" she squeaked in disbelief.

Rick leaned into the doorframe, his shoulder pressing against the cracked wood. "Well, not instantly, no. We invited everyone to a meeting at our offices, chatted with them, offered them the relocation package. It took a couple of months, but they eventually got pretty excited, once we tweaked and refined what they wanted. We have a lot of perks with this package."

More to herself than to Rick, she muttered, "Huh. So you're not booting people out on their ears while they cling to their Hummel collections." Because Mrs. Marshall had a Hummel collection spanning an entire wall, and if push came to shove, she'd sit on a wrecking ball in protest while the building came down around her.

Rick looked at her as if she'd lost her mind. "Don't be ridiculous. I'd never do something like that. I care about these people, Poppy. I treat them in the same way I'd want to be treated in my senior years. Why do you think I get invited over for kielbasa and sauerkraut?"

She knew she was harping, but she had to try to understand why no one had told him Lennox Griffith wasn't the occupant of 7E. Had no one in the entire apartment building stood up for her? Mentioned she was out of town?

Even though she owed back rent, had she been gone just another week, she would have come home to a leveled lot of dirt and no one would have said a word.

"So no one said anything about this…Lennox?"

"We didn't ask about Lennox. It's not the job of the residents to keep track of the people in the building or the paperwork that goes with them, but we also assured them we'd contact everyone. And that's what I'm doing right now, making one last attempt to find Lennox." He pulled a set of keys from his pocket.

"You have keys to her apartment?"

"I do. So if we could get on with this—"

"Wait!" Poppy yelped, throwing a hand up in front of his face to prevent him from entering. She wanted to at least explain what he was stepping into.

Like the life-sized picture of her in her Daisy Dukes sprawled on the hood of an old Ford Granada, courtesy of Hank and Red. Her only defense being, it was her one claim to fame and when she realized she'd never be on a marquee or billboard in Times Square, she'd hung it up on the wall directly across from her doorway.

And just as she was about to do that, incident number two of Here, Have Some Uncontrollable Magic, occurred.

There was a rumble of thunder, low and distant, the floor beneath her feet quivered a smidge, and then—wham.

Rick turned to stone.

* * *

"Ahahahahahahaha!" Nina cackled as she eyeballed Rick's form, etched in stone, as perfect as it had been in life. Each line in his face, each fissure had Poppy's heart crashing against her ribs for fear he'd crack in half.

Nina reached out to ping his cheek by flicking her finger, but Poppy caught her. "No! What if he cracks?"

As she'd prayed all her neighbors were napping or out, Poppy had texted Nina and crew to come help, with trembling fingers and a pulse beating so hard, she thought it might break her eardrums.

From Nina's shoulder, Calamity yawned wide, assessing. "Whelp, this is some shit, huh?"

"Some shit?" Poppy almost screeched, rubbing the spot on her wrist where her familiar brand had creepily gone red and itchy. "*Some shit?* Are you kidding me? This is *the* shit, Calamity. The shittiest shit. How do we fix this? We have to fix this!"

Calamity scurried down along Nina's body until she was at Rick's feet, circling and sniffing. "Good question. But be very, very careful. If you break him, well, let's just say, Rick won't ever be the same. Wink-wink."

Break him? Oh, sweet and sour, that was really a thing?

Wanda reached for her just as Poppy sucked in a whoosh of air, steadying her, as she had from the very start. "Everyone just relax," she said so complacently, it only ratcheted up Poppy's fear.

"Relax? Are you kidding me? He's a statue! Like, an honest-to-God garden ornament! That's not something you see every day, Wanda!" Poppy knew her hysteria was mounting by the second, but holy cats. Rick was a statue!

"Actually," Wanda said, smoothing a hand over Poppy's arm, "we rather *do* see stuff like this every day, honey. As a for instance, just last year we saw all sorts of reincarnated Greek gods who tried to kill us. There was a Cyclops, too, wasn't there, Marty?"

Marty rolled her eyes, the memory obviously still fresh as she bobbed her sunshine-colored head. "I think so. I don't remember. It's all sort of a mixed bag with Brenda the Good Witch and those whacked Russian mobster bears. Ugh—those bears with their, "We vill kill you! And your leetle dog, too!" she cried, complete with Russian accent.

Nina grinned as she, too, took a stroll down Memory Lane. "Let's not fucking forget the vampire supremacist. Jesus and fuck, he was cracked, right?"

Everyone nodded their heads in agreement as though they were recalling an old high school cafeteria incident, not someone she'd just turned to stone.

It was too much information. Too much crazy to wrap her head around. Bears and gods and vampires. This was as close to cracking as she'd come, and as her hysteria bubbled to the surface, she looked to Calamity. "Do something!"

The feline stretched, lazy and slow. "Yeah. Not exactly sure what to do here."

Poppy swallowed hard, her hands going clammy. "You don't know how to fix this? You're the one who hangs around witches all the time! How could you not know how to fix this? Use a spell! Whip up some tsetse fly wings and spider venom—*do something!*"

Oh my God. There had to be something!

"Shhh," Marty reprimanded, holding a finger to her mouth and hitching her jaw in the direction of Arnie Banks, who was making his way down the length of her hallway, probably on his way to a rousing game of chess with Mrs. Bernbaum.

In one fluid motion, Wanda grabbed the key from the floor and jammed it into the keyhole, pushing the door open as Nina steamrolled Rick, grabbing his stone form around the waist with a grunt and running like a quarterback to the goal line while Marty stretched her arms wide to block the door before she slammed it shut with the high heel of her boot.

"Hey, there, Poppy-girl!" Mr. Banks called out, lifting a gnarled hand. "I thought that was you. Cain't see a damn thing anymore. Where ya been, good-lookin'?"

Breathe, Poppy. Breathe.

Pasting a warm smile on her face, she held out a hand to him and squeezed his fingers in hers. "On the road with a show. Don't you remember? I told you all about it before I left. You promised to keep my seat warm down in the garden while I was away." Pausing, she gave his wrinkled cheek a kiss. "It's so nice to see you, Arnie."

He scratched his snowy-white head, still thick with plenty of hair to go around, the confusion in his twinkling hazel eyes very clear. "Don't recollect it. But did ya hear?"

Now was her chance to find out if it was just Leona who was dazzled by Rick and his good looks and charm, or if everyone really did want to leave Littleton. "Hear what?" she asked, leaning into him, his Old Spice cologne thick in her nose.

Straightening his ice-blue sports coat from the seventies, one of the many things she adored about him, Arnie grinned, his white dentures extra white against his spray-tanned skin. "We're movin'!"

"Aw, I'm sad to see you go. Where ya goin', Arnie?" she asked, continuing to play dumb.

His smile grew, the skin of his cheeks stretching, making his tanned skin shiny. "Great Neck—got a cute little place that includes cable. Can't wait!"

There was a rumble from behind her door, and someone yelled, maybe Nina. "Jesus Christ and a bag of cement! Be careful!"

Poppy blanched, redirecting Arnie's attention as it strayed to her door. "But *why* are you leaving, Arnie? I thought you loved it here. It's right near the senior center where that cute Miss Leslie goes to bingo, and then there's your favorite dry cleaners—you know, the one that always presses the crease in your pants just the way you like. And let's not forget about the best corned beef and pastrami sandwiches at Giuseppe's on Avondale. Why would you leave all that for Great Neck? What's in Great Neck anyway?"

He paused a moment, as though he had to think about his reasoning, and then he said, "Because it's what I want to do. I can do what I want to do. I'm plenty old enough to make my own decisions."

His words almost sounded agitated to Poppy's ears, defensive even, which was completely unlike Arnie. She wanted nothing less than to agitate him, so she smiled again in reassurance and nodded.

"Of course you are, Arnie. If you're happy, I'm happy. You are happy, *right*? You're okay with this whole relocation thing? Uprooting your entire life and so on to move to Great Neck?"

He rocked back on the heels of his white loafers. "Happier than when Ford made the Thunderbird."

Arnie's response sounded almost canned, but his smile was the same smile that had soothed her when she'd broken up with that self-absorbed jerk Keith Tidsdale after he discovered she wasn't connected enough to get him a gig in the chorus of *South Pacific*.

Poppy sighed in frustration. Why was everyone so damn happy? There wasn't a disgruntled senior in the lot? No one was spearheading a campaign against Corporate America?

Arnie nudged her and winked. "So where *you* goin', Cookie? What's your plan, Fran?" he teased.

Yeah. If only she had one of those. "You know, I'm not sure just now, Arnie, but I'm sure gonna miss you guys—"

"Hey, McGuillicuddy! Get your tuchus in here pronto!" Calamity yelped from inside her apartment.

Damn. Rick. She'd forgotten about Rick. What were they going to do about Rick?

But Arnie clearly saw her distracted distress. "You go on and be with your friend, kiddo. I got stuff to do anyways. Make sure you drop by before D-Day, huh? So we can say goodbye." He cupped her cheek with his weathered hand and grinned, patting her face with affection.

Poppy gripped his wrist and cocked her head. "D-Day?"

"Demo day, honey. We're all gonna camp out at the diner and make it a thing so we can watch 'er fall!" he declared, his voice chock full of excitement as he waved goodbye to her and sashayed down the hall with a little soft shoe.

They were going to demolish this building and Arnie and gang were going to make a party of it?

All right, enough was enough. She had to get to the bottom of this, but not before she did something about Rick

As Captured in Stone. Pushing the door open, she didn't even give herself the chance to enjoy returning to her apartment, no matter how fleeting the return might be.

Her entire life was in this place—all her Playbills, her memorabilia from each show she'd ever had a part in. Her wigs and false eyelashes, her eclectic and completely worthless collection of boas, her dime store-ish bobbleheads.

But she couldn't see any of that.

All she could see was Nina the vampire, standing just beneath the poster of her for Red's Rides and in front of Rick, still encapsulated in stone. More of that panic gripped her intestines.

Nina pointed at the blown-up picture of her on the Ford Granada and grinned a devilish grin. "Niiice shorts. But I'm super fucking keen on the red gingham shirt tied at your belly button, *y'all*," she teased, making Calamity, who'd taken residence on the battered armchair in her tiny living room, snort.

"Ladies!" Wanda admonished, clapping her hands. "Now isn't the time! If we were in crisis before, it was nothing compared to what just happened. The man's a stone, for heaven's sake. Knock it off with the jokes. Besides, Poppy looks perfectly lovely in gingham. Totally in her color wheel."

Again, a shot of panic sliced through her veins, making her heart pound in her ears as she gazed upon Rick in stone form. If nothing else, he sure was quieter, and oddly as handsome in still life as he was animated.

Gripping the back of her chair, she held on for dear life before she asked, "Now what?"

"We got trouble. Right here in River City. With a capital T, that rhymes with Rick and stands for holy shtick!" Calamity sang out.

Poppy shook her head, her knuckles white from clinging

to the chair back. "Ha and ha. While I appreciate the *Music Man* reference, just spit it out, Calamity. What happened?"

Marty popped out from behind Nina, her face distorted with worry. "Well, here's the thing. As I was trying to keep our cover from being blown, I lost my footing. I'm usually as graceful as a cat, despite the fact that I'm a werewolf, *but…*"

Poppy wanted to scream. Instead, she fought the rising tide of a headache and could only manage to whisper, "But what?"

Marty's beautiful face scrunched up into a wince as she bit her lip and pulled something from behind her back, holding it out to show Poppy.

No.

Nonono.

That wasn't his…

Yes. Yes, that's exactly what that is, Poppy.

Nina grabbed at Marty's hand, latching on to it and raising it up in the air.

Then, to Poppy's horror, the vampire puffed her cheeks out and deepened her voice. "Hi, my name is Rick The Dick. Got an itch?"

Calamity began to giggle, the sound rising from her throat and swirling about the room as she rolled to her back and almost fell from the chair laughing.

Then Nina turned Marty's hand toward the werewolf's face and rubbed the spot under her chin. Mimicking her friend, she batted her eyelashes in a flirty manner, waving Marty's wrist in the air once more. "Hey, Rick The Dick! I'm Marty the werewolf, and I don't think this is in your color wheel, *mijo!*"

Her words made Calamity squeal with more laughter, higher-pitched and bordering hysteria.

If Poppy were the fainting type, she'd welcome such an

event right now. It would block out the horror of the scene before her.

Nina, holding Marty's fingers—fingers that were wrapped around Rick's hand.

His carved-in-stone hand.

The concrete hand that had broken right off at his wrist in, if she did say so herself, a pretty clean line.

"Waitwaitwait!" Nina yelled to Marty, holding up her cell phone. "Selfie!"

Jesus. Did she have any Band-Aids?

CHAPTER 8

"So, are you mad?"

"You mean that I have packing tape wrapped around my wrist to keep it in place?"

Poppy winced, shoving the tips of her fingers between her lips. "Does it hurt?"

Rick held up his arm, the light from her window glinting on the crude packing tape they'd used to patch him back together. "Why would my wrist virtually cracking off my arm hurt, Poppy McGuillicuddy?"

"I apologized. I did. I even offered to go to the realm and tell them I'm the shittiest in the history of shitty familiars so they'd reassign me."

His eyes met hers in one of those sizzling assessments he was so gifted at. "A deal's a deal. You have one week. I'd never renege. And surprisingly, to answer your question, no. It doesn't hurt. Though, it's a bit awkward if my back gets itchy." He made a comical reach for his back, the crooked angle at which they'd taped his wrist on making it almost impossible to use his fingertips.

"I'm sure Calamity will find a remedy. I just know it. It's got to be in the *Big Book of Witches*."

Calamity had summoned some book on magic, an enormously thick, dust-riddled black book with pages so brittle, they crackled as she turned them, and she and the women were now poring over it in an attempt to fix Rick's wrist. But Poppy wasn't hopeful. Not after the grunts and groans of dismay coming from her couch.

Rick's nod was curt and clearly skeptical. "I'm sure she will. In the meantime, how about you explain to me this Lennox thing—which you could have just told me, by the way. I mean, if you're done turning me into garden fixtures, that is."

Yeah. There was still that. "Listen, here's the score. I leased this apartment from my friend, Lennox, whose real name is Ethel Leeman."

"Another actress, I take it?"

"Yeah. Anyway, when the lease ran out, Mr. Rush didn't ask me to sign any official papers or anything. We just sort of did a handshake kind of deal on it, and I paid my rent every month on time, no matter what. So I guess he didn't tell you Lennox didn't live here anymore. Though, I'm not sure why. He knows all of us. He cares about all of us. Even if he was angry with one of us, I can't imagine he'd just not mention he was selling the place."

"Like I said, he had the stroke just after he signed the papers to sell. So if he was going to tell you, he either didn't have time or it slipped his mind because you were gone. But I promise you, Poppy, I made sure he was comfortable with the terms of the sale. I'd never take someone's home from them."

But you're taking mine...

She made her way into her cramped kitchen and opened a cupboard, looking for some coffee mugs. Glad she'd cleaned the cracked Formica countertops with the yellowed edges before she'd left.

"And that's very noble of you. I'm not questioning whether this was on the up and up. I'm just wondering why Mr. Rush finally agreed to sell. I know he didn't have any children or grandchildren to leave this building to, but he loved this old place. He worked hard to maintain it—he called it his baby."

Rick's smile was genuine, one she felt from the top of her head to the tips of her toes. "Yeah. He did, and it shows. He's a great old guy. Lots of stories about the war and the good old days. I enjoyed my time with him."

As she pulled out some mugs and pointed to the coffeepot to indicate she'd make coffee, and Rick nodded a resounding yes to some caffeine, Poppy decided it was time for even more honesty.

"So there's more. I'm three months behind on my rent. Which could explain why I was excluded from the relocation package. I'm guessing your numbers person got in there and saw as much and decided to skip my offer. Which is totally fair."

But Rick used his good hand to point to the pile of mail on the floor by her door, scattered in every direction after the melee of getting him inside. "You definitely would have been offered a relocation package, Poppy, missed rent or not. ARMD absolutely doesn't play dirty. Maybe it's in that pile there, but I can check on it with my assistant, Heather."

She shook her head, pouring water into the coffeepot. "I probably can't afford wherever it is you offered to relocate me to anyway. But if it's the last thing I do, if I have to dance at Mitch's A-Go-Go in a platypus suit, I'll pay the money I owe. I always pay the money I owe. Eventually…"

Rick barked a laugh, throwing his dark head back on his shoulders, revealing his tanned throat as he sat in one of her cracked blue vinyl kitchen chairs. "No platypus costumes for you, young lady. I'm pretty sure we can figure something out."

As the scent of coffee filled her little apartment, and she was reminded of how much she loved this cracked and peeling space, she shook her head. "Nope. Mr. Rush deserves the money. He was really nice to me while I struggled these last couple of years. He gave me more breaks than I care to count when times were lean. Well, they were always lean, but you know what I mean. Even if it's just left in an account for him somewhere—for medical care or physical therapy or whatever he needs, it's not a fortune, but it's his, and I owe him that kind of respect."

Rick watched her as she poured the coffee and offered him some powdered coffee creamer. "Have you always been an actress?"

She grinned, taking a place opposite him at the table. "You mean a poor has-been with no solid plan other than a bright-lights-big-city dream?"

"I mean, is that what you strictly do for a living?"

"Well, it's not a living by any stretch. Believe that. But I love it. It's what brings me peace. Fulfills me, even if it doesn't fill my bank account." She paused a moment, running her finger over the rim of her mug. "However, I've learned that making a living isn't the same thing as making a life."

Ricks sat up straight, capturing her gaze with his, his eyes intense, his jaw tight and pulsing. "Maya Angelou, right?"

Poppy blinked, cringing at the intensity of his gaze. "What?"

"What you just said," he pressed, leaning forward. "That's a quote from Maya Angelou."

Surprise made her frown. "Is it?" Where had that come from? Had the spirit of sage advice and sound wisdom possessed her? She didn't know any Maya Angelou quotes.

"It is. My—" Rick shook his head. The moment they'd shared seconds ago had clearly passed, and whatever he'd been about to say, he'd decided against. "Never mind." Rising, he looked at the women and Calamity, still flipping the pages of the enormous book. "Ladies? It's time we took this show back on the road. I have to get back to my place for a meeting with Avis."

"But your hand. How are you going to explain that to your partner?" Poppy asked, rising, too.

His answer was clipped and short. "He's a warlock, too. He'll get it."

Well, that was one less explanation to squirm through. But why was Rick so stiff and closed up whenever they talked about magic? In fact, didn't he say he'd made it a point to work with only humans?

Gazing at the pictures she had scattered over a shelf under her kitchen clock made Poppy's heart tighten further. She had tons of them, from snaps of her family back in Cincinnati to all sorts of pictures of her in some of the shows she'd done.

"Do you want to gather some things to bring back to my place? Clothes? Maybe your Red's Rides poster? I think it could work on the wall of your bedroom. You know, right over the head of the bed?" he teased, lightening up a little.

Biting the inside of her cheek, Poppy squirmed. Damn that poster.

But she had an idea—one she was sure he'd agree to in light of the fact that he resented her being in the shed. "Why don't I just stay here? I could show up at your house like a job. You know, nine-to-five kind of thing? You didn't love the idea of me living at your place anyway. This way I wouldn't be in your hair." All that amazingly glossy black hair.

But Calamity was on the table in a flash, her kitty paws

thumping Poppy's fingers. "That's not how this works, Poppy. You have to be on call at all times. Until the bond is officially broken by the powers that be, you absolutely must stay close. You don't think I roam around with that volatile nut because I want to, do you? I'd rather graffiti bridges and go through a gang initiation."

"Bite me, Calamity!" Nina growled from her place on the worn couch.

Looking around, her heart hurt with loss. Her apartment wasn't much to look at aesthetically, but it held so many dear things.

"Isn't there some spell I can conjure to zip me to his place every morning? I mean, if I can turn him to stone, surely I can appear and disappear. How hard can it be?"

"That was a crazy accident. I don't even know how or why it happened. In fact, I don't know how the hell I even managed to turn him back." Then the feline looked at Rick's wrist, still hanging by a thread. "Well, mostly anyway. Look, Poppy, the gig's the gig. End of. You gotta be wherever he is."

Catching her by surprise, Rick nodded his agreement with a grin. "Plus, a deal's a deal. One week was the deal."

"You're right," she answered softly, her response tinged with regret as she swallowed back the threat of tears.

She couldn't afford this place anymore even if it wasn't going to end up demolished. She'd known that the moment she'd stepped off the bus to go to Mel's party. Still, it hurt to leave her small haven. It hurt more that everyone was so excited to leave theirs, too, and she was baffled by the very notion.

Rick placed his good hand on her shoulder, the warmth of it, the compassion of his light squeeze before he let go, making her choke up. "I know this is hard, Poppy. If you want, I'll come back and help you pack up your things personally. You can spend some time here, and we'll figure the rest out. I promise. I made it right for everyone else, I will for you, too."

"Don't make promises you can't keep, pal. You forget you only have one working hand?" she joked, shrugging off his touch as she headed for her bathroom to gather toiletries. She didn't want pity or a free ride or anything she didn't earn.

But it was decent enough of him to offer. It was a side to him she rather liked. She knew it was genuine. She felt the truth of his sincerity to her core.

When she reached the bathroom, Poppy closed the door, leaning back against it and closing her eyes. The sounds from the street below, the scent of her favorite perfumes and soaps surrounding her, all played a part in reminding her everything was about to change. Reaching for a towel, she inhaled a shaky breath and willed herself not to cry.

Something was very wrong here. Very, very wrong.

"WE HAVE MATCHING HANDS, *AMIGO*," Rick said on a laugh as Carl, Nina's zombie, held up his wrist to show off the blue metallic duct tape keeping his index finger in place.

"Know how he got that?" Nina asked, though it was obvious she was using this moment to teach Carl something.

"How?" Rick asked. "Bet it was fighting off some evil foe."

Carl snorted.

But Nina gave him a stern look and shook her head in the negative. "Climbing a damn tree. I've only told him eleventy-bazillion times he's breakable, but he's all about reading Robin Hood these days. So Errol Flynn decides to climb our oak tree in the backyard last week, and now look. All hacked up again."

Rick's laughter rang out. "What's next, buddy? Robbing the rich to give to the poor?"

While Poppy was absorbing this not only new, much lighter attitude of Rick's, but also the fact that there was a zombie, gentle as a lamb, in the middle of Rick's kitchen, everyone milled about.

Nina had arranged for a man named Archibald to bring Carl to her while her daughter, Charlie, went on a father/daughter trip with her husband Greg.

And the awe and wonder Carl had brought with him, the complete sincerity in his crooked smile and kind eyes, floored Poppy. She loved him almost on sight.

What floored her more? How gentle Rick was with Carl. He'd made it a point to be sure he was comfortable as they'd commiserated over their war wounds. He'd listened patiently as Carl—who, according to Nina, was slowly learning to speak sentences—told him about the book he was reading.

The Three Musketeers—which Rick wholeheartedly supported, as a fan of Alexandre Dumas himself. While they chatted, Carl stroked Calamity's back and listened closely to Rick's words.

And for the moment, everyone was getting along, and it was all peachy keen. But the unsettling noise in her stomach, the buzz in her head, wouldn't let her leave this thing about her apartment and the flagrant acquiescence of the seniors to vacate alone.

She needed time to sort this out. Time to reflect on Arnie's almost rehearsed words. She wanted to talk to all of her neighbors, see if they really felt the way Arnie did.

Sure, free cable was a great thing, but to leave the home you've loved for forty years because of it was a stretch for Poppy.

Rick's front door opened and a very blond, startlingly handsome man, in a dark gray suit with a multi-colored tie, poked his head around the door and called in a very proper British accent, "Rickster?"

Rick's head popped up, and he hitched his jaw. "C'mon in, bro," he called, waving this new person inside.

Instinctively, she knew who he was. An immediate warmth flooded Poppy, straight to her bones. This was Rick's friend Avis, his partner. The man he trusted enough to own a business together. His affection for this man skittered across Poppy's heart.

But was that instinct? Did it really take a genius to figure out the man was Avis? Was the feeling she had really Rick's? After all, Rick had said he had a meeting with him here today.

But she wasn't sure that was how she'd identified him. It had more to do with a strong wave of emotion. An emotion tied to the word friendship. The word popped into her head as though she'd seen it written on a chalkboard. It rooted around in her heart, making her grip the counter as Avis strolled in, a smile on his handsome face, a face as light as Rick's was dark.

"Am I interrupting something? Heather said we had a meeting today at two here at the house. And bollocks, chap! What the bloody hell happened?" Then he shot a look at the women in the room. "Pardon my foul language, but I can't leave your arse unsupervised for even a day, can I?" he asked, his tone teasing as he pointed to Rick's wrist.

Rick slapped him on the back with a fond grin. "We do have a meeting, and I'll explain all this in a minute. For now, Avis, this is everyone. Everyone, say hello to Avis."

As introductions were made, and Avis gripped each woman's hand in greeting, spreading his charming English accent around like whipped butter on toast, Poppy watched. Watched as he flirted, watched as he winked, watched as he made jokes with even Nina—who behaved like Nina.

Cautious and skeptical, but it wasn't long before he made her smile.

When he finally made his way to her, he held out his hand, the perfectly even skin of his fingers wrapping around hers, causing Poppy to literally fight a shiver—a violent shiver.

Huh.

Gone was the warmth and in its place was a chilled sense of dread.

"Charming to meet you, Poppy."

Her eyes met his green ones. No. No, it wasn't charming to meet her at all. His mouth said it was, but his eyes said something entirely different.

Shrugging off the ugly vibe, and giving him her best movie-star smile, Poppy said, "You too. It's nice to attach a name to a face."

"Have you known Rick long? How have we missed meeting each other? How did I miss meeting someone as utterly bedazzling as you?"

She stared back at him, watching the wheels of his mind turn, feeling the strangest vibration course through her once more. "Nope. We've known each other just a day."

Driving his hand into the pocket of his sharply tailored trousers, he asked, "So how did you meet my chap Rick?"

"Magic," she replied, keeping her answer purposefully mysterious.

He cocked his head, making the fall of his thatch of blond hair sweep over his forehead. "Magic?"

Straightening her spine just like she'd been taught in all those years of ballet class, Poppy took on a haughty air, pretending she was someone important, like royalty. That always helped her when she felt uncomfortable, and she definitely felt discomfort.

"I'm his new familiar."

A flicker of confusion, brief as it was, flashed in his green eyes before a smile spread across his lean face. "A new familiar? How smashing! I'm thrilled for him! Especially seeing as he lucked out with one who's so pretty."

Leaning back against the counter, Poppy nodded. "That's good to hear. I have so much to learn about him, so I'll be around a lot. It's nice to know someone as close to Rick as you are is easy to get along with."

As she spoke the words, she heard the pitch of her voice, noted it held a slight threatening tone, but she didn't understand why.

Rick nudged Avis and pointed to the end of the warehouse where his office was. "We need to get some stuff done. Quit flirting with the lady and let's do this."

Avis nodded his head, his expression teasing and bright. "Right. Sorry. I was all caught up in hearing about how you have a new familiar. Oh, the secrets you keep, friend."

Rick laughed as he grabbed a briefcase from a shelf by the front door and headed toward the end of the house. "I just bet you were, buddy. Told ya, I'll explain that. Move it, Mackland."

Backing away, Avis kept the smile on his face. "Anyway, such a delight to meet you, Poppy. I must go feed my workaholic beast, but I hope we get the chance to chat again soon."

Without thought, without filter, Poppy responded, "Count on it."

And as she watched his broad back, almost as broad as Rick's, turn to a pinpoint of color before he rounded the only corner in the warehouse, she discovered she'd been holding in another violent shiver.

Chills assaulted her skin, goose bumps running the length of her arms and along the back of her neck, making her hair stand on end.

Avis Mackland wasn't pleased to meet her. He didn't want

111

to chat with her again. He'd be happy if she fell off the face of the earth.

She knew this. Knew it as certainly as she knew how to tie her shoes.

Avis Mackland was a snake. A total and complete snake with a cultured British accent, and his best friend, Rick, his business partner, his roommate in college, hadn't a single clue.

Pip pip and cheerio.

CHAPTER 9

"So, jolly good show, brother! Way to score!" Avis congratulated him once they were in the privacy of Rick's office.

He sighed, dropping into his office chair. Avis was nothing if he wasn't a player. He loved women. Rick couldn't fault him for that. He loved women, too. He just didn't love them in multiples, or behind their backs while he loved someone else.

Avis played the field more than the entire NFL. And that was fine by Rick. As long as he showed up to work and kept making them money and he kept his drama off their work field, Rick kept his mouth shut.

Grabbing a pen, he flicked the top of it over and over. "She's not a score, pal. She's my familiar. A familiar I don't want, but who's here whether I like it or not."

Avis scoffed. "Then I'll take her off your hands. She's got a bottom like a round—"

"Knock it off, Mackland," Rick warned, his tone serious. He was never fond of how Avis objectified women, and he'd said as much on many occasions. But Poppy was different. He'd like to chalk that up to the fact that she was his familiar, but the protective side of him railed against the notion. "She's not a piece of meat. There's some respect due here. And you already have a familiar. You don't need another one."

"Hah!" Avis barked. "You mean I have someone who's always lagered up and makes an appearance maybe twice a year? I don't even know where the living hell Judith is right now—haven't seen her since last spring."

"Lucky you," he muttered, staring at his jacked-up wrist.

"So how are you going to handle this, old chum? You know damn well the PTB will sprout moths out of their dusty arses for days if you complain."

He did know that. He'd been ready to risk that until he'd spent some time with Poppy today. He liked her spunk. He liked how much she cared about the people over at Littleton. He liked that she wanted to pay Mr. Rush back no matter what it took.

He liked her...her aura, and he hated to admit as much. He'd been so defensive when she'd been thrust upon him with no warning; he really had been an asshole.

And she'd told him so. He liked that, too.

"Still not sure how I'm going to handle it. She's no Yash, that's for sure." Though today, she'd reminded him of his familiar, made that tug in his gut burn with awareness.

Avis slid into the chair opposite his desk with a chuckle. "Damn right, she's no Yash. She has a helluva lot more hair and her legs are perfection. No comparison t'all."

Looking his partner directly in the eye, Rick narrowed his glare, leveling it at Avis. "I said lay off the comments about her body."

Avis threw up his hands as white flags. "Chill, brother. I

was simply joking. But how about you tell me what she did to your body? I smell magic of some kind or another, though it's quite strange."

Strange was an understatement. But Calamity was correct. He absolutely did feel the connection to Poppy. He wasn't sure the connection wasn't muddied with other feelings, but they had connected when she'd blown the lights out in his kitchen and when she'd turned him to stone.

Which was actually kind of funny.

So Rick shrugged. He wasn't ready to be completely open about what was going on inside him just yet. "We had a bit of a collision over at Littleton. Can't exactly explain it other than it was pretty bizarre."

"Littleton? She was at Littleton with you?"

"Well, yeah. She's my familiar, remember? We're in the getting-to-know-you phase."

Avis leaned back in the chair, crossing his ankle over his knee. "And how do you feel about her replacing Yash?"

"I don't feel anything about Yash. Yash was a dirty son of a bitch." He ground the words out, even if he really did feel something about his disappearing familiar. Utter and complete betrayal—a desolation so deep, it still stung.

"You have to let go, friend. Especially the talk of despising your magic."

"I don't despise my magic, Avis. I just don't want it used in my everyday life. We can't meld with humans, do business with them on a day-to-day basis, if we're casting spells on them, forcing them to do our bidding. It's not right."

Avis rolled his eyes. "A little magic never hurt anyone," he drawled, snapping his fingers and making a waterfall appear in the corner of the office, the sparkling gush of fluid spilling out over his floor.

"You know it's not my bag, buddy. Our magic is weak

compared to our female counterparts. It's rare to find a warlock who can do more than some stupid card tricks or make waterfalls appear anyway, and you know it. We're the lesser of the two genders. But let's not forget, magic can wreak all sorts of havoc in your life."

Avis shot him a sympathetic look. "And it killed your mother. I know the story, friend. I understand your reasoning."

The reminder of his mother, Delfina, stung. Yes. Magic had killed his mother, and Yash had picked up the pieces of that broken little boy, sewn him back together again, raised him with all sorts of wise words and mother-of-the-earth intentions—and then duped him.

Never again.

"Give the old bloke a break, would you? I still say something happened, chap. I daresay no magic on earth, no matter how powerful, could have torn that man from your side. He was bloody attached to your hip like some sort of Siamese twin."

Rick held up a hand. He wanted to thwart the onslaught of defenses Avis had cooked up in his mind on Yash's behalf. No matter what the case was, no matter how Yash had disappeared, he'd still stolen money from their company.

"Don't bother to defend. We've been down this road, and it has the same conclusion. We lost an assload of money because of Yash. End story. Now, onto other, more pressing matters, like Littleton. Did you have any idea the person listed as 7E's occupant was incorrect?"

Avis's head popped up from scrolling his phone. "Say again?"

Sifting through the papers on his desk, he dug through them, separating them by date. "Yeah. We have a Lennox Griffith listed, but it's actually Poppy who lives there."

Avis gazed at him from his seat in the chair. "Poppy? What an incredible coincidence."

As Rick explained the events of the day, he found himself almost a little too exuberant when referring to Poppy, making him firmly clamp his lips together.

He wasn't ready to like her just yet.

* * *

"S'up, Stone-Maker," Calamity chirped as Poppy unpacked her clothes and began putting them into the armoire, tucked away in the corner of her new bedroom.

She let the joke go in favor of the distraction from her thoughts. "Just thinking."

"About?" Marty asked, poking her head around the corner of the room.

She shook her head, wiping her hands on the thighs of her favorite pair of ripped blue jeans before she sat next to Wanda on the edge of the bed. "Not sure I can articulate just yet."

She wanted to be sure she had her ducks in a row before she came out swinging. Yet, the longer she thought about Avis, the more she recalled the terrifying vibe he'd sent out, the more she wanted to confide in someone. She just wanted the words to be right.

"I fucking hope you're thinking about doing more magic tricks because I'm here to tell ya, you're GD awesome," Nina said on a snort, positioning herself against the wall opposite the bed.

Carl wandered into the room, cocking his head to indicate he'd like to sit next to her. She patted the surface and smiled as he scrunched in between her and Wanda.

Thumping her thigh, he murmured, "Like you," and followed up with his adorably crooked grin.

Poppy grinned back, hooking her hand through the crook of his arm. "That's so nice to hear, Carl. I like you, too."

"So what's going on in that brain of yours, Poppy? Talk to us," Wanda encouraged, licking the tips of her fingers before passing a bag of chips.

She grabbed one and nibbled at it, trying to define what she was feeling without sounding like some crazy alarmist. "Something just feels off. It's the best way to describe it. Totally off. I can't explain it, I have no reason for it, it's just wrong."

Calamity settled onto Carl's lap, rubbing her cheek against his chest. "That's just you adjusting to being a familiar. It happens all the time. We all go through highs and lows while we get used to our assignments, Poppy-Seed. I think the powers that be forget we each had lives apart from one another. They just throw us the eff together and expect us to get each other. Just because the fates say we should be paired, doesn't damn well mean we'll totally understand every foible and bad habit. Maybe when all this is done, I'll lobby for some reform."

Sure, that could be the case. Who was she to say what one felt when they were turned into a familiar? Maybe the rush of instincts and emotions had something to do with how off she felt. But that just didn't sit right. "Maybe," she answered, grabbing a handful of chips.

"I daresay, if you spoil the fantastic meal I'm making out in that wee kitchen for your welcome-to-the-fold dinner, I shall reserve the right to clock you in your lovely head," Archibald scolded with a teasing grin.

She loved his gently aged face, the crisp black suit he wore with a smartly tied silver ascot. She loved that he was no-questions-asked inclusive. At a time when she was feeling pretty alone, missing her family, unsure how to call them and explain all that had happened, they were filling a need in her like no other.

Pressing a hand to her throat, she affected her best southern accent. "You're making *me* dinner? Whatever did I do to deserve such kindness, sir?"

Throwing a dishtowel over his shoulder, Arch raised a jaunty eyebrow. "Frankly m'dear, I don't give a damn!"

Nina slapped him on the back, dropped a kiss on his shiny head and said, "Worst accent ever, Arch," as everyone laughed.

But Arch swatted her with his towel and grinned as he looked to Poppy. "Are we inviting Master Delassantos to our feast? Have we given him the thumbs-up yet or are we reserving judgment? The texts I received from Miss Nina about him were anything but kind."

"Of course we're inviting him," Marty declared with a chuckle. "He's part of the family now whether he damn well likes it or not. And trust me, he's already warming to you, Poppy-Seed. By week's end, he'll be all over this familiar thing. Mark my words."

Yeah, and she had one week to show him what being part of the family was about by telling him she thought his best friend and partner was a bad, bad dude.

"Or all over *her*," Calamity teased. "Seen the way he looks at her unfairly perky rear-end? Phew. Can't believe you didn't catch fire yet, Pops."

Blushing, she flapped a hand and rolled her eyes at the cat, ignoring the giddy rush the idea brought. Because it was crazy. Rick was no more attracted to her than he was to Arnie.

"Enough already. I've been at this job one day, and you're already shipping us. We hardly know each other."

Arch gave them a crisp nod and clicked his heels. "Then I

shall extend our invitation to the butt-watcher and add another plate to the roster." As he went off to tend to whatever was creating the delicious scents wafting in from the kitchen and filling the tiny house, Poppy shifted on the bed.

Nina crossed the small space between them and ruffled her hair. "Listen, Ball Crusher, if you don't want to talk about whatever's eating you up, you don't have to. I see you all over here fretting and shit. But when you're ready, we'll be here. Okay?"

Poppy nodded, clinging to Carl's arm. "Thanks, Nina. I appreciate everything you guys have done. I just need to get my footing. But I want you to know, you're all really pretty great people to just drop everything and help like you do."

Nina flicked her shoulder with her fingers. "Fuck that. I'm a total bitch," she crowed. "Don't go spreadin' rumors sayin' any different now." But she grinned.

And so did Poppy. And as she tucked her misgivings away for the moment and prepared to share a meal with these people, she sent up a thank you to the universe in a moment of deep gratitude.

* * *

SWIRLING the burgundy wine in her glass, Poppy sipped at it, stuffed to the gills after an amazing dinner of roast chicken in lemon sauce seasoned with sage and thyme, and the most tender baby potatoes to ever grace her tongue.

Nina was off in a corner, practicing her wand magic with Calamity, alternately setting random things on fire or turning them to thick globs of ice, while Wanda, Marty, and Carl snuggled under a heated blanket on an outdoor couch, flipping through a magazine about planes.

She held up her glass and saluted Arch, who sat next to the women on Rick's patio by a wide brick fireplace, the hearth festively decorated with pumpkins, mums, and a free-standing skeleton.

"That was an amazing meal, Arch. Thank you."

He lifted his wine glass, too, tipping it at her with a genuine smile. "'Twas my pleasure, Miss Poppy. Welcome to our ragtag band of merry paranormals. Here's to many more meals shared with us just like this one!"

Rick rubbed his stomach, leaning back in the chair he'd pulled next to hers. "Wow. Glad I got an invite. I haven't had a meal like that in forever."

Nodding, she had to agree. She lived on salads and bag after bag of cheap pork rinds with the occasional apple thrown in for good measure. "It's really beautiful out here," she commented with a contented sigh, looking up at the string of globe lights hung in the shape of a square and wrapped around steel stakes driven into the ground.

Huge black iron candelabras held flickering stump candles, giving off the scent of vanilla and pumpkin spice. Purple and orange lights adorned the back of his house around the windows and woven into the bushes. Ghosts made of some sort of cloth swung from limbs on the big tree near the woods edging his property, and there was the most fabulous freestanding witch, complete with cackle when you walked past her, by the table where they'd dined.

"One of my favorite places to relax and have a beer. I don't get to do it as often as I'd like."

"I can see why you'd want to. You've made it a real haven." The patio was broken up into small groups of weather-proofed furniture in bright reds and teals, just like the interior of his house, and very unlike the décor in the shed.

"It's nice, seeing it filled with people like this. It was what I'd intended when I designed it, but work gets the best of me most days, and I never seem to find the time to entertain."

Right. Avis the snake had mentioned something about

workaholics and Rick. "So, I don't know if you noticed, but you're really into Halloween." She pointed to the jack-o'-lanterns scattered everywhere. Yet another side to him she'd been totally unprepared for. He'd really gone all out with the decorating.

He laughed. "Well, it is the song of our people."

Poppy snorted, tucking a blanket around her waist, snuggling deeper into the soft material. "So witches and warlocks are really into Halloween? I guess I've watched too many movies. I got the impression you guys hated the commercialization of it all."

"Well, you know what it's like. Traditionally, I mean not the costumes-and-candy, commercial kind of Halloween. There's lots of folklore and such surrounding the day, of course, but it's a lot like Christmas for Christians. Only it's Samhain and such. But in the interest of blending with humans, mostly I just like seeing all the kids in their costumes trick or treating, and there's nothing I like more than a cool skull."

"You give out candy to the kids in the hood? Stop. You're making me like you. I won't have it," she teased, poking his shoulder with a playful finger.

"*Full-size* candy bars. Assholes have hearts, too."

She gasped and feigned over-the-top surprise with a hand to her throat. "Color me aghast."

"This year, a blood moon's supposed to appear on All Hallows Eve. You know what that means."

A shiver skittered up Poppy's spine. "A blood moon? Sounds rather ominous."

Rick cocked his head, leaning forward, his eyes going dark and hard. "Sounds ominous?"

She gazed back at him, frowning. "Yeah. I mean, anything with 'blood' in it sounds ominous, don't you think? So explain to me about this blood moon."

"Explain?"

"Again with the communication problems. Am I the one who's speaking a foreign language now? What. Is. A. Blood. Moon?"

Sliding to the end of his chair, his strong thigh muscles flexing as he braced himself on the edge, he asked, "Why don't you know what a blood moon is, Poppy?"

Oh, damn. He looked serious. "Is this some kind of history test? Did I fail?" she joked, twisting the length of her braid in her free hand.

"This isn't a history test. It's your heritage. As a familiar, you should know what the blood moon means."

She was growing more insulted by the second. How the hell was she supposed to know about the moon? "Well, I don't. I mean, I'll go right back to the shed now and Google it, if it's so important to you, but I have no idea what it means."

"Again, as a *familiar*, you should know," he insisted.

"Okay, we're going around in circles here," she accused, her voice rising. "I'm a familiar, not an astronaut. I know not thing one about the moon other than Neil Armstrong planted a flag there. So chill out already and tell me."

Setting his wine glass on the table next to him, he said, "We're obviously missing some kind of link here. If you were raised in the white witch way as a familiar, you should know what the blood moon means, Poppy."

Oh. That explained it. "Phew. So intense. Ease off there, warlock. I can explain why I don't know what the heck you're talking about."

"Oh, no. Wait. Let me guess. You missed the class on the blood moon because you were on an audition for *Grease*? Or were you doing another local commercial for Maury The Mattress Guy?"

"You know, funny you should mention *Grease*. Do you

have any idea what goes into teasing your hair that high? I had knots for days."

"Yeah. I got chills, they're multiplyin'. Get to the explanation, please."

"Like I said, that's easy. I just became a familiar yesterday evening. It was an accident."

"And you failed to mention this...*why?*" he asked, his voice rising.

Poppy blinked in astonishment, her voice rising, too. "I did tell you I was a newb." Hadn't she?

"Hey! What's the ruckus, you two? Jesus, I'm trying to turn water into wine over there. Can't you see that takes concentration?" Nina yelped, suddenly standing between them. "It's like you damn well want me to set your fancy house on fire, Ricky baby."

But Rick hopped up out of his seat, his eyes filled with anger. "What I *want* is someone to explain to me why no one ever mentioned a single word about Poppy being fresh off the familiar turnip truck?"

"But I told you I was new at this. Why do you think they're all here with me?"

"I thought they were your friends! And yeah, you said you were new at this, but I didn't know you weren't born a familiar! I didn't know you didn't know anything about familiaring!"

Oh, dear. Had they skipped that part? She hadn't done it on purpose. In fact, it now occurred to her, she'd been so wrapped up in proving herself, in nailing this familiar thing, she'd maybe forgotten a detail or two.

Sliding out of her chair, she stepped around Nina to look up at him. "Okay, so I'm new-new. What's the big deal? I can learn. I'm a quick learner. Just ask Miss Debra at Dee-Dee's School of Dance. I learned the soft-shoe in like three days."

"I don't care if you found the equation for the meaning of life in three days, you have no idea what you're doing!"

Sure, that was fair. She didn't have any idea about anything having to do with any of this. Moving from foot to foot, she nodded her head. "And that's very fair. I don't know anything about witches and blood moons and flippin' whatever else is involved in Sow's Hain—"

"Samhain!" Calamity shouted, correcting her pronunciation as she circled her feet.

"Whatever!" she shouted back, the emotions of the day and the tone of Rick's discontent taking its toll. Sucking in the cold air, she forced herself to stay reasonable. "Listen, Rick, this was all an accident. I'm a familiar because I was in the wrong place at the wrong time, okay? Two days ago I was a broke dancer in the chorus of a show that ended early and without a paycheck. Today, I'm a familiar, if this mark on my wrist is any indication, and I'm doing my best to do right by you and whatever else I'm supposed to do so I don't end up in the Bad Place."

"Do you have any idea all the things that could go wrong because you don't know what you're doing? Like this, for instance?" He held up his wrist, the one they still hadn't figured out how to fix. "So, here's the score. Tomorrow morning, I'm calling Familiar Central."

"But we had a deal!"

Jamming his hand into his jean pocket, his angry eyes glittered beneath the pale moon. "And I went into that deal with the idea that you knew what the hell you were doing because you'd been raised around magic and witches."

Yep. That was the metaphorical sound of her last straw breaking. "You know, I almost wish it were your head instead of your wrist that cracked off, you elitist jerk!"

Of course, the moment Poppy threw those words into the wind was the moment she heard a cracking sound.

Sharp and resonant, it echoed throughout the patio and whistled through the trees at the edge of Rick's backyard.

After that, she didn't hear or see anything else—the world and everything around her simply went dark.

CHAPTER 10

"*P*oppyyyyy! Where are you? Answer us, Poppy honey!" Wanda's voice trilled out into the cold night air, swishing in her ears.

"Swear to fucking Christ, I'll kill you if we don't find her. You hear me, *Rick?* Kill you. Like smash the shit out of your skull and hip-hop in your frickin' brains! She was just trying to do the right thing like a champ, and you've done shit-all but bust her ever-flippin' chops since she started. And I'm gonna see to it you pay for that. So you'd better damn well pray to whatever it is you crazy motherfucker warlocks pray to that we find her!"

Oh, that was Nina, and she was mad. Though, Poppy found she rather liked the vampire's anger in her favor.

But where was she, and why did her head feel like it was going to pop right off her shoulders? Letting her hand stray to the area surrounding her, she squeezed her fist when she happened on something soggy. Clenching her fingers, she reached around her, skimming the surface. Leaves, she was lying on leaves, and something was poking her in the back.

Then dampness permeated her cold nose, and there was another sharp poke of what was surely a branch.

"Poppy-Seed!" Calamity shouted. "Please be out here somewhere! Give us a yell!"

There was the scamper of little feet in frantic fashion, and crunching leaves, signaling Calamity was somewhere close.

"Popp-eeeee!" someone else howled, slow and stilted, with an emphasis on the letter E. "Come...nooow!"

Carl...aw, that was Carl. She'd know him anywhere, and she wanted to answer him. She wanted to call out, but her head throbbed with the beat of a thousand drums and the mere thought of screaming back left her immobile.

"Poppy! Oh, thank God!" Marty. That was Marty. Her sweet lilt laced with relief as she scooped Poppy up in her arms was a welcome sound. There was a rustle of fabric as she yanked off her jacket and wrapped it around her. "She's over here! I've got her now!"

Feet. Tons of pairs of feet pounded the ground, making her headache throb in time.

Soft as a baby's backside, Marty's hand roamed over her face. "Are you okay? Look at me, sweetie. Open your eyes now and look at me so I know you're okay."

Forcing her eyes open, Poppy groaned when someone shone a flashlight in them, the abrasive glare making her wince. The trees above her, their limbs creaking in the wind, bounced in the inky sky. Woods. She was in the woods somewhere.

Calamity climbed into her lap, pressing her round head into Poppy's jaw. "Aw, Jesus and illicit fornication, Poppy-Seed, you scared the shit out of us! You okay?"

Gripping Marty's arms, she nodded. "If it's possible, I have a headache bigger than even Rick," she joked. "What happened?"

Nina knelt down on her haunches, pushing some stray

strands of hair from Poppy's face before she ran the back of her knuckles over her cheek. "Not a fucking clue, Ball-Crusher. One minute you were there, the next you were flying across the damn sky like some kinda human cannon-ball. I've seen some shit, but that was crazy. It was like some damn invisible hands picked you up and launched your ass out here. We just followed the streak of light."

Which was when she remembered what she'd said before everything went black. She forced herself to a sitting position, shrugging her way out of Marty's steel grip. "Oh my God, Rick! Did his…" No. She couldn't say it. "Does he still have his…"

"Head?" Rick asked, coming into view, his large form blocking out the moon as he knelt next to her.

She bracketed his handsome face with her hands and yelled, "Yes! Oh, thank God you still have your head!"

He gripped her wrist and smiled sheepishly. "I do. Not that I deserve it, but I still have it."

Poppy scoffed, shoving his face away with a light push of her hands and mock disgust. "Oh yeah. You were being a jerk. I almost forgot."

But he didn't let go of her wrists. Instead, Rick pulled her closer, his nose almost touching hers. She smelled the faint hint of wine on his breath, they were so near. "I'm sorry. My only explanation is I have a long, not-so-great history with magic gone wrong, and sometimes that history gets the better of me. I overreacted."

Upon reflection, she had to at least apologize for not telling him the whole story, but she'd been so focused on doing this right and then the thing with her neighbors and her apartment, and who she'd been before this became lost in the shuffle. But it certainly hadn't been intentional.

"I'm sorry I didn't give you the whole story. It wasn't intentional, just circumstantial," she whispered, her body suddenly warm and tingly with all sorts of heady vibrations and electric pulses.

Cupping her jaw, Rick sighed. "How about we start over?"

"Bacon?"

"Bacon?" he repeated.

"You could make me bacon. Bacon makes everything better."

Rick chuckled, the sound low and deep in his throat. "Bacon it is."

"So deal's back on?"

"Like Donkey Kong," he replied on a snicker.

Nina tickled the inside of Rick's ear with a broken limb. "Hey, back up, buddy. You're getting pretty cozy there. It's damn cold out here. We need to get the kid back home and figure out what the hell just happened. Can't do that if you're tryin' to stick your tongue down her throat. Now move, Slick-Rick, or I'm gonna give you a case of genital warts that'll end up on some medical mysteries show."

Poppy giggled as Rick backed off and grabbed her hand, pulling her upright. She swayed to and fro, leaning into the strength of his grip, her head still light and fuzzy. But she squared her shoulders and sucked it up.

"When we get back, I'll tell you everything. Then there'll be no loose ends."

"Fair enough, and then we're going to examine what happened here tonight. Familiars certainly have magic, but a magic this powerful? One that could send you clear across the woods? I have to wonder what's happening."

She squeezed his hand, liking the feel of his slightly callused palm against hers, and nodded with a shiver. But she put on a brave front with a smile. "Let's do this."

As they picked their way back to his house through the woods, everyone lost in their own thoughts, Poppy clung to

Rick's hand, trying not to think about what this all meant without having some solid answers.

To speculate could only make her already vivid imagination get away with itself. She'd spent way too much of her childhood pretending to be one fictional character or another, and making up stories in her bedroom mirror as she practiced for the long-awaited time when she'd leave Cincinnati forever to become a famous actress.

It was better she didn't think too hard on this. Like for instance, maybe there was some evil force out there that didn't want her around, and it was lurking in the shadows, waiting to snuff her out.

But that was crazy.

And dramatic.

Yes. That was crazy dramatic.

* * *

THE NEXT MORNING brought only more questions as they ate breakfast around the kitchen island before preparing to head off to Rick's office.

"Okay, so we have two instances now that have been detrimental. My wrist, which, hey, Calamity, thanks for reattaching, and this thing with Poppy last night. We should be calling Familiar Central, because something's not right," Rick commented over his scrambled eggs.

Calamity had finally found a spell to literally knit Rick's hand back onto his wrist. It had been a little horror movie-ish, but it had worked.

"Oh, I called their asses, all right, and you know what they said after keeping me on hold for half an hour? Someone would get back to me. They're backed up with this blood moon prep."

Now Poppy nodded, forcing her eyes to look away from

Rick's handsome face as they ate. "My flying Wallenda act aside last night, and speaking of this blood moon, could someone explain it to me? I have no clue what any of this means and your Wi-Fi sucks. I can't get a signal on my phone to save my soul—which might need saving after last night. But you know what I *did* find out? I found out you witches are crazy bitches. Did you know that witches allegedly stole penises and kept them as pets? Like, according to this article, some guy wrote about how they made your stalks of love vanish and kept them in what this guy called a nest? I don't know if it's true, but if it is, what kind of medieval whacky is that?"

Rick squirmed in his chair, his laughter thin. "Feel like maybe you went a little overboard on the research there. Maybe you should stay away from Google and rely on us for correct information."

"So it's not true? How do you know? Were you there?" she asked, dropping her fork on the plate. "Because I'm not keeping anyone's junk in a nest."

"Good thing you're a familiar and not a witch then, huh?" Calamity snickered from her plate of fresh salmon, courtesy of Arch, who now slept in Rick's armchair after making them all breakfast.

"Here's something I was wondering. Did you smell the magic last night, Calamity? Like just after Poppy cannon-balled through the air?" Rick asked, popping a forkful of eggs into his mouth.

Calamity brushed up against his arm, rubbing the length of her body against him. "Damn right I did. It was ugly magic, for sure. That kind of magic contains only one thing. Malice and it's meant to harm. But why? Why would someone want to hurt Poppy?"

"Yeah. Why would someone want to hurt me?" she asked,

picking up her plate to bring to the sink in the center of the island.

As the daylight streamed in through the tall windows opposite his kitchen, misty-gray and chilling, she finally wondered out loud what they'd all been wondering, but hadn't articulated.

"I think we need to call the Doc," Nina said, cutting Carl's broccoli. "Maybe she can give us some fucking information on what the hell is going on, seeing as Familiar Central's so damn busy."

Poppy held up a finger after she slung a dishtowel over her shoulder and grabbed a sponge to wipe down the counters. "Right. Which brings me back to the blood moon thing. What's the deal? Do I need to get a new dress? Why's everyone in such an uproar over it?"

Rick brought his dish to the sink and rolled up his sleeves. "It's on Halloween this year—or Samhain, as we celebrate, often mispronounced as *Sam Hain*. It represents the death of one cycle and the birth of another, but it's also when the veil to the other realms is at its thinnest."

Poppy gulped as Rick squeezed into the space at the sink, his hip pressing to hers. "Meaning?"

"Meaning, all sorts of things can push their way through the veil. Halloween is already rife with plenty of shenanigans. Sometimes, what you see on TV is really real. But add in the blood moon, and it can get scary. Magic becomes more powerful, entities become bolder, spirits take their shot at breaking through. I'm just saying, things happen."

Handing Rick a dish, Poppy frowned. "So what's pushing through the veil that has Familiar Central so freaked out?"

He stopped rinsing the dishes and looked at her. "Well, demons for one. All manner of evil for two."

Flapping her hands, she sprinkled water in his face. "Is that all? Hah! What's the big deal about a little ol' demon?"

Marty's chair scraped against the floor as she reached over and dropped her plate in the sink. "Well, if we were talking about *our* demon, Darnell, it'd be no big deal at all. He's the sweetest man alive. But Darnell's also the exception to the rule. Have we called our boy today?"

Nina nodded, holding up her phone. "Yep. This sounds like it's right up his alley. Figured we'd better get him here pronto. I'm also gonna call the doc. She should at least be able to help with this bad magic shit. I'm not crazy about the kid up and disappearing the way she did last night. I can't fight what I can't fucking see."

"Good idea, Beastmaster! Now you're thinking like a witch," Calamity crowed. "Maybe she can cast a protective spell or something to help keep Poppy from harm."

"You have a demon?" she asked, though not nearly as surprised as she'd been just two days ago.

Wanda chuckled, handing over her coffee mug. "Well, we don't *have* one-have one. He's not like a pet, he's an integral part of our crew. Gentle as a lamb, fierce as a hungry tiger. He's one of the very reasons we're still here to tell our tales of adventure."

She stopped dropping dishes into the sink for a moment to ponder. "So a good demon?"

Wanda smiled her sweet smile and bobbed her head, folding her hands in front of her. "The very best demon."

Rick remained quiet during their conversation, and she sensed his reluctance in waves of discomfort. The thread was strong, wrapping around her heart and tugging.

So she elbowed him in the ribs, more because she rather liked touching him than to get his attention. "You okay with all this magic and demon stuff?"

His wide shoulders lifted in a shrug, but his eyes had a faraway, haunted look. "Why wouldn't I be?"

Blowing her hair from her eyes, she shook her head.

"Nah. Don't pretend like you didn't tell us last night you've had some bad experiences with magic. If we're gonna do this, Rick, or at least give it a fair shot, you have to be straight with me. Besides, in case you were wondering, I can feel you're upset. I don't know if that's what I'm supposed to do as a familiar, but I can, and it has to do with your heart. So I'm just checking on you. You don't have to tell me what soured you to your people, you just have to be honest that you are, in fact, sour."

His lips began to thin, but she gave him a stern look. "I mean it, Rick. Don't clam up on me now."

"It's a sore subject for me."

"The journey of a thousand miles begins with one step," she encouraged, drying her hands on the towel and taking a step back from him.

Everything about Rick was delicious. The way he smiled when he really meant to express his happiness. The way he looked at her with those intense dark eyes. The way he smelled. The way he'd protectively held her hand last night as he'd brought her back to the shed, and stayed by her side until they'd finished explaining how she'd come to be his familiar and who the OOPS girls and Calamity were.

But she wasn't only feeling what he was feeling; she was feeling things *for* him. Things she was uncomfortable feeling in the midst of all this turmoil. It was probably a hard-and-fast rule somewhere in the Big Book of Witches that familiars and their warlocks shouldn't have lustful thoughts for one another—she'd do well to remember that.

He stopped rinsing the last dish, interrupting her thoughts, and capturing her eyes with his gaze, a gaze no longer so far away. "Lao Tzu."

"Huh? Is that another magical, mystical, demon-freeing night I have to be afraid of?"

Rick gave her a crooked grin, but his dark eyes were full

of questions. "No. It's who said the quote you just repeated. The journey thing."

Where had that come from anyway? But she shrugged it off. "Oh. Well, Lao was a smart cookie because it's true. So how about you don't do the man thing and deny your squishy feelings anymore? At least acknowledge they exist. Because they do, and they interfere with our progress if you can't at least own them. It gives me a point of reference when you turn into a crabby ass."

He took a step forward, getting so close she could count the navy-blue lines on the fitted green shirt he wore. "Are we making another deal?"

Poppy's lips were suddenly dry, her throat tight. "If that's what it takes."

"Okay then, deal. I'll no longer hide the fact that I'm opposed to magic in all forms."

"You sure weren't opposed to using your magic when you froze Nina…"

He grinned, the white flash of his teeth and the deep brackets on either side of his lips making her stomach turn a flip. "Have you encountered her in threatening pose?"

Poppy giggled, swishing the towel in the space left between them as though she might ward off his sexy with mere fabric. "That's very fair. She can be very *Fight Club*."

"Yeah. She sure can. It happened without me thinking, though. She was there, and a woman to boot, a very angry woman. I would never hit a woman, but she was coming at me, full thrust, so I stopped her."

"In her tracks. It was quite impressive. She hasn't stopped bitching about it since it happened. But here's a thought. Maybe you could use your magic for good sometimes and you wouldn't hate it quite as much."

He stared at her for what felt like a hundred years before

he said, "Maybe I could, Poppy McGuillicuddy. Maybe I could."

His phone rang then, breaking the spell of whatever was happening between them, reminding her once again, she had no business having lustful thoughts for a man she had to spend the rest of her life spouting advice to.

But shoot, he was really good to look at, which was going to make her own journey that much more difficult.

CHAPTER 11

*A*s they headed down the long corridor at Sunset Ridge Nursing Home, Poppy tried to keep her nausea at bay. She'd experienced this deep unrest from the moment they'd pulled into the parking lot of the home, with its beautiful oak trees lining the entry, the rolling green hills littered with fall leaves, and the quaint brick building housing the seniors.

Everything should be fine. The setting was lovely—Mr. Rush couldn't have picked a better nursing home in which to spend his golden years.

Yet, she couldn't define this wave of panic filling her as they neared Mr. Rush's room. She'd asked Rick if she could take some time away to see him, so she could at least explain what happened and how she fully intended to pay back the rent she owed.

But Rick had insisted he drive her after last night. He wasn't taking any chances leaving her alone until they had time to talk to this doctor, January Malone, Nina, and Calamity mentioned as someone who might be able to help.

He'd declared himself glue, and he was sticking to her no matter what.

His words had warmed her from the inside out, and it was silly and girlie and ridiculous to give them any more attention than was due. Despite her strong attraction, Poppy had to remind herself they hardly knew each other, for gravy's sake.

Rick was a good enough guy, and that was all this was. She saw that now, felt it in her bones as she'd gotten to know him.

He wouldn't want to see her hurt, his sense of integrity was too strong, but it had nothing to do with anything else or she'd feel that, too, right? She had to stop creating romantic scenarios in her mind before it did them harm.

She renewed that vow as they walked together, her taking care not to brush against him as they plodded toward Mr. Rush's room and focused on seeing her landlord again.

According to Rick, via Mr. Rush's doctor, he understood everything going on around him. He just wasn't able to articulate as such in words, though he was working in physical therapy every day. But if he could understand what was happening and could hear her, that was all she needed.

As their feet ate up the white tile, Poppy smiled at how active and happy the seniors they passed were. Everyone was smiling and waving to her as they went about their day.

And that was an enormous relief. Rick had told her he'd ensured Mr. Rush's facility was one of the best, and he hadn't been kidding. From the rec room in bright, happy colors with plenty of sun and board games in every corner, to the dining room with vaulted ceilings, fabric napkins, real china and plenty of staff to care to the seniors' every whim, to the nurses who were incredibly sweet and informed, he'd been nothing but truthful.

Still, just as they approached the door to Mr. Rush's

room, her stomach revolted, heaving and rolling. She stopped, gripping the handrail on the wall, beads of sweat forming on her forehead.

"Hey, you okay?" Rick's concerned face loomed in front of hers, swaying to and fro in her blurred vision.

Swallowing hard, she breathed in and out, something she'd done a lot of since this all started. Poppy held up a finger. "Just gimme a sec."

What the hell was going on?

Rick leaned into her, offering support with the strength of his bulk, and she found she was grateful. There was a moment when she thought she might pass out from the cold sweat under her thick jacket.

But it finally passed and as she straightened her spine, wiping her clammy hands on her faded jeans, she looked up at him. "Sorry, I was just a little warm there. Let's go see a man about some late rent."

He smiled at her, brushing a stray strand of hair from her face in an intimate gesture she instantly blushed over. "You're a good egg, Poppy McGuillicuddy."

Pushing the door, Rick held it open for her. As she entered the sunny room, positioned directly in front of a park-like setting just outside the window, Poppy had to fight a gasp.

Rick had also warned her that Mr. Rush had lost a great deal of weight since his stroke, and to be prepared for the physical changes. At the time, she thought she had mentally geared herself up for seeing him as anything other than the lean man who was as spry and sharp as a twenty-year-old.

In fact, she'd given Rick a great deal of credit for keeping such close tabs on a man he'd only done business with. But to actually see Mr. Rush, sitting in a wheelchair, the left side of his gentle face slack, his cheekbones almost poking from his skin, Poppy really had to draw on every skill she'd ever acquired as an actress.

Yet, his glistening blue eyes lit up when he saw her, and he grunted.

So she smiled, wide and as bright as she knew how. "Mr. Rush! Holy cow, are you a sight for sore eyes!" Taking the chair opposite his wheelchair, she reached for his hand, the skin papery dry. "You rook mahhvelous!" she declared, doing her best impression of Billy Crystal's infamous Fernando Lamas.

He frowned at her and blew a raspberry as though to dispute her claim, the wrinkles on his forehead creasing into his snow-white hairline, but his eyes were warm and smiling.

Never kid a kidder, he'd always said. She tapped his wheelchair with her fingers. "Okay, so you've got some new hardware and you could use a haircut, but you're still as cute as ever."

Mr. Rush snorted, his fingers trembling when he tried to grip her hand.

Rick leaned down, patting Mr. Rush's hand with his tanned one. "Good to see you, sir. I trust they're treating you well?"

Mr. Rush nodded, and she was happy to see his eyes also lit up for Rick.

Tucking the blanket on his legs tighter around his waist, she asked, "How's the food here? Please tell me they don't give you the dreaded mushy green beans and applesauce?"

He snorted again and shook his head in the negative.

Patting his cold hand, she grinned. "Phew. Good thing or we'd have to riot, right? Maybe naked? Invite Mrs. Fedderman over? You know how much she loves to people-watch from her window in the buff."

Rick laughed a deep chuckle of understanding. "Nobody knows that better than me."

Poppy snickered and leaned back, taking in the cheerful room in soothing blue with framed, abstract artwork. "So do you need anything, Mr. Rush? Is there anything I can bring you? Do you have all your John Grisham books here?"

Mr. Rush nodded, lifting his bony finger to point at the closet in his room.

"Perfect. So, you wanna take a walk? I'll drive," she joked. "It's a pretty great day out. A little nippy, but I know how much you love this sort of weather. We could sit under that tree and have some hot tea?"

He lifted his arm and snapped it back with remarkably great reflex, the corner of the right side of his face lifting in a shadow of a smile as he mimicked a whip.

"Excellent, I'll grab your jacket and then you can lead on, my liege!"

"I'll get the tea," Rick offered. "I want to pop into the nurses' station and be sure you're behaving yourself, Mr. Rush. Okay?"

Translation—he was going to look in on Mr. Rush's care and be sure he was getting what he needed. Gosh, he was really nice when he wasn't being an asshole. He made her heart go all pitter-pat and soft.

Mr. Rush appeared okay with Rick's suggestion, so Poppy popped the brakes off his wheelchair and wheeled him out into the hall, talking as she went and updating him on everyone back at Littleton.

She pushed them out into the sunshine and made a hard right to the park-like area, where picnic tables were scattered, and the sun peaked through the amazing canvas of color from the leaves.

Taking a seat on a bench, she looked him in the eye. "Do you like it here, Mr. Rush? You can be honest with me. Rick tells me you're pretty happy here, but he's sort of biased, you know? If they're cruel to you or mistreat you or feed you all your meals from a blender, speak your piece. Just nod once for yes, you like it here, or twice for no, and if you hate it, I'll find a way to get you out."

The snow white of his hair bounced in the breeze when he nodded once, leaning into the effort by pushing his shoulders forward.

Poppy let out a sigh of relief and leaned back against the picnic table behind her, closing her eyes and inhaling the fresh scent of fall. "Phew. I didn't know what I was going to do if you hated it. I'm good, but I don't know if I'm good enough to sneak you out of here without getting caught."

He made a burbling sound in the back of his throat and lifted the half of his face still capable of moving in a smile.

"I know you're laughing because you just had a frightening mental image of ninja Poppy, pushing your wheelchair at high speed, tryin' to break you outta this joint."

Mr. Rush lifted his hand and thumped the wheelchair's arm, letting his head fall back on his shaking shoulders to indicate he had, indeed, pictured her making a break for it, and it was hysterical.

Leaning forward, she tucked his hand under the warm blanket and looked him in the eye. "So, listen Mr. Rush, I came to apologize to you. I still owe you three months' rent, and you were nothing but nice to me about it. I thought I'd have it all when I got back from the show I was on the road with, but the guy running it ran off with what little profit we made and bilked us all."

His groan slipped from his slack lips, and he attempted a sad/angry face, his lower lip jutting outward in a pout.

But Poppy shook her head. "Yeah. Boo-hiss, right? But forget that part. That's not your problem, Mr. Rush, and I'm not here to give you any kind of excuses. I just wanted you to know that no matter what, I'm going to be sure you get that money. You were always so kind to me—when I was down, when I'd lost yet another audition. You never let me give up on my dream even though I should have given up on it a hundred years ago. But I appreciate you so much. I appreciate that when I was late with my rent, you let it slide more than once. I appreciate that you let me stay long after I should have gone so you could rent the apartment to someone more reliable. You're a prince among men, Mr. Rush, and really, that's rare these days."

Mr. Rush winked, but shook his head and grumbled.

"What? You're denying you're a prince among men? Baloney, I say!" she cried out, laughing when Mr. Rush shook his finger at her. "Don't try to deny it. You know how awesome you are. We all do. Speaking of 'we', are you really okay with selling the building?"

At first she hadn't planned to broach the subject at all, thinking maybe it was better to let Mr. Rush alone, but this niggle she had wouldn't let her be. This twist in her stomach, this strange foreboding all still bugged the hell out of her when she recollected her conversation with Arnie Banks.

But upon her question, Mr. Rush sat up in his wheelchair, rigid and tense. His papery-thin skin went pale but for the two bright spots of crimson on his cheeks.

That swell of nausea assaulted her again, making her grip her stomach just as Rick came out of the building with two cups of steaming tea in his hand.

But now, seeing the faraway look in Mr. Rush's eye, she couldn't just let this go, and she had to make it fast before Rick was within hearing distance. "Mr. Rush? Nod if you're really okay with selling the building. If Rick pressured you or harassed you at all, tell me. *Please*. I can't help but find it so curious everyone just agreed to this. So give me a sign, any sign, and I'll see to it they stop the demolition."

Mr. Rush looked right through her, but he didn't budge, frightening her.

Her heart began a steady thrum of panic as she stared back at him, considering going to get a nurse. "Mr. Rush? Can you nod yes or no? Are you okay with the sale of the building? Once for yes, twice for no."

His nod happened with a slow downward descent of his head, but what Poppy couldn't get past was the dead look in his eyes. It was as though someone had come along and literally erased all emotion from them.

"I have tea, milady," Rick said as he approached, a smile on his face. He held up the cup before passing one to Mr. Rush, helping him wrap his fingers around the Styrofoam before passing hers over.

She watched Mr. Rush over the rim of her cup. Watched how he watched Rick with admiration. So she let go of her crazy notion Rick had anything to do with pressuring the man to sell Littleton.

Holding up her cup, she clinked it with Mr. Rush's. "Here's to Littleton. Long may she live in our hearts and memories!"

The moment the words fell from her mouth was the moment Mr. Rush appeared to return to their conversation, as though someone had beamed him back up. His shaky hand pressed his cup against hers in return, the amber liquid of the tea sloshing along the side.

As Rick helped him steady the cup and sip his tea, Poppy's anxiety grew in leaps and bounds. That ugly feeling that something was so wrong plagued her.

As Rick chatted amicably with Mr. Rush, Poppy observed, hoping to find something, any little hint, anything of any substance to lend this crazy, unexplainable fear.

She was on to something. It burrowed in her bones. She felt it. Knew it. She just didn't know what that something was.

By hell, she'd find it though.

She'd find it.

* * *

A FIRE BLAZED in the shed's fireplace, crackling and warm, the blue and purple embers spiking and spitting.

Calamity sat on the white stone hearth, curled up, her eyes closed, purring her contentment. After another phenomenal dinner, Carl, Arch and the girls all sat around the tiny kitchen island playing cards.

During dinner, she'd thought long and hard about Mr. Rush and the bizarre way he'd reacted to her questions about selling Littleton, and she'd continued to come up dry. But the worry for him and her neighbors remained, and she couldn't shake the feeling.

To take her mind off things, Poppy decided to dig into the Big Book of Rick, dropped ceremoniously in the pile of trash the first night they'd met.

"Mind if I sit with you?" Rick asked as she tucked her legs under her on the couch.

"Sure," she said absently, sliding to the other side of the cushions so he wouldn't end up too close.

His nearness made her giddy, maybe even downright swoony, and it would only take a toll on their relationship. She only had a little time left to prove to him she could work in his life, and she was determined to do such without muddying the waters with romantic notions.

But he leaned in and tapped the wad of papers she was reading, strung together with, of all things, punched holes and twine. "What's this, Miss McGuillicuddy?" he asked, his lips much too close to her ear.

Poppy kept her eyes on the stack of papers. "Homework."
"For?"

Tapping the papers, she looked up to find him studying her intently. "It's the big book of you."

"Me?" he gasped in mock outrage.

"Uh-huh. From Familiar Central. Calamity says they send one for every new familiar. Sort of a getting-to-know-you manual. I'm only just now getting a chance to read it. It's supposed to unlock all your secrets," she teased.

"That entire waste of a tree is about me?"

She grinned, pointing to the highlights of his life's history in one paragraph. "*Si, señor* Ricardo Delassantos—who, by the way, was born in a small town in Mexico to Delfina and Eduarte Delassantos—moved to America with his parents when he was just a year old. Broke his leg when he was eight after jumping off a swing in the park, attended Kendall High School, was voted best all-around athlete, and graduated with high honors."

His face said he was impressed. "Absolutely true."

"Went on to attend Princeton University, where Mr. Fancy-Schmancy worked his way through school by slinging hash at a local diner and working for a moving company. Graduated with a degree in engineering, loves vintage cars, dabbling in the stock market, and ice hockey. Some of his favorite things are: horror movies, hot dogs, chocolate fudge brownie ice cream, pears, animals of all kinds and the color red."

Rick grinned, the deep grooves on either side of his face flashing as he reached over her arm and tapped the papers again. "All very accurate. Though, I waffle between red and blue."

"Wait, it also says you like Brussels sprouts—as in, you eat them, willingly?"

He chuckled, leaning his arm on the back of the couch so close to her shoulders, she almost couldn't think. "With relish. I mean, not actual relish, but you know. I dig a good Brussels sprout."

Poppy made a gagging noise and wrinkled her nose. "Ick. Though, I admit, I love sardines."

Now Rick made a gagging noise with an exaggerated shiver. "Fish in a can is disgusting."

Laughing, she said, "So it also says you worked your way through Princeton? Who does that and doesn't die from sleep deprivation?"

He winked, absently twisting a strand of her hair around his index finger. "This guy. I'm not saying it was easy, and I did get a partial scholarship, which helped, but it's where I always wanted to go to college. So I made it a priority."

"A man with a goal. I admire that." And she did. Anyone who stuck out more schooling after graduation was a saint as far as she was concerned.

"You had a goal, too. A goal you're still working toward."

Poppy snorted, making a face. "That's really generous of you, but I think my goal was a little less realistic than yours. Or a lot. The chances of me becoming a huge star have narrowed to nil at this point. Plus, look at me, then look at you. We can hardly compare the two. I'm thirty-four, and I have nothing. You're thirty-five, and you have everything." *Everything.*

He leaned back, the red shirt he wore gaping at the throat to reveal his smooth chest. "Everything is subjective. I have a lot of work to fill my days, but not a lot else."

"You do work a lot. You could certainly use some balance. Like the occasional party or two."

"I think Avis has that covered for the both of us," he joked, and there was no malice to his words.

His words were fond, and that made her squirm. She'd *bet* Avis had it covered. Scumbag...

"So you met Avis at Princeton, right?"

"Yep. He was an exchange student from London. We hit it off from day one."

"What? Like in polo class or something?"

Ugh. His loyalty to Avis troubled her deeply. Something in her wanted to scream, "He's a fraud!" but she had no proof to back that up, and if she was to get to know Rick, she had to know and accept everyone in his life, too, until she had some kind of proof her intuition wasn't just a fluky result of becoming a familiar.

Rick barked his laughter. "Not exactly. More like English Lit, and he was way better than I ever was at that class. Our professor was one tough dude, but Avis charmed the stodgy right out of him."

"So was it some crazy coincidence you ended up finding another warlock at a place like Princeton?"

"I'm pretty sure it wasn't a coincidence. The powers that be are good at putting our kind together to keep us with others who are like us."

Like us. He'd said that with vague disdain. She needed to find out what his dislike of magic was about. What had happened to make him so bitter? She didn't want to read about it, she wanted him to share. His hatred of magic was part of what made him tick, and she wanted to understand.

"So does Avis hate magic like you, too? Did you bond over that?"

"Nope. Avis is all about the magic. He'd love it if we were able to do more. But as you know, our female counterparts are the real warriors in our world."

Poppy grinned harder. "Ah, and you say that without malice. I like it."

"It's how we're raised from birth."

"So Avis enjoys the use of his magic?"

"Almost to his detriment and it always involves a woman.

Though, in his defense, when he came to Princeton, he'd been hurt pretty bad by a relationship. "

Maybe this was a lead to why she was so turned off by Avis. Maybe it was nothing more than he was a womanizer. "Interesting. What happened?"

"He's never really talked about it much, other than saying someone he loved deeply burned him."

Rolling her eyes, she wrinkled her nose at Rick. "I'm so surprised you never talked about it. Men."

"It's just not how we roll, *bonita*."

The word *bonita* reminded her of his very light, only occasionally detectable accent. "So you came from Mexico with your parents at a year old. Yet, you still have a hint of an accent."

He bobbed his head, his dark hair falling toward his chin. "Though both of my parents spoke English fluently, they encouraged me to speak Spanish at home. I think it sort of stuck with me. It reminds me of them, I guess. It gets thicker when I curse in Spanish."

His parents, both deceased; felt like a sore subject. Maybe one best left for another getting-to-know-you session. They were in a nice, noncombative place right now, and while she was all for pushing him to open up to her, she wasn't for pushing him over the ledge.

Instead, Poppy asked the question burning on the tip of her tongue ever since she'd picked up the Rick Manual. "So it says here Yash was the name of your last familiar. Mind if I ask what happened?"

Because he hadn't said a word about any other familiar in his life. In fact, she hadn't even thought about asking if he'd had others.

But this Yash was listed as his familiar since Rick was a child. He was her predecessor. Surely he had something to say about him?

Yet, that was the moment Rick tensed up, his body language changing in the blink of an eye as his fingers tightened in a clenched fist and his jaw hardened. "I don't mind if you ask, I'm just not ready to answer."

Oh, okay. Here it came. That close-mouthed, withdrawn, I-can't-go-there-just-yet shtick. She braced herself when she said, "Look, we can keep things as superficial as you'd like, I guess. We can talk about your love of heinous little balls of green puke. We can talk about Princeton. We can talk about '56 Chevys. But we can't really understand each other, really get to a place where I understand your reactions and motivations, if you don't divulge."

Instead of loosening up, he became more rigid and unyielding, letting go of the strand of her hair he'd been playfully twisting around his finger and sitting back against the couch.

"Yash is a closed subject."

As Poppy was about to get more insistent, the doorbell to the shed rang, startling her.

"Got it!" Nina bellowed, her husky voice ringing through the small living room.

As they both sat in tense silence, Poppy simmering and Rick clamping his lips up tighter than if a vise had been slapped on his mouth, Marty, Wanda, Carl, and Calamity were all sound and motion, welcoming someone inside.

A pretty woman with round glasses, her chestnut hair in a fishtail braid over her right shoulder, held out her hand to Poppy. "Hi, Poppy. Sorry it took me so long to get here, but as you know, blood moon prep is upon us. Some patients are more freaked out than others. Anyway, I'm January Malone. A therapist and a witch." She followed her introduction with a smile, making her pretty face even prettier.

Poppy hopped up and took her hand, smiling in return.

"You're the person who referees between these two, right? Where's your headgear?"

January grinned, crossing her arms over her chest, the sparkle of her wedding ring offset by the purple sweater she wore. "I left it in the car," she said on a chuckle but then her nose wrinkled. "Calamity?"

"Yeah, Doc?"

"You smell that?"

Calamity circled January's ballet-slippered feet. "Pizza. I smell pizza. With anchovies. Did you and Mr. Doctor have pizza for dinner?"

Bending at the waist, the doctor scooped up Calamity and tipped her chin. "Mr. Doctor doesn't eat food, remember? And that's not what I mean. Sniff Poppy." Holding the cat up, she put her directly in front of Poppy.

Calamity took a deep whiff, her whiskers tickling Poppy's face. "Ooooh. Aw, yeah. Damn, Doc. That's what I was afraid of. It ain't good at all. I was hoping I was wrong, but Rick smelled it the other night, too. So we called you to be sure."

Panic began to swirl in Poppy's belly as she looked from January to Calamity and their stricken faces. "What?"

January set Calamity down and took Poppy's hand. "Why don't we sit?"

Rick, who had risen when January entered, stuck his hand out. "Rick Delassantos. Pleasure to meet you."

January took it and gave it a firm shake then turned her gaze back to Poppy. "Can we sit?"

But Poppy shook her head, jamming her hands into the pockets of her jeans. "Nope. Just hit me with it. I can take it."

Nina gave her a thump on the shoulder as Carl grabbed her hand with his stiff one and tucked her near. "Sit, kiddo. Don't be a fucking hero."

Now her stomach twisted into a knot so tight, she thought her belly might explode. "Just say it."

January put a hand on her shoulder and squeezed as she looked her straight in the eye. "You're surrounded by hatred right now."

Hatred? Her chest grew tight as her legs grew wobbly. "And?"

"And it wants you out of the picture."

Now her throat dried up, too, and her heart began to crash against her ribs. "Like, out of the picture move to Canada? Or out of the picture as in it's curtains for you?"

Now January planted both hands on her shoulders as Rick pressed his hands into her waist. "As in, out of the picture someone wants you dead."

CHAPTER 12

"I think I need to sit," Poppy murmured, reaching blindly for the first thing to support her, but Rick grabbed her around the waist from behind and brought her back to the couch, setting her down and sitting next to her.

He grabbed her hand and looked to January, who'd taken the armchair opposite them. "Do you know the origin of this hate?"

She shook her head, her eyes sympathetic and round behind her glasses. "I don't. I can't pinpoint it. I might be able to summon something with a spell, but whoever is behind this won't easily be revealed."

Marty slid a cup of tea in front of Poppy. When she didn't respond, she physically took her hands and placed them around the cup then sat on the side of the couch and wrapped an arm around Poppy, letting her chin rest on the top of her head. "Drink, honey. Drink and breathe," she whispered.

So in this crazy new society, and in her deep desire to understand these people whom she'd call her own, she decided to face this head on and not only attack it but understand it. "Please explain what you mean when you say I'm surrounded by hate. I don't understand how you can see something like that."

"As I said, I'm a witch, Poppy. I can see auras, and your aura is mingled with someone else's. But sometimes, because I'm certainly not the most powerful witch, I can't always see the person belonging to the hateful aura unless they're right in front of me. Like, in your case, your aura is light and breezy. You've had hard times, but your passion, your creativity keeps you tethered to the joy of life. You never give up. You have a good heart. You're loyal and kind, hardworking. You throw yourself into whatever it is you do, and you do it with all your heart. You're all things good, and when I look at you, I see that—so clearly, so brightly. There is no malice in you.

"But there's an aura, one lurking in the shadows of your own aura, and it's angry. So angry. I'd go so far as to say malevolent. It's ugly, and for whatever reason, it wants something extinguished to feed its anger. I suspect this is why you were launched into the woods the other night. It was an attempt to purge hatred—to appease it. It's a temper tantrum of sorts."

A shiver assaulted her, threading throughout her body in tremors. "So what do I do? How do I combat this hate? One I can't see? Who could possibly hate me enough to want me dead? I mean, sure, there are people who don't like me. We all have our haters, right? But this is a little extreme, and I'm going to be honest—no one has attempted to take my life until I got here and became one of you."

"I won't lie, Poppy. Your new world, Rick's world and mine, is filled with plenty of good, but there's also bad, too."

Yeah. This was so much good. "Which leads me back to

my original question. What do I do to stop this? Will there be more attempts on my life?"

"Not if I can help it," Rick said, his face a tight mask of anger.

"This is my fault," Calamity said mournfully from her feet. "All my damn fault. I'm sorry, Poppy. So damn sorry."

Closing her eyes, she reached down and scratched Calamity's ear. "No blame, Calamity. It was an accident. I know that." Then she lifted her chin. "So auras and evil on the back burner for a second, how did I turn Rick to stone and tear up his ceiling in his kitchen with just the wave of my hand? I thought you guys had all the power and we were just supposed to advise you? Why is mine so strong?"

Smiling, January leaned forward, her eyes twinkling from behind her frames. "Because sometimes, when a match like yours is made, it's fated, and you get the double-whammy effect. Rick's magic, plus your very new, very fragile and out-of-control magic, make for some very solid magic."

"Hah!" Calamity chirped, jumping to the kitchen island where Nina sat and lifting a paw. "Up top, Half-Breed. I knew it! The two of you together are magic times ten!"

Nina fist-bumped Calamity and winked, her grin wide. "You called it, you pain in my ass."

Rick scooted forward on the couch, steepling his hands under his chin. "So my magic is stronger when I'm with Poppy. The question is, how do we control it so she's not turning me into something you'd find in the Home Depot garden center?"

Looking down at her hands, Poppy nodded. "Yeah. I think some control might be in order. That was probably the scariest half hour of my life. Though I won't deny, it *was* a little cool. So how do I get a grip on this and keep from hurting someone?"

January gave her another one of those soothing smiles.

"We teach you, of course. We teach both of you to harness your energy as a duo and manage it."

Yeah. Just like Batman and Robin. Rick surely would be up for harnessing the magic he hated as a team, right?

"So what do we do until then, January? How do we figure out who this malevolent aura is and how do we stop it?" Wanda asked, threading her arm through Arch's.

"If only I had the answer. First, we need to identify it and find out if it's personal or some misguided spirit with a grudge."

"Of course it's personal. It launched me into the woods," Poppy reminded, twisting her clammy hands together.

"That's not what I mean, Poppy. What I mean is the act itself. Could be the anger this aura is presenting has nothing to do with you and everything to do with simply lashing out."

"So maybe someone doesn't necessarily want *me* dead— just a death in general?" Still, to think this aura was attached to her had Poppy far more freaked out than anything that had happened since this all began.

January blew out a breath of air, her lean cheeks puffing outward. "Maybe. But that doesn't feel right. I know it's scary, but the attack *does* feel aimed at you. However, if you can't think of anyone who wishes you ill, the scenario of a temper tantrum, revenge with no care for collateral damage, does fit. But that this aura also wants death, whether that's aimed at you personally or not, it's still death."

Poppy gulped, wiping her clammy hands on her thighs. "Okay, so here's an outlandish thought, why don't you witches and your magic spells and incantations call this thing up? Like, 'Hey in there! Come out, come out wherever you are and stop beating up Poppy! What'd she ever do to you?' You know, like a good old-fashioned exorcism?"

Calamity scoffed, her whiskers bobbing. "Because we don't summon spirits, Poppy-Seed. Or at least neither

January nor I do. And you're not freakin' possessed. It's not the same as having an aura haunt yours. Auras are slippery sumbitches. They attach themselves to you and hook their claws into your soul."

"If you two can't do an incantation to summon this, we could still damn well put in an emergency call to Familiar Central and tell them about it, couldn't we?" Rick asked, his anger clearly bubbling just below the surface. "We could get someone here who does specialize in it. As in pronto."

January rolled her eyes as though he were crazy. "Rick, you know what this time of year is like without the blood moon. But with the blood moon upon us? Where are we going to find someone to identify an aura when it's all hands on deck at every portal?"

"Portal?" Poppy squeaked. God, there was so much to learn. Portals and auras and double magic and fate. She was quite suddenly more overwhelmed than she'd been so far in this process.

Rick folded his hands in front of him and gave a curt nod. "Yes, portals. There are many. Some lead to good places, some to not-so-good places. As I mentioned, the blood moon thins the veil and opens up this world to evil from other planes. Everyone who has even a modicum of power is going to be in combat mode come Halloween."

Poppy had this image of ghosts flying around in a midnight sky, circling for their prey. Sort of like Ghostbusters, but maybe less jokey.

"Okay, so we wait until after Halloween to call Familiar Central and rid me of this aura. It's not far off. We just watch out for bad auras, right?"

No big deal. Just watch for totally invisible entities.

"To be safe, until we can get some answers, I'm going to do a protection spell on you, Poppy. I don't know the strength of the aura. I might not be the strongest witch, but I'm no weakling."

Yes! Yes, a protection spell, a whatever spell. Whatever would help, Poppy was down for.

Clapping her hands on her legs, she rose, ready to attack this and move on to the next problem. "Okay, so what do I do? Do I have to gather moths' wings? Do we need a cauldron with bubbling green goo? Frogs? Oh, please don't say frogs. I love frogs. They have those cute little legs and beady little eyes. I had a pond behind me where I lived when I was a kid, and I'd die if we had to sacrifice a frog."

Both January and Rick barked a laugh. "No frogs," January reassured. Rising from the armchair, she approached Archibald and gave him a quick hug. "So, Arch? Got some raspberry Kool-Aid?"

* * *

"Kool-Aid? Like for real, the kid is gonna drink a frickin' metaphor?" Nina asked, her dark eyes skeptical.

January chuckled. "For real, Vampire. It's just to hide the taste of the spell, but it works every time."

January pulled a packet from her medical bag containing a powdery substance and dumped it into the glass of dark pink liquid. With her index finger, she made the water swirl until it was a deep vortex of color.

The good doctor's calming tones, her honesty about this aura haunting her, her soothing nature, all served to calm Poppy. She didn't doubt January was a solid therapist, and when all was said and done, when things had evened out a bit and her world wasn't so filled with chaos, she planned to make an appointment with her.

Until then, Poppy prayed this protection spell would do

the trick, and she was going in with total trust. Whatever it took to rid herself of the evil attached to her.

Closing her eyes, January squared her shoulders and said, "Spirits know this, know this well, protect Poppy with this spell. Harm be hindered, chaos be gone, keep her safe from dusk till dawn!" She let her hand fly open, her palm over the glass, before she removed it with flourish and snapped her fingers.

The pink water hissed and bubbled momentarily, creating a white froth. As quickly as the liquid stirred, it also calmed, eventually going still. The doctor opened her eyes and smiled at Poppy and pointed to the glass. "Chugalug, baby."

Nina, Marty, and Wanda, along with sweet-sweet Carl, pounded their fists on the kitchen island like they were all in college and sang out, "Drink! Drink! Drink!"

Laughing, Poppy lifted the cup to her lips and threw it back, guzzling the drink until it was gone while everyone cheered—even the very proper Arch.

The moment she finished, she stuck her tongue out, scraping her knuckles over it with a gag. "Gah! That's awful! What is that?"

Rick leaned down and whispered in her ear, "Goats' eyeballs. Dried, of course, and maybe some virgins' tears. I hear those are very powerful."

Nudging him in the ribs, Poppy giggled. "You better shut—"

Those were the last words to exit her mouth.

What came out after that was her dinner, on a hot, acidic spew of liquid, spraying from her mouth like a fountain.

Her belly protested the contents being ripped from her, heaving and rolling with acrid swells. Leaning forward, Poppy gasped on a sharp intake of breath and wrapped her hands around her waist as a white-hot flash of electricity zigzagged through her, making beads of sweat pop out on her forehead.

Her eyes went wide in panic and fear. She couldn't speak. She couldn't ask for help. She couldn't do anything but fight a scream from the agonizing pain rising from her stomach and lodging in her chest.

The lights in the shed flickered, the small chandelier over the entryway swaying so hard, the sheetrock began to pull away from the ceiling. The floor beneath them rumbled, at first distantly, then growing louder as it picked up steam, crashing in her ears, matching the pounding tide of her pulse.

And with that, Poppy heaved again, this time her stomach almost turning itself inside out, the violent hacking stealing her breath.

She fell forward toward the island countertop, almost cracking her head but for Carl, who threw himself in front of her, gripping her shoulders as she dropped against him, unable to get her legs beneath her.

His awkward, stiff arms went around her immediately as her face cracked against his thin chest. "Popp-yy!" he stammered, the alarm in his voice crystal clear.

She heard Nina yelp, "What the fuck is going on, Doc? What the hell did you give her?"

And then Marty screamed, "What in the living hell is *that*?"

Poppy wanted to look up. She wanted to know what the hell *that* was, too. She wanted to know why there was a hint of terror in Marty's voice, but she couldn't because whatever had rooted in her gut was now screeching from her mouth.

Her head fell back on her shoulders as Rick grabbed for her from behind, his strong hands supporting her helpless form. Her throat began to swell like a balloon until she thought surely her skin would split, her legs going rigid, the muscles so tense, they were sure to snap.

And then she retched, retched like no college coed before, her mouth opening so wide, it was as though someone had pried it open with a crowbar. A taste so foul, so ungodly, flew from her throat, and she was helpless to stop the coming wave.

"Help her, for Goddess's sake!" Rick shouted, his voice hoarse and cracked, his grip on her tight as her body shook until she swore she heard her bones rattle.

Vaguely, she heard January and Calamity begin to chant as the shed shook and shuddered, rocking and lifting with creaky groans. "Evil be gone, we refute your hold! Evil leave us, no longer so bold!"

More hands were on her as Rick continued to hold her from behind, rocking back and forth when she collapsed against his chest, whispering soothing words.

Whatever they'd done, whatever those words evoked, the evil clearly did not have its cooperative pants on today, because everything just became worse.

A low hum, like a transformer sizzling before it blows, began an upward climb of noise, tearing at Poppy's ears until the sound was all she could hear.

It whirled in her eardrums, pounding, ripping, punching its way to a frenzy, clawing at her, pulling her from Rick's arms until, in a whoosh of air, it lifted her upward...

The intent obvious—crush her against the ceiling.

Everything happened in slow motion, the weightlessness of her limbs, her awareness that if she didn't do something to stop this, she'd end up embedded in the sheetrock above her, the notion that whatever had a hold on her left her feeling dirty and ashamed.

"*By all that is mine, I order thou to release!*" Rick roared, so loud the shed reverberated with his demand.

"Arch! Look out!" Poppy heard Wanda cry out in distress before there was a loud thunk of what sounded like body-to-body contact and Nina was screaming, "I got her!"

Then she was falling, her limbs thrashing, her stomach dropping in similar fashion to that of riding a roller coaster. Arms caught her, the strength of them secure and comforting in their capture.

Nina grunted in her ear as they fell to the floor in a heap, knocking the wind out of her.

Rick's was the first face she saw, his eyes masked in worry. Pulling her upward, he enveloped her in his arms, the scent of his cologne settling in her nose as he pressed his lips to the top of her head. "Jesus, Poppy. Are you okay?"

Her head fell back, limp and dizzy, but she managed a nod, her stomach hot with the ache of vomiting. "I think my intestines need to be stuffed back into my body. Is that a thing? I mean, can that actually be done? Somebody call the witch proctologist."

His laughter slithered into her ears, almost making her smile, except her lips felt like someone had taken a shoehorn to them and stretched them out. "I think you still have your intestines. I don't know how that's possible after what just happened, but I think you're good."

She wanted to struggle out of his embrace, certain it was inappropriate, and January would report back to the powers that be that she was a dirty-dirty whore, but she had nothing left.

It had all flown out of her mouth.

"Give her to me, Rick," January demanded, pulling Poppy from Rick's embrace and saving her the embarrassment of a weak show of feministic strength. "Poppy, oh Goddess! Are you okay?"

As the doctor's face came into focus, her hair wild about her face, her glasses cracked, Poppy forced a smile. "Duh. I just puked a demon. I think the purge is complete. What's not okay about that?"

"Fuck, you're GD awesome!" Nina crowed, looking down at her with a hint of admiration in her eyes.

"Is everyone okay? Carl? Archibald?" Poppy asked, attempting to sit up, only to be settled back against January with a gentle hand.

January patted her shoulder with a light touch. "Everyone's fine. Just catch your breath."

Calamity scampered near her head, pressing a paw to her cheek, making a clucking noise. "I'm sorry. I suck the ass of an elephant for getting you into this, Poppy-Seed. I'm the crappiest of crap. But I'm gonna tell ya the truth. We got big trouble."

January bit the inside of her cheek, enforcing Calamity's claim. "She's right. We got trouble."

"Should I have a scotch in hand when you define 'big trouble'?"

Marty and Wanda helped January lift Poppy to her feet and brought her to the couch, where Rick plumped a shredded pillow behind her.

But Poppy waved them away. "Don't fuss over me, just tell me what big trouble is."

The silence to follow was deafening.

"I'm not hearing an answer."

January knelt in front of her and took her hands. "The aura I told you about—the malevolent one? That's what you vomited."

She searched January's eyes, not understanding the fear she read in them. "But that's good, right? Rick told it to let go and it did. So all gone, no? Sort of like an exorcism."

January shook her head, gripping her fingers. "No. It's not all gone. That was only a taste of what it's capable of. My protection spell should have at least kept this thing at bay.

But it broke through the spell, Poppy. I've never seen that happen before."

Poppy blanched, the remaining acrid taste on her tongue souring her stomach all over again. "And that means?"

Licking her lips, her face lined with concern, January held fast to her hands, her fingers digging into Poppy's. "Whatever this force is, it's latched onto you, and it's not leaving. I've never seen anything so powerful. But worse, I don't know how to get it out of you."

CHAPTER 13

"Ghostbusters?" Poppy asked, only half joking. If there was a crisis group for newly minted paranormals, why couldn't there really be a group who busted ghosts?

But January didn't laugh, and neither did Calamity nor Rick, which didn't bode well, she suspected. "I need to do some research on the obscure, but while I do, I want you to promise never to stray far from anyone. You can't be alone with this entity."

"Done deal," Poppy agreed, hoping she didn't sound desperate and petrified, even if she really was.

But the doctor gripped her hands harder. "I mean it, Poppy. Keep someone with you at all times until I figure this out. This isn't something to play with. You *need* someone who can help, or at least call for help if it attacks again. The ladies are tough as nails, don't get me wrong, but this doesn't just require brawn. It requires a spell or a summoning, or... I'm not sure. Something stronger than I've got, that's for sure. Are we clear?"

"She won't have to worry about that, January. I'll stay

close." As if to prove his good intentions, Rick wrapped an arm around Poppy, pulling her to his side.

"*Okay?*" January asked again, peering into her eyes.

Poppy nodded outwardly, but on the inside, the inside not torn up by this aura she'd puked, she was terrified. "Okay."

Squeezing her fingers one last time, January rose, smoothing her skirt. "I need a laptop from someone, please."

"And coffee, I've no doubt, Mistress January," Arch, Johnny-on-the-spot as always, offered.

She smiled and gripped his upper arm, running an affectionate hand over his battered ascot. "You're a prince among men, Arch. Yes, please. Coffee is necessary if I'm going to keep my eyes open."

Arch and January scurried off into the kitchen, picking their way over the strewn throw pillows and overturned end table.

"Calamity? Ladies? Let's see how we can aid January," Wanda suggested, giving Poppy's head a stroke of her hand before she left for the kitchen as well.

Nina chucked her under the chin. "Jesus, that was something. All that green and yellow puke comin' out of your mouth like some freight train bound for hell. And look at you—still walkin' and talkin'. You're the shit, kiddo."

Green and yellow puke certainly was a testament to one's constitution. She grabbed Nina's wrist and squeezed. "Thanks for catching me. I owe you one."

"You owe me shit. Glad I was there," she muttered before taking her leave to join everyone else, so clearly uncomfortable with praise.

When it was just she and Rick left, the silence didn't become as uncomfortable as she'd thought it would after their conversation about Yash. Instead, he kept his arm around her and pulled her back to lean against him.

"Was it really green and yellow?"

"I think there was some red in there, too. But I can't be sure. It all happened in a split second of sound and color."

"You think anyone thought to YouTube it?"

His laughter rumbled deep in his wide chest. "Feel like that might create some widespread panic, you know?"

Relaxing, Poppy inhaled a soothing breath. "Yeah. That's fair. I think I might need to go brush my teeth."

"I think I'd support that choice."

Now she laughed, letting her head fall to his shoulder as she looked up at the cracked ceiling. "Ever tasted an aura?"

"Can't say I have."

"It's far more disgusting than your Brussels sprouts. In fact, I'd rather eat a barrel of those green balls than puke an aura ever again. But my eternal thanks for making that thing let go of me. How'd you do it?"

"I think it was us a whole, Poppy. It's the only explanation. I've never had that much power before. I think what January says is true. Our power together is strong. I felt the current."

"But I didn't do anything but flail helplessly like a fish out of water."

"But did you feel the magic?"

"I felt the burn on my tongue like a nuclear bomb had gone off in my mouth, but I can't pinpoint the same feeling I had when I turned you to stone. I think I was too caught up in the pain of my intestines being ripped from me via my throat at that point."

He squeezed her tighter. "It was there, Poppy. I felt it."

"And you're admitting it?"

He sighed, turning her to him so her cheek lay on his chest. "I'm admitting it. I don't have a choice but to admit what was right in front of me. That aura could have killed you. The hell I'd let that happen."

His words warmed her in a place deep inside where she'd never felt this kind of warmth before, and it left her almost breathless. "I appreciate you protecting me, but I don't want you to go against your principals on my account."

"This thing with magic, my dislike of its use, goes back to my parents…"

"Doesn't what puts us on the therapy couch always lead back to our parents?" she teased, hoping he'd see his explanation didn't have to be a tense conversation.

"Maybe it does, but in this case, magic killed my mother, and eventually my father."

She sat up, placing a palm over his heart. "Oh, Rick. I'm so sorry."

"My parents were good people. When they immigrated here to the states, it was on the promise my father's best friend would help get him a job at the paper mill he worked for."

Hackles rose on the back of her neck. "Was this friend a warlock?"

"He was, as was his boss, who took a shine to my mother. The long and short of it is, the bastard cast a spell on her, a cleaving spell. A spell you're helpless to fight against, even though you're aware of everything happening to you. You can't speak in protest. You can't do anything but ride the tide."

Poppy gripped his hand, fascinated by the contrast of their skin. "He didn't. Oh, God, he…"

Rick nodded, his slick black hair gleaming in streaks under the lights. "He did. She left my father and me for this guy. She had no will to stop it, but I saw it in her eyes, I saw how he'd turned her into a helpless puppet on the outside. But inside? She was dying."

"And your father's magic wasn't strong enough to remove the spell, was it?" she asked, her voice low and hushed.

"No. And every day, he'd see Mama at work while his friend's boss dragged her around like his toy, and it broke him, brought him to his knees until he couldn't even get out of bed some mornings. But he eventually found someone he thought could break the spell."

"Who?"

His head hung low, his chin at his chest. "Me."

Oh God. No. Please don't tell me Rick was responsible for his mother's death.

Gulping, she was afraid to push any more. "Don't. Don't tell me if it's too painful. Please. I don't want to make this any harder."

But Rick shook his head, his lips in a firm line of determination. "Nope. You're right. You have to know what happened. I don't know why my father thought I could break the spell. I was just a kid with typical, very minimal warlock powers. But Papa swore he'd prayed to the Goddess, and she'd told him I was the savior to this problem. Looking back now, from an adult perspective, I truly believe he was delusional at that point. With his grief, with his fear. He wasn't sleeping or eating…but I didn't have anyone to turn to. I didn't know *who* to turn to anyway."

Poppy closed her eyes and absorbed the information, but she didn't speak.

"Anyway, convinced I was the one who'd be able to break the spell, Papa taught me the incantation. I read it over and over again. I practiced doing all the right things, using all the right sacrificial objects."

"And you did it because you were a good kid and you were just doing what your father told you to do. You know that, right?" He had to know that.

Rick's fingers flexed in his lap, the veins beneath his olive-colored skin pulsing. "Rationally, I absolutely do. But it doesn't change the fact that when I read this incantation, when I summoned this dark force that was supposed to break the spell and release my mother, it didn't break the spell. It didn't break the spell because my magic was weak, and no matter how much I practiced, I'd have never been able to pull it off without help from someone with stronger magic."

Biting the inside of her cheek, Poppy tucked her chin beneath the neck of her sweater. "What did it do?"

"It stole my mother's heart. Ripped it right from her chest," he rasped.

As though a sonic boom of information had fallen into the room, Poppy fought a gasp. She gripped his hand and squeezed with everything she had in her. "I'm sorry, Rick. I..." Words failed her.

"And then my father's boss killed him for taking my mother away. A woman who had no defense against him."

Now she *did* gasp, instantly stuffing her knuckles into her mouth to quell the abrasive sound. "What happened to his boss? Surely you people have some kind of punishment for this? You guys can't just go around murdering people and getting away with it, can you?" She was outraged by the notion.

"Oh, he was punished, but the damage was already done. Both my parents were gone, and that's when Yash came into the picture. He was sent by Familiar Central to take care of me—and he was probably more a foster parent than a familiar until I got older."

Her eyes opened in surprise. Just as she was catching her breath from his last admission, he said, "But in the end, Yash stole millions of dollars from Avis and me and took off. Haven't heard from his since."

She sat up and looked him in the eye, unable to hide her astonishment. "Okay, whoa. Slow that roll. Your familiar stole money from you after he'd been with you all these years?" No wonder he had trust issues.

Rick's eyes became hard, simmering with anger. "He did. This was his place, by the way. I had it built for him when I began making serious money. It was my gift to him for taking a kid and turning his life around—giving him a place to call home. Yash called this his sanctuary—his bliss. A place he could go when he needed silence and solace, a place to reflect. And he shit all over it."

Huh. Poppy heard the words, but she was having trouble placing stock in them...and that didn't make a lick of sense. She didn't know Yash from Adam.

"Why did he steal money from you? What was his motive after all those years?"

Rick shrugged his shoulders, the anger in his eyes tinged with sadness. "I have no clue, but it's irrefutable. I found it all on a thumb drive. He'd almost left it right out in the open—it was as though he'd wanted me to find it. I'm assuming he thought he wouldn't be caught. Cleared all his personal effects out of here except the one thing that damned him."

"And you didn't think maybe the thumb drive was a plant? Because it was so obvious?"

"I did at first. Believe me, I didn't just automatically assume Yash was a lowlife. We'd spent too many years together not to give him the benefit of the doubt. But then I couldn't figure out who'd do something like that. Incriminate Yash? Frame him? There was never a single bit of evidence to suggest it was anyone but him. So maybe he just got careless. Or maybe didn't give a damn whether I found the thumb drive or not. And still, if he was framed, where the hell did he go?"

So a man who'd spent all of Rick's life with him, quite out of the blue, steals his money and blows the Popsicle stand without looking back? Had he pretended for all these years to care for Rick?

But the proof was all there, according to Rick.

"So the assumption is he just up and left?" That was incomprehensible to her. She couldn't wrap her mind around that kind of betrayal. If Calamity had done nothing else, she'd impressed upon her loyalty to your assigned warlock—*forever*.

"Yep. Gone for good," was Rick's response, wooden and dead.

Tears stung her eyes—tears for a little boy caught up in his father's madness and an evil warlock's lust for a woman he shouldn't have been able to have. Tears for his loss of someone who'd saved him and just as surely had dropped him like a brick from the top of the Empire State Building.

"Jesus… I'm flabbergasted. I…I don't know what to say. What do you say to that kind of betrayal? But I understand now. I get it, and I'm really sorry I pushed."

As suddenly as he'd begun, Rick was done. Patting her thigh in conciliatory fashion, he slid to the edge of the couch. "It's over now, there's nothing that can be done about it anyway. Yash is in the wind and the money went with him. We've recuperated. I'm going to go see if there's something I can do to help January. I won't let anything happen to you, Poppy. I promise."

With that, he was gone.

But she was left with a million questions. But there was one thing she was very clear about—he had a right to rebuke magic in his life. He'd been burned in the worst possible tragedy, and she felt every ounce of his rage, his grief, his unrelenting sense of betrayal by the people in his life who were supposed to protect him.

A tear slid down her cheek as she watched him mingle with the women, pouring himself a cup of coffee and draping a casual arm over Carl's shoulder. A tear of desolation for a little boy who'd lost everything and regained his worth by making piles of money and never letting anyone in.

Poppy swiped at the tear in frustration. For now, she had to set aside the grief she somehow intuitively shared with Rick. She had a bigger problem on her plate—her life.

Something or someone wanted her dead, was the general consensus. Whether by proxy or she was the aura's target, remained unclear. Either way, her life was in danger, and she didn't know how to stop it.

Tucking her legs beneath her, gazing at the mess of the shed, she wondered about Yash and his about-face betrayal. She wanted to pry, but it was clear Rick didn't want to offer much more at this point.

Yet, there was a part of him unwilling to let Yash go— unwilling to believe his betrayal was real. She felt that, too. Felt it hard, deep and sure.

How did she find out what really happened to Yash?

Avis? Would he have more objective insight? The very thought repulsed her.

She'd like an explanation for *that*, too. Why did Avis make her want to drive a stake through his eyeball?

Tucking that emotion away, Poppy attempted a rational approach—get in touch with Avis and grill the dick until he was puking the information she needed. She didn't want to go behind Rick's back, but there wasn't anyone she was aware of closer to him than Avis.

So that settled that.

Not to self. Make a date with a dick.

anuary nudged her shoulder. "You okay?"

"I think my eyeballs might fall out of my head, but I'm mostly okay." The microwave clock read three a.m., and they'd been scouring old books and the Internet since shortly after nine.

"Now if that happens, I *know* I can put them back in your head," January joked, tucking her hair behind her ear and stretching her arms.

Poppy gave a tired laugh, rubbing her hands over her eyes as she slid her upper body forward on the island countertop, letting her head rest in her arms. "Being a familiar is hard."

January stopped surfing some website about spells and gazed at her. "In all this madness, I forgot to ask how you're holding up, Poppy. It's not like you came into this already a paranormal. You have to be in shock."

"I don't know if shock is the right word. I guess finding out some of this stuff is real was definitely shocking, but when it happened, there was this weird feeling in my gut. Like I knew what Calamity was saying was true. You know? I dunno. I can't explain it. I'm suddenly getting all sorts of weird vibes I never had before."

Leaning into Poppy, she rested her chin on her hand. "Want to share?"

"Do I get a free session if I do?"

January laughed, taking a bite of a chocolate chip cookie Arch had made a batch of in order to keep busy. "Gosh, I just can't shake the damn therapist thing, can I? Is it the glasses?"

"It's definitely the glasses."

"So the vibes? What's happening? Tell me."

Maybe it would be good to just tell all. Spit it out and get 'er done. "I feel things. All sorts of things, especially relating to Rick. For instance, I feel his deep sense of loyalty to his friend and partner, Avis. As another example, I knew Nina could be trusted almost from the moment I met her. I know something's going on with Wanda she can't identify. I knew Familiar Central was real. I knew—"

"Wait. Back up. You can feel Rick's emotions? Are we talking literally?"

Now she tensed, sitting up straight. "Is that a bad thing? Wrong?"

"No. No. But it's unique for such a new relationship. As familiars, you get to know your assignments over time. Sometimes there isn't even a connection at first. I've had my familiar Farley forever, and every once in a while I still stump him. To feel emotions like someone's loyalty and trust so instantly is huge, Poppy. It means you have the gift of intuition, which only enhances my thought you two were fated."

She knew a little about what that meant after watching some movie or another. Or was that empathic? All these witchy catch phrases were too much to absorb.

"So now I'm an intuit, too?"

January smiled, warm and so supportive, Poppy's heart

clenched. "Yeah. And it can be pretty great. It has its pitfalls, too, I'm told. Not everything is rosy."

There was validation in that sentence. Maybe she wasn't so crazy after all. "Okay, so can I confide something in you then? Will you promise to keep it just between us?"

"As long as it does no harm to you or others, yes. Of course. I'm here to help in any way I can, Poppy. No matter what."

She sucked in a breath. "Good, because this has been killing me from the moment I met Rick's partner, Avis. He's bad juju. I can't pinpoint why, I have no proof to back it up, but I feel it, so strongly it almost doubles me over." She pointed to her sore gut and reiterated. "*Feel* it."

"Oh boy," January muttered. "A man and his best friend are delicate issues. Definitely presents a problem. Maybe it's all the other stuff going on mingled with these feelings?"

"Like the aura stalking me?"

January paused, giving her a thoughtful look before she said, "Could be. Sometimes everything gets muddied, and you need to isolate each incident with some critical examination."

"That makes complete sense. A meltdown of my senses is a good explanation, but I have one more question." Poppy explained her apartment building and Mr. Rush and all her neighbors, and the definite feeling something was very wrong at Littleton. "Could those waters be muddied, too—because I'm so upset that everyone is skipping off to greener fields like they didn't spend most of their lives at Littleton?"

"That's definitely a possibility, Poppy. You're almost extra-sensitive at this point. Maybe you're picking up on everything as you adjust to this way of life. I mean it's pretty big. Everything that's happened up to this point has been nothing less than life-altering."

Wiping the crumbs from her cookie into her hand, Poppy considered. "So an overreaction?"

But January's shake of her head was firm. "No. I wouldn't say that. Never doubt your intuition entirely. Don't dismiss, but it could be a magnification because this Avis sounds like a misogynistic swine."

She laughed, but it was tinged with this inexplicable bitterness she couldn't shake off. "Oh, he's all sorts of cheerio and tut-tut," she replied in her best British accent. "But since I met him, I haven't been able to shake the feeling he's a creeper."

"Then revisit them often. Don't let them go, but keep your eyes and ears peeled. Call me if you need me. Always. Okay?"

Relief to have confessed her feelings flooded her. She'd needed to confide in someone. But there was still more. "Also, one more thing."

"Shoot," January said.

"I like Rick."

"That's a good thing, isn't it? Shouldn't you like your warlock?"

She'd been battling this feeling all night. How was she going to spend the rest of her life with a man she found wildly attractive and not somehow inject that into everything she did?

"I'm pretty sure I shouldn't like him quite in the way I like him. I like him in the biblical sense. In biblical proportion."

January blanched, but it had a sympathetic vibe. "Is this making it difficult to do your job as his familiar?"

"Well, I'm pretty sure when I should be helping him, I shouldn't be ogling his body parts while I do. If I'm to do right by him, I don't know that I can if my advice is clouded with my dirty-dirty thoughts."

"Damn, you're a good person, Poppy. You know that,

right? I can think of some who'd continue on and guide with a manipulative slant in their favor. But not you. You should be really proud of who you are—of your integrity."

Poppy's cheeks went red. "Don't give me too much credit here. I *am* the person who purposely sent a check to the electric company made out to my water company to stall my electricity being shut off."

January giggled. "That's called survival, not manipulation. Your integrity remains intact."

"So what happens to me if I confess to Familiar Central? Do I still go to the Bad Place? Calamity said I shouldn't complain ever."

"You're not complaining, honey, you're owning your feelings and doing what's in the best interest of your assignment."

"But does it still mean the Bad Place?"

"I'm going to be honest here, I don't know, but I promise you this, I'll go with you when you talk to them. I'll be your advocate, and I'll do everything in my power to keep you out of the Bad Place if this is what you really want to do."

"It's kind of the right thing." She hated it, but it was unfair to Rick to do anything else.

"Promise me something though? Let's wait until after Halloween, okay? Let me get past this blood moon thing, and I'll take you on my broom personally."

"Shut up. You have a broom?"

"She does not have a GD broom!" Nina called from the other side of the room, pushing her hoodie from her face to glare at them.

Now Poppy laughed, despite her misery and fear of the unknown. "I'll wait then."

"You're an angel."

"And you're really nice, January. Everyone is really nice. Thank you. I appreciate your advice."

January hitched a thumb over her shoulder to where Marty, Nina, and Wanda were cleaning up the debris of her attack. "These three and Carl are something, aren't they?"

Her heart warmed, growing tight in her chest. "Yeah. They really are."

No matter what happened with Rick, she knew she'd remain in touch with these people for as long as she walked this earth.

And even if that meant giving up the position as Rick's familiar, she was still walking away with something good in her life, and that was so nice.

* * *

POPPY SAT in the diner across the street from Littleton for her meeting with Avis while Nina and Marty sat a couple of booths away. Wanda sat in the park with Calamity, watching Littleton, her eyes far away.

In the interest of honesty, she'd told Rick she was going to continue to do her part as his familiar and get to know the people in his life. That included his employees and Avis.

She'd even managed to inform him without a sneer when she'd said Avis's name. So while Rick went to check on her neighbors and tidy up last-minute details for the demo, she'd taken the opportunity to invite Avis for coffee.

And he was fifteen minutes late. Five more and she was going to hunt him down and choke him with a happy "cheerio."

Marty tapped her wrist and an imaginary watch, mouthing, "Where the hell is he?"

She shrugged, giving the waitress her order for coffee, even though her stomach was still in complete turmoil, and it wasn't just because she'd hacked up a demon last night.

When the doors to the diner swung open, bringing with

them a chilly breeze, Poppy intuitively knew it would be Avis striding through the cluster of white vinyl booths. She knew because he gave her a chill like no other.

Don't let your feelings cloud your judgment, Poppy. Stay aware, but stay cool.

Rolling up the sleeves of her flannel shirt, Poppy took that thought to heart as she waved to Avis with a half-smile.

"There you are! How delightful to be asked to coffee by such a dish!" he exclaimed, way too cheerful and exaggerated for her taste. But objectivity was the name of the game here.

She wanted to find a redeeming quality in Avis—for Rick. "Hey, thanks for meeting me."

His eyes widened, his grin following when he reached over and patted her hand. "Anything for Rick. That you're not hard on my eyes makes this little meeting a plus. So what can I do for you, Poppy McGuillicuddy? How can I make your transition into familiar-hood with Rick easier?"

You could start by letting go of my hand, thus removing this feeling I'm somehow dirty. Pulling her fingers from his, Poppy tucked them in her lap and decided to get down to business. She wasn't going to pussyfoot around with him.

"Tell me about Yash."

Avis's shift in position was ever so slight, the change in his face, the clouding over of his eyes just as brief. And then his face went sad, almost comically mournful. "My poor chap Rick. I suppose he told you what happened?"

"He did." And that was all she was saying. She was curious to hear Avis's take on Yash, and she didn't know why a statement from him made a difference, but there was this voice deep inside that told her it did—that he might have vital information about the familiar.

He sucked in his cheeks, giving his face an unintentionally long, menacing look. "You're a woman of few words, aren't you, Poppy?"

Leaning her chin on her hand, she purposely wanted to show him she was relaxed. "I just believe in getting to the point. So what was Yash like?"

Pressing his hand to his chest, he sighed. "I loved Yash as much as Rick did. When he all but disappeared, I was heartsick."

Liar! The word flashed before her eyes with such clarity, Poppy almost ducked, and the smarmy, ugly tentacles clawing her insides latched on tighter.

"But he took your money, too, didn't he?"

Avis blustered, yet his eyes were cool. "That's almost irrelevant. The money wasn't so much a betrayal as the lies. I thought Yash had Rick's best interests at heart always. He was Rick's closest confidant. I didn't know if Rick would ever recuperate after such an agonizing break in trust."

"So you believe Yash stole ARMD's money and took off without a word? Just like that? It seems so out of the blue. So random after being with Rick for so many years. Why would he do such a thing?"

Leaning back against the booth, Avis nodded solemnly as his fingers toyed with the paper napkin. "Tell me something I don't know. No one was more surprised than I, except for maybe Rick himself. We were both blindsided. But I'm not one hundred percent convinced Yash's intentions weren't true."

Her eyes zeroed in on Avis's handsome face, alarm bells singing their song. "Meaning?"

"Meaning I think it was something more. Something he couldn't tell anyone. Something utterly *dreadful*."

Cue evil music. Avis was just shy of maniacal laughter as he used the word "dreadful." Yeah, Poppy didn't doubt whatever had happened to Yash was dreadful, but were there no clues? No telltale signs?

"So you think something nefarious happened to him? How does that explain the missing money?"

Avis rubbed his hands together and grinned. "Nefarious is such a tasty word. And frankly, I don't know. Call it my gut."

"So you believe in Yash's innocence?"

"Will this conversation be all about Yash? I thought you wanted to get to know *me*," he teased, batting his eyelashes.

As the waitress dropped her coffee in front of her, granting her a reprieve from Avis's question, he dismissed her offer to take an order.

Adding sugar to the dark liquid, she stirred, deciding to keep her acting shoes on when she answered him. Summoning her best Jessica Rabbit smoldering gaze, Poppy winked. "I guess it depends on how interesting *you* are. Are you more interesting than a familiar who steals millions of dollars and betrays the boy he's virtually raised? For instance, this woman Rick mentioned who broke your heart just before you began attending Princeton. We could talk about that…"

Avis threw his head back, the weak sun glinting on his blond hair from the window beside their booth. "Hah! Touché, beautiful lady." But when his eyes came back into focus, they were hard chips of ice. "What did he tell you?"

"Basically nothing other than you'd been hurt deeply."

"Bah! At the time, and taking into account my age, yes, it was quite a drama, I'm sure. But it's long since over."

"No lingering feelings for your lost love?"

His lips wanted to show their disapproval, but Avis wouldn't allow it. "All water under the bridge."

His phone rang then, chiming out the familiar tune "Thank You For Being a Friend," and he held up a finger to plead for a moment, the smile never leaving his face. "Of course, chap. I'm on it. Give me five, and I'll be right there." He clicked off his phone and smiled. "That was our man of the hour. I'm afraid I'll have to cut this short. Shall I keep this meeting our little secret?"

Sipping her coffee, Poppy shook her head. "Nah. I don't mind if you tell him. I don't want you to be dishonest on my account." *Not any more than you already are.*

He swatted the table with a pair of gloves he'd pulled from his pocket. "Good show then. Lovely to have spent some quality time with you, Poppy. Let's do this again soon? Maybe with Rick?"

Smiling, she bobbed her head. "Sure."

He rose, sliding out of the booth with the grace of a cat. "Cheers!" he called, and then he was moving back between the booths toward the door.

Nina and Marty were in his side of the booth in two seconds flat, each looking at her with the big question on her face. "So?" Nina asked. "Is he a douche or is he a douche?"

Poppy wasn't sure she could find the right words to express her feelings about Avis at this point, something she appeared to struggle with lately.

Marty reached across the table and grabbed Poppy's wrist. "Poppy?"

Letting out a breath she didn't even realize she was holding, she made a face. "He's the biggest douche ever. As in, the douche of a lifetime."

"And you're sure, honey? I mean positive? This is his best friend since college."

Nina flicked her fingers in Marty's face. "Yeah, she's sure, Fakey-Locks. Can't you see the look on her face?"

Flattening her palm on the Formica table, wishing Avis's face was beneath it, she agreed with Nina. "Yes, I'm surer than sure. He's a scumbag, and I don't know what he's done, but he's done something. It's something dark and ugly and cruel."

Marty tugged at her purple scarf, loosening the knot. "I

just thought of something. Do you think he's this aura January's talking about? The one that's attached to you?"

She hadn't made that leap, but it made sense. Complete sense. "You think he's jealous? Rick's been familiar-less for a while now. Maybe he thinks I'm taking up too much of Rick's time?"

"Maybe he needs his fancy British ass whooped?" Nina asked, pushing her sunglasses back on her nose.

"I think we need to talk to January before we do anything. If Avis is the aura, or whatever we're calling that green and yellow cloud of toxic waste that came out of you last night, we need to be sure we handle this the right way," Marty said.

"I think Marty's right. So no ass whooping just yet. But the more I think about it, the more what Marty says works."

"Then let's go see a witch/doctor about a fuckhead," Nina said.

Poppy would laugh if she weren't so worried about telling Rick how she felt. She couldn't just accuse Avis of something with no proof and expect Rick to believe she had a gut feeling she was right.

That was ridiculous.

On the other hand, this was one more thing off her plate.

Date with a dick achievement unlocked.

$\mathcal{A}$ s she sat amidst boxes in her soon-to-be-former apartment, preparing to load them up and send them to storage, Rick slapped the last sealed box with a final grunt. "I think we got it all. Every single bobblehead known to man," he teased with a grin.

"Bobbleheads give me life," she defended, forcing her eyes from devouring him in his navy-blue sweater and black jeans.

His grin made her heart skip a beat. "I heard all about it as you gave direction on how much bubble wrap I should use to pack them properly."

"Listen, you complain, but how would you feel if all those fancy vases in your fancy house ended up in little pieces? My bobblehead of Beyonce would never forgive me," she joked.

Laughing, his eyes scanned the boxes piled high by her bathroom door. "You know, you don't have to put this all in storage, Poppy. I have plenty of room at the house."

Yeah, but there wouldn't be any room left at the inn when she confessed her feelings about Avis. He'd want out, and after an unsuccessful attempt to reach January to get her council on whether Avis could be the entity, Poppy realized it didn't really matter anyway.

She still thought Avis was up to no good, and if he wasn't the aura, she still had to confess to Rick her bad feelings about him.

And as Calamity had warned, he wasn't going to like that shit. She'd talked to the girls and Calamity about her suspicions, and while they agreed she had no proof, they also agreed honesty was the only way.

But she'd already made a decision after talking with January last night that would solve everything. She had to tell him how she felt and she had to do it soon. Letting another day go by with him thinking she was sticking around after the date for their deal was up was wrong. He was officially off the hook after Halloween.

Looking out the window at a slew of moving vans, loading up box after box for her neighbors, every last one of them virtually skipping out the door, smiling and laughing, she closed her eyes to keep from crying.

Was no one even a little upset? Was Arnie not at all distressed that he'd probably never have another chess game with Mrs. Bernbaum? Did Leona really want to go to a strange country all by herself just because she loved empanadas and had learned two phrases in Spanish?

But as she watched them, their eyes gleaming, their faces bright, she couldn't deny no one appeared to care.

Blowing out a breath, Poppy plunked down on her couch and grabbed a stray pillow, resting her cheek on it. When she'd walked into the building after her meeting with Avis, prepared to pack up her things for the last time, she'd had that same feeling of desolation she'd had when she'd been here the other day.

What? What did it mean? January had said not to ignore

her intuition, but she'd also told her to examine her feelings and their possible magnification.

Was she magnifying this feeling of dread? Were all the things she'd experienced since this had happened compounded by the strangeness of her new world?

Rick dropped down next to her and asked, "You okay? I know this is an emotional day for you, Poppy, but I promise everything's going to be okay."

"Thanks for helping me pack. You didn't have to. I know you're busy."

He ran a finger down the length of her nose. "It's the least I can do in light of the fact that I'm stealing your apartment right out from under you."

"I need to talk to you about a couple of things."

He smiled his devastatingly handsome smile. "All ears."

"Listen, Rick... I can't be your familiar."

His eyebrow rose. "Um, you didn't even give it the full seven days. You're giving up already, *señorita*?" he teased, using his index finger to playfully poke her shoulder.

"I'm going to hit you with some honesty. Like brutal honesty. You ready?"

Leaning back, Rick nodded, crossing his arms over his chest. "Sure," he replied with a stiff tone—one she sensed would become defensive when he heard what she had to say.

"I like you. Once I got past your very unwelcoming response to my arrival, you turned out to be an okay guy." She bit the inside of her cheek to ward off the humiliation of this conversation.

"But?"

"But. I..." She sighed, letting her head hang to her chest. Honesty was the best policy. No room and board was worth this kind of dilemma. So she leaned back, too, and looked him square in the eye. "But I like you too much."

He rolled his tongue in his cheek. "Can you ever like a

person too much?"

"You can when you're supposed to be their advisor, but you're thinking very un-biblical thoughts about them. Or maybe they are biblical. I'm not sure. I just know, they're a little unsanitary." She bit her lip on her last words and winced, waiting for his reaction.

And Rick said nothing. Absolutely nothing. Which might have hurt her ego had she not already decided he probably didn't feel the same way. Surely, with all this connectivity between them, she would have felt something if he had.

For all his teasing and flirting, he wasn't into her like that, and that was okay. There'd been plenty of guys who hadn't been into her when she was into them.

She'd live. She didn't like that she would right now, but as a rational adult, she knew that would pass, and while she'd probably always be attracted to Rick, she could handle it if the only time she had to see him was over a bubbling cauldron at the witches and warlocks annual gala.

As he was about to speak, Poppy held up a hand—a cautious hand, because her hands were pretty good at creating mayhem these days. "Just let me do this without interruption. I think we both know familiars and their assignments can't possibly work if one of them is having feelings that aren't familiar-ish. How can I, as your familiar, advise you in relationships if I'm thinking...er, impure thoughts? Think about how crazy awkward that would be. Every time you had a date, me all pouty and jealous of the other women in your life? That's not going to work for me. I don't do jealous. It's an ugly emotion I have no time for."

He grunted, but he still didn't say a word. Opening his mouth, he frowned when nothing came out. Which was indeed odd. Using his finger, he pointed at the interior of his mouth.

Now Poppy frowned, confused. "Laryngitis? Does laryngitis happen that quickly? You were just talking a minute ago."

Rick's eyes were confused, too, when he lifted his wide shoulders in an "I don't know" way.

She flapped a hand at him. "It's just as well. I only need you to listen anyway. Just know that you're a good guy, and magic and your warlock legacy can be good things, too. If you let them, anyway. The nutbag warlock who killed your mother was an evil piece of shit and just one bad guy in a sea of a million good guys. Don't give up the ship."

He shook his head, his lips now clamped bizarrely shut. He pointed to them in a gesture she didn't understand, using his eyes to attempt to communicate something.

So she cocked her head at him and patted his thickly muscled leg. "I get it. A sudden onslaught of laryngitis. Please just let me finish; I'm doing this for you. Because it's the right thing to do. Because it's unhealthy to stick around and play at advising you when I don't want to advise you. I don't know if I *always* won't want to advise you, but for now, I don't. I want to...uh, do things with you. I tried. I really tried. I ignored my attraction to you. I plodded forward, but I'd be a shitty person if I didn't own my stuff. So just let me own my stuff."

"Mmmm!" he managed, his eyes even wider when they caught hers.

Poppy nodded her head and swallowed the lump forming in her throat. "Yeah. Mmmm. Anyway, I hope your next familiar works out. I hope you really give whoever it is a genuine shot. Don't be an asshole next time around. Not everyone's as forgiving as me. Not everyone's as desperate as me, either. All I heard was room and board. Your next familiar might own a palace and tell you to go shit yourself, buddy. Keep that in mind when he or she arrives—"

In a swift move, Rick stopped her ramble by gripping her

shoulders and driving his lips against hers, effectively shutting her up.

And boy, did he know how to shut a girl up. As his lips touched hers for the first time, Poppy sighed, and when his tongue slipped between her lips, she saw stars and colors and vivid images of her beneath Rick, naked and needy.

Pulling away, he gazed at her, a question in his dark eyes. She knew what he was asking—if he had her permission to continue.

But there was no question about this for her. No matter the outcome, she wanted Rick to make love to her. Call it impulsive, because they'd only just met, call it crazy, but everything about his body so close to hers felt right. She'd deal with the repercussions later.

So in response, she kissed him again, melting into his hard frame, running her hands along his arms, relishing the muscle beneath her fingertips.

He groaned, reaching for the top of her shirt, popping the buttons until her bra was exposed. Rick brushed his fingers over the swell of flesh, making her nipples harden to tight peaks as he unhooked the front clasp of her bra.

As her breasts spilled out and his thumbs brushed against her skin, Poppy moaned, too, wrapping her arms around his neck until they were pressed together tight.

And then their hands were roaming, exploring, undressing until they were both naked. Poppy forced her eyes open so she wouldn't miss seeing every inch of his rippling body.

His shoulders were broad, his olive skin stretched tight over sinew, dipping inward, then bulging out. Her fingers traced the ridge of each of his abs, luxuriating in his moan as he pushed her back to the couch and slid his hand between her thighs, running his tongue over her neck, nipping at her earlobe.

When he grazed her clit, Poppy's eyes rolled to the back of her head, the pleasure so exquisite. Her hands reached for his cock, hard, thick, hot with desire, stroking him until he wrapped his fingers around her wrist and stilled her.

Sliding along her body, he wrapped his arms around her waist, slashing his hot tongue over her breast, bringing her nipples to hard nubs, making her cry out and drive her hands into his thick hair.

Heat pooled between her thighs, wet and slick, and she knew she had to have him inside her now. Forget the fore-play, forget the pretense, she just wanted him to bury himself in her depths.

Just as he was kissing his way down along her belly, she dragged him upward and looked him in the eye, lifting her hips and encouraging him to drive into her.

Rick lifted himself up onto his palms and stared down at her, poising at her entry, but she didn't need to ask what he wanted to know. She simply knew.

Without a word, she wrapped her legs around his waist, hooking her ankles together and bracketing his face with her hands before pressing her lips to his once again.

Their gasps mingled, their hands entwined as Rick drove into her, stilling, settling, letting her adjust to him.

And it was amazing. A revelation. A multitude of roller coaster emotions she decided not to question or analyze. In this moment, Rick was deeply imbedded in her, and she wanted him like no other before.

Pressing her body into his, Rick drove his tongue into her mouth in time with his thrusts, stroking, pushing, giving, taking, until the swell of orgasm began its upward climb.

Her hands went to his back, kneading the thick cord of bunched muscles, digging her fingers into his flesh as the white-hot heat of release called to her.

Another slick thrust and Rick was tensing, too, their

bodies rocking, his hips pressed tightly to hers. He ground against her, tearing his lips from hers and burying his face in her neck as they drove toward completion.

And when she came, her chest heaving against Rick's, the scrape of her nipples against his smooth skin driving her mad, she cried out, bucking against him in a wild thrash of light and color.

Rick tensed then, too, his thighs, crushed to hers, flexing and releasing as he took one last thrust before groaning out his pleasure at release.

Driving her arms up under his, Poppy burrowed against him and sighed, closing her eyes and smiling.

BUTTONING HER FLANNEL SHIRT, Poppy realized she had one more thing to do, and she hated doing it, but in the interest of forewarned, she was going to plow forward.

As she looked at his perfect body, reveled in the amazing lovemaking they'd shared, she sighed. "There's something else I need to talk to you about."

He gestured to his throat, still unable to talk. Which, in this case, might be a good thing...still odd, but nonetheless, a good thing.

Cupping his jaw, she ran her thumb over the stubble there, loving the feel of his skin against her fingertips, wishing they could stay like this a while longer. "I have a bigger dilemma than even the one I'm having with your hot self. And by the way, I'm not holding you to the dirty-dirty sex we just had. Even though it was pretty damn good."

He chuckled, but it came out as a dry hiss as he grabbed at her fingers and kissed the tips.

She wasn't sure if his chuckle meant this was a great way to pass the time, and he was okay with her backing out of their warlock/familiar relationship or he had something else to say.

So she reiterated. "I mean that. No strings, no promises whatever. I mean we just met. Maybe this was just a thing I needed to get out of my system? Either way, I'm an adult. You're an adult. That's not what I need to get off my chest right now. But I do need to get something off my chest."

He shook his head, running his hand over her arm affectionately—which again, she wasn't sure meant he was down with no strings attached, or against it, but that was neither here nor there at this point. Or it wouldn't be in a minute.

"Okay, so can I get you to lend me your ear?"

Rick rolled his eyes and smiled as if to say, he had nothing but an ear to lend.

"It's about Avis," she broached with cautious care.

His head cocked at an angle as he, too, sat up and pulled on his sweater. As though he thought they needed to be dressed to have this conversation. Once he'd fully dressed, he held out his wide palm and gestured for her to continue.

Zipping her jeans, she slipped on her clogs and looked down at the floor. "Boy, I suck at dicking around. Look, I'm just going to be straightforward with you and get right to the point."

He grinned his consent by grabbing her fingers and leaning down to press another delicious kiss on her lips, almost deterring her from telling him what was on her mind.

But a sense of urgency took over. Looking up at him, she planted a hand on his wide chest and said, "I don't like Avis. He's not a good person."

Now he frowned, dropping her hand. "Mmm?"

"You heard right. He's not a good person. Call it intuition, call it my gut, but I know I'm right. I can't prove it. I don't know why I feel this way, but trust me, he's a wolf in sheep's clothing."

She avoided adjectives like "misogynistic shitface" and "twatwaffle" out of respect for Rick, but they were certainly on the tip of her tongue.

His eyes narrowed as he planted his hands on his lean hips and gave her a questioning glare.

"I know, I know. You want proof. I don't have any. I'm just telling you, it's what I've felt from the moment I met him. I didn't tell you because I didn't understand it. I still mostly don't. But I'm right. He's no good for you. He's shady, Rick."

He grabbed his phone and punched something in before lifting his hard jaw. She saw all the things he wanted to say but couldn't. She saw his denial. She saw the words of support he would use if he hadn't lost his voice. She saw the defense she knew he'd use in favor of Avis. But it didn't matter.

Avis was bad mojo.

But her heart began to thrash even as she planned to stick to her guns. The sour look Rick gave her, the look of utter surprise, sliced right through her. So she attempted to soften the blow. "Look, I know he's been your best friend since college. I know he's like family, but—"

She stopped talking then when her phone pinged an incoming text—but there was no point in finishing. Rick's face, if not his text, said it all. His disappointment, his hurt was plain to see. He loved Avis. She was saying shitty things about someone who'd been in his life for a very long time.

But his next words, written calmly and meticulously, chilled her. "I need to wrap my head around this, Poppy, and right now, I don't think I can."

Then he turned on his heel and walked his perfectly perfect ass right out of her apartment door.

End conversation.

CHAPTER 16

"*Y*ou okay, Kitten?" Wanda asked, dropping down beside her on Rick's lush patio couch, where she sat in companionable silence with Carl, watching leaves fall by the outdoor fireplace.

Wanda held up a blanket with a smile, encouraging Poppy to sit under it with her. "Poppy?"

Weeell, I just had sex with my assignment. Incredible sex. But when all was said and done, and I told him I was feeling some weird feelings about Avis, he got a little bent out of shape, and we had a fight—a very quiet one, but a fight nonetheless--and then he left early this morning without speaking a word to me.

But she wasn't ready to talk about their encounter yesterday yet. She'd spent all night long fretting over it, fretting over Rick's reaction to her feelings about Avis.

Today was Halloween and this blood moon everyone kept talking about was happening. After tonight, she could go off to Familiar Central with January and fix what was broken. Then everyone could go back to their families.

She snuggled under the blanket and sighed. "I'm fine.

Really. Who wouldn't be fine with Carl for company? Does it get any more handsome than this?"

Carl thumped her arm and grinned his crooked grin before pushing his hands back into the pocket of his hoodie. "Nicccce," he husked out.

Impulsively, Poppy leaned up and kissed his lean cheek. "Thank you, Carl. Let's always be friends, okay?"

He placed his dark head against hers. "Yesss."

Nina's head poked out of the shed then, her face full of worry. "Carl? Where the hell are you, buddy? Jesus and lost and found, you gotta stop running off!"

"He's with us, Vampire!" Wanda called out before pointing to the shed. "Better go see what she needs, sweetie."

Carl slipped from the couch, leaving just her and Wanda.

"Wanna talk about what's upsetting you so?"

When she'd awakened this morning, one of those instincts she was still adjusting to, had struck her and it had to do with Wanda's relationship with both Nina and Calamity. It had to do with Wanda dismissively pooh-poohing Nina's concerns about over indulging Calamity's misbehavior and why she was giving the adorable feline such enormous leeway.

Tucking the blanket around Wanda's chin, she said, "Nope, but I do wanna talk. Got a minute?"

"I always have a minute, Poppy. What's up?"

She'd been feeling this weary sort of worn-out vibe from Wanda since they'd met, and she had this crazy idea she wanted to share. "You're sad, Wanda. Mind if I ask why?"

Poppy didn't want to intrude, they'd only known each other a scant few days, but for once, outside of Nina's riveting, though almost-comical outbursts and Marty's beautiful but chaotic swirl of activity, Wanda deserved someone to see she was in need.

She'd never say as much. In her eyes, that was complaining, and Wanda Schwartz-Jefferson didn't complain.

She was grateful for her life, her world and everything in it. In fact, she experienced extreme discomfort when she even considered saying what she was feeling out loud in order to avoid appearing ungrateful.

Wanda sighed with a small smile before she said, "This intuition thing is definitely your bag, Poppy McGuillicuddy."

She smiled and grabbed her new friend's hand. "Yeah, tell that to the boss. He seems to think I'm a complete moron for calling his douchebag business partner a lying dick. If I could just prove he's a lying dick..." Poppy shook her head. This was about Wanda. "Forget that and talk to me. I feel a deep disturbance in you, but I can't pinpoint what's causing so much unrest."

Her shoulders sagged, and she patted Poppy's hand with her gloved one. "You know, sometimes, I don't even know if *I* can pinpoint it. It comes and goes. Lately, it comes a lot more than it goes. I'm supposed to be the nurturer—the peacemaker. It's a label I've had since we all hooked up. Somehow, I'm just compelled to keep Marty and Nina from killing one another. It's what I do. It's what I've always done since we met almost nine years ago. But I find more and more, I want to kill them rather than fix them."

"So you're tired? Maybe not so much of the role, but of the lack of appreciation they give that role? Because I want you to know, they respect the hell out of you for putting up with them. Still, I can only imagine what it's like to get between a werewolf and a vampire when they want to eat each other's faces off."

Wanda barked a laugh and squeezed her hand as the crisp autumn air whirled around them. "They don't really want to eat each other's faces off. They love each other. I love them. I love them maybe even more than some of my own family except my sister, Casey. But I need something, Poppy. Something more I can't put my finger on. *Something* right on the tip of my tongue...I just don't know what. I mean, I have so many amazing things in my life. I want for literally nothing. I have an incredible husband, the girls, and the tons of friends we've made along the way while we cobbled together OOPS. It's selfish to consider I need anything else."

"Yeah. You're the most selfish person I've ever encountered, Wanda. I mean, all selfish people drop everything they're doing and rush to the aid of someone they don't even know in order to help them. God, when will you ever think about anyone else?" Poppy teased.

Wanda's smile, so elegant and beautiful, wisped across her face before she sobered. "I guess I don't think about that as being unselfish."

"Maybe that's why you're where you are now."

Wanda looked at her, her unlined eyes confused. "I don't get it."

Poppy knew what Wanda needed—knew it in her soul. But as taught by Calamity, she was only a guide to an end game. She couldn't force the answers down Wanda's throat. Wanda had to find them on her own.

"Maybe you need something just for Wanda sometimes, and I'm not talking about shopping or a dress or even a hobby. I'm talking about something that fills you up, makes you want to get out of bed each morning."

"I thought OOPS did that for me. I love helping people. I'm not as crazy about the scrapes and bruises and the occasional ruined outfit, but there's almost nothing that gives me greater satisfaction than getting people through a paranormal crisis in one piece, helping them find their fates, leaving them happy and healthy. I've made so many wonderful friends because of it. How can I feel anything else but fulfilled, Poppy?"

Poppy smiled now, too, leaning back against the bench they sat on, watching the bright colors of fall drift to the ground in the swirls of leaves. "Yeah. You're amazing at it, too. If I could choose a mother outside of my own, the very awesome, though sometimes smothering Rose McGuillicuddy, I'd choose *you*, Wanda. You're smart and funny, and above all, you're nurturing and supportive."

Wanda cocked her head, her eyes far away. "We can't have children. As wonderful as my life is, it's the one thing I wish were different."

"You'd make an incredible mother."

"You think?"

Wrapping an arm around her slender shoulders, inhaling the scent of Wanda's lightly floral perfume, Poppy nodded. "Oh, I don't just think, Wanda. I *know*. I know you're all things good—all things kind. Maybe you just need to hear someone say it out loud."

As they sat together and watched the leaves drift and the chilly midday wind blew, a tear slid from Wanda's eye. One she didn't bother to dismiss or ignore. One from deep within, from the core of her enormous heart.

Wanda was realizing it was time to tweak the direction of her life. Maybe take a small detour and see what was around the bend.

And that was exactly as the universe planned.

WHAT IN ALL of fuck had happened to his voice?

As he scribbled out his signature on yet another work order for the demolition of Littleton, he used his eyes to apologize to one of the demo guys.

But the hearty man with shoulders as wide as a redwood slapped his back. "No worries, Boss."

Running a hand through his hair, Rick tried once more to speak but could do nothing more than hiss a crackly response. Which brought him back to his conversation yesterday with Poppy.

Damned if he understood what she'd meant about Avis, but damned if it hadn't left him tossing and turning last night. Her words had been clear as day. She didn't like him. She thought he was a bad person.

But she didn't know why, which made no sense. He liked this woman far more than he'd planned on originally. Yes, she'd been crazy attractive from the get-go, but he hadn't planned on her stirring up feelings the way she did with her funny jokes. He didn't plan on her attractiveness ramping up a hundred notches while he'd watched her humble herself from the window of the nursing home to Mr. Rush about her overdue rent. She had a deep sense of integrity, and it was something too often ignored in this day and age.

Then there were her incredibly sensible quotes. Quotes eerily similar to Yash's quotes. In fact, at one point, when she'd quoted Maya Angelou, it was the exact quote Yash had often used—he'd maybe even used Tzu's. Still, it was uncanny.

Rolling his head on his neck to ease the growing tension there, Rick forced the image of a beautiful, naked, incredibly sexy Poppy from his mind and focused instead on the frustration he'd felt when he was unable to express himself.

He, too, was in the wildly attracted zone. He'd wanted to tell her that until his throat seized up like a car engine. So instead, he'd kissed her in the hopes she'd feel what he was feeling.

He wanted to ask her not to make any rash decisions until this demo was over and he could take some time off to spend with her.

He wanted to tell her about the visions he had of them

sharing a bottle of wine, having dinner, getting to know one another, and yes, digging deeper into him rebuffing magic in general. But the Avis thing was an enormous problem.

And he'd be fucked if he knew what to do about it. Avis had been through it with him. Every exam, every late night while he worked at a diner as a short-order cook and Avis helped him study over customers' hamburgers, every good deal they'd made together as a team and every last shitty day he'd had since Yash abandoned ship.

He wasn't just going to up and ditch all that history because Poppy had some "feelings" she could neither identify nor back up with any proof.

But he couldn't discard them either—because he found he cared what she thought. He wanted to get to know her.

He wanted.

He just didn't know how to address her problem with Avis. He didn't even know where to begin, it had caught him so off guard. But the second he got a break here, he was going to hunt her down and find a way to ask her to stay—at least until he had a voice and they could have an actual conversation.

Speaking of, he pulled his phone from his pocket, deciding to at least send Poppy a text, asking her to stay. He pulled up her name and typed out, *Please stay* for the umpteenth time, only to have it refuse to send.

"Rickster!" Avis shouted as he made his way across the entry of Littleton with a sweep of his long trench coat and a wave. "How are you, old man? Still having trouble with the throat?"

Rick nodded, still baffled by this sudden case of laryngitis.

Avis slapped him on the back, peering down at Rick's phone. "You need to see a physician, my friend. And is that our Poppy you're texting? Is my boy in like?"

Rick grinned at him, but then he remembered how Poppy felt about Avis and toned it down, shrugging his shoulders.

"I knew it!" Avis declared. "I saw the way you were looking at her, you dirty dog! Why don't you go? I can certainly handle this alone. Everything is ready, and everyone is out of the building. No stragglers at all. As a matter of fact, they're all meeting up at the diner across the way to watch the demo. Codgy old busybodies," he joked affably.

But Rick shook his head in a vehement effort to remind Avis they were in this together. Besides, he wanted to be available to the people of Littleton if they had second thoughts—to reassure them everything would be all right.

Avis held up a gloved hand. "Don't say another word..." He paused and gave a hearty laugh. "Sorry, bloke. I meant, don't trouble yourself with an explanation. I understand why you'd want to bugger about until the demo is done. For the tenants, yes?"

Rick nodded his confirmation. How could Poppy not see that while Avis could be a real cad when it came to women, he also had a big damn heart?

"You always were an old softie, and I'm in full support. Now, I have to get moving and be sure the city isn't going to thrust their greedy little hand out any farther for more last-minute permits. Call me later?"

Rick gave him the thumbs-up sign and smiled.

"Good enough. We're going to be very rich soon, Rickster, my boy. Very rich indeed!" he cackled.

The prospect of the money they'd make from building these condos had at one time been insanely appealing. But today, none of that interested him. Not the dollars, not the exhilaration of a new project.

As he looked at Littleton, with its charming gardens and weird stone spiral on the roof, he experienced a stab of sadness he didn't understand. But it was there, and it was demanding he pay attention.

* * *

OH MY GOD!" Poppy called out from the bedroom in the shed, pushing the white and gray-lavender comforter out of her way. "I think I found something, ladies!"

She'd awakened today with an ominous emptiness in the pit of her stomach and a heavy heart, and that sense of pending doom hadn't left her all day long. It eased as she'd sat beside Carl outside and chatted with Wanda, probably because those were all things that brought her joy.

But as the day crept into late afternoon and Nina and Marty prepared to do a quick round of trick-or-treating with their girls, that doom grew.

Calamity skidded into the room, sliding right into Poppy, who sat on the floor in front of some drawers beneath Yash's old bed. She hadn't really bothered to look around much since she'd been here. Moving in had felt like an invasion of someone else's space. Add to that Rick's original dislike of all things familiar, and she'd avoided even unpacking her overnight bag.

This had been Yash's, and his imprint was clear. But today? Today he was everywhere. Every single thing she looked at in the shed screamed his name in big, bold letters.

"Whatcha got there, Pop Star?"

She pointed to the hidden bottom she'd mistakenly come across when she was looking for her ballet slippers. Arch had tidied up, and she couldn't find them anywhere. The bottom of the drawer, lined in a velvet lavender material, had bubbled up and the strange notion she had to pull it back at all costs, the surge of urgency, made her do just that.

"Look!" she waved a hand at the scads of pictures and papers.

"You think this is all the Yash guy's pictures of Rick?" Marty asked, coming to sit next to Poppy. "If he took off like a bat out of hell, I guess the dirty SOB didn't want any reminders of the boy he raised like his own."

But Poppy shrugged her shoulders. She heard the words, the tinge of venom associated with them, but that just didn't sit right.

"Let's find out." Sifting through the pictures, Poppy couldn't help but smile, her heart clenching. There were tons of them. Rick in a Boy Scout uniform. She almost laughed out loud. Of course, he'd been a Boy Scout.

Rick in a Santa hat next to a stack of partially opened presents, wearing a pair of batman pajamas. Rick building a snowman, his nose red from the cold. Rick with a big turkey drumstick. Rick getting his high school diploma. Rick with Avis wearing hard hats at what looked like an earlier development project. Rick surrounded by a circle of small children with a building of some kind in the background. The back of the picture read, *Africa, 2011.*

"He built things in Africa," she whispered softly, staring at Rick, sweat glistening on his forehead, his dark hair slicked back.

"Well, our Rick isn't such a dick after all, is he?" Wanda said, tapping the picture with a smile.

And the final pictures, Rick with a man in a dark brown robe with an embroidered pattern down the front, that looked exactly like what Poppy had pictured someone doling out advice would wear. His face was kind amidst the wrinkles lining his cheeks, his eyes shining and happy, his snow-white hair but fringe surrounding his mostly bald head.

In one picture, he had his arm around a young Rick, protectively tucking him to his side. In another, Rick's head was thrown back as he laughed, apparently at something Yash had said or done. Yash sat next to him at a table, his hand stretched across the surface to rest on Rick's, his eyes laughing, too, his smile wide.

There were easily twenty or so of Rick and Yash, and even one of Yash by the shed, tending the gardens she had earlier enjoyed sitting beside.

But it was the very last one she touched that caught her attention. Fanning her hand over the pile, she revealed a picture of Avis, Rick, and Yash, standing in front of Littleton.

Her heart began to drum up a beat of raging panic as she looked closer, leaning forward at the waist. Everyone was smiling but Yash. In fact, he looked quite pained. Reaching out, she picked the picture up to examine it more closely—which was exactly the moment her stomach began to roll much in the way it had when she'd puked an aura.

A groan slipped from her lips as her fingertips burned and she fought a scream of agony as the white-hot pain seared through her belly, forcing her to roll to the ground.

"Poppy?" Marty bellowed, grabbing her shoulders. "Poppy! What's happening?"

She gripped the picture harder, her fingers clamping onto the shiny paper so hard, the bones in her fingers cracked, and her arms shook.

As quickly as it began, as severe as the pain became, it just as swiftly dissipated before the picture caught fire.

Poppy's fingers let go in reflective response, flexing outward until she hissed a protest.

"Fire in the hole!" Calamity yelped with a hiss, bringing Nina from around the corner.

"Got this!" Nina yelled as Poppy dropped the picture, and the vampire yanked her wand from behind her back, aiming it directly at the flames.

The spray of yellow mist from her wand extinguished the

fire in a mere second, the remaining smoke wisping to the ceiling in threads of acrid black tendrils.

"Holy great balls of fire! You did it!" Calamity exclaimed, prancing about. "You fucking did it! You put out the fire, Nina! I told you all those hours of hard work would pay off, Half-Breed!"

But Nina, so obviously not one for praise, stooped beside Poppy and planted a hand on her shoulder. "You okay? And what the fuck just happened? That damn aura again?"

She shook her head in astonishment as she lay on the floor, dazed. "It was that same pain again, and...I don't know. But I *do* know what just disintegrated in my hand was a picture of Rick, Avis, and Yash at Littleton. Yash knew about Littleton?"

"Did you ask the British Boob about Yash being there? When did he disappear anyway?"

Marty helped Poppy sit back up with a grunt. Looking at Nina, she made a face. "No. I didn't even think about it. I also didn't ask my favorite warlock. Getting Rick to talk was like trying to pry open a can of beans with your fingers. What he did tell me was hard enough to get out of him, but if I'd pressed any harder? I can't even imagine how withdrawn he'd become. He all but walked away from the conversation as though I should just leave things alone. I didn't get every detail. I was so blown away by what he told me about his mother and father, I almost couldn't speak. Stupidly, I left things alone. Because I thought I'd have more time to dig. But it's no wonder he's not all 'yay, familiar' after what he did share."

Nina's nostrils flared. "So the picture? Is this like some kind of nutty-ass sign? Why the hell is a picture bursting into flames? How does this tie into this dude Yash? Does it tie in at all?"

The moment she wondered the same was the moment

she was reminded of the expression on Yash's face. It had stuck her as pained. "You know, Yash didn't look happy in that picture, and in every other picture, he's either smiling or at the very least, looks peaceful. What about that picture made him so unhappy and why am I feeling this impending sense of doom?"

Wanda, who'd also raced to her side but had remained as quiet as she'd been through almost this entire journey, cocked her head. "Explain doom."

"I've been feeling it for a while now. At first, it started with the idea Nina would leave me here alone—"

"It was just a joke, Tiny Dancer."

Poppy held up a hand. "No, I know that. In fact, as part of this familiar bundle package, I intuitively knew you wouldn't leave me on my own. I didn't know I'm also intuitive until January explained, but when she did, it all made sense. But the doom thing began as early as that moment, and it's just been building since. At my apartment, I felt it, too. Like something is wrong, but I don't have the tools to figure it out. Then today when I woke up, I was overwhelmed by it, consumed by it. The thing is, I just don't know what to do about it."

"So this was going on before the aura thing?" Wanda inquired.

"Yes. Definitely yes."

"And you didn't tell us you were feeling this way, *why*?" Calamity asked.

She sighed, exasperated by this unexplainable rush of ugly fear. "Because how do you describe a feeling without proof there's a reason for a feeling? Lots of people say I have a bad feeling. I just didn't know with me it really meant something." Leaning back on the bed, she winced at the pull on her abs.

They were still a bit sore from the other day, but this

encounter hadn't helped. Something shiny under the small dresser across from the bed caught her eye. Well, maybe shiny wasn't the word she was looking for.

Sparkling was better, muted, but sparkling.

Getting on her knees, Poppy scooted to the dresser and slid her hand beneath, sweeping the floor until she knocked the item out the other side.

Eyeing it, she realized it was a crystal of some kind, a blue, prism-like crystal in the shape of a teardrop.

Wrapping her fingers around it, Poppy was instantly slammed back against the side of the bed.

"What the hell is going on?" Nina yelled as a scramble of feet thundered in Poppy's ears.

But the chaos and the pain of the crash were vague and distant as the crystal grew warm in her hand and her eyes clouded, her vision becoming blurry. That crazy low rumble began in her ears again, pulsing, growing stronger.

The word *Littleton* popped up in front of her like a neon sign, flashing and blinking a furious rhythm just as the whispering began. "*Littleton! Littleton! Littleton,*" the ironically soothing voice hummed.

"Do you hear that?" she called out to the girls and Calamity.

"Hear what?" Marty yelped, her voice frantic.

"*Rick, Rick, Rick!*" the voice whispered, swirling in an ominous throb in her ears. Poppy jolted upward, throwing her hands over her ears to stop the maddening chant, tears forming in her eyes.

More flickering images flew in front of her, heinous images of death, pain so ugly, she had to close her eyes to block it out, and all the while, the words, "*Littleton! Littleton! Littleton!*" screeched through her brain.

"Stooooop!" Poppy screamed, so loud her throat ached. "Stooooop! *Please, stop!*"

"Jesus Christ!" Nina yelled, grabbing her by the shoulders and pulling her close to her chest. "What's happening?"

As suddenly as it began, the chant stopped.

Gulping for air, Poppy struggled out of Nina's arms, looking right at her. "Littleton! I have to get to Littleton!"

CHAPTER 17

"*I*'mma tell you one last time, Ballerina, slow the fuck down, or I'm gonna put you down. I'm all for a good hunt, but not when your life's in the mix. Now sit your ass down on that couch and shut your flappy lips before I sew them shut," Nina ordered, her face cross.

"We have to go to Littleton *now*!" Poppy insisted, so panicked, not even Nina's threat made her think twice. Rick was at Littleton. She was certain. Something awful was happening with him. She needed to see to his safety.

Nina shook her head, flashing her fangs in a threatening manner. "Um, no. We need to wait and hear from the doc. She said today was the day for the crazy. Like, the ultimate crazy. We're not letting you go stick your nose into that crazy until we can get her advice. And Darnell'll be here any minute to help. You're not going to Littleton alone. End of. Now, swear to Jesus, Slick, you make a break for it, I chase you down like a tiger chases a gazelle in a Discovery Channel documentary, and trust this shit, I'll catch you."

Marty grabbed at Poppy's arm, her face so full of concern, it almost made Poppy tear up from her frustration. "Just give us a second to get in touch with January, honey. *Please.* We have to have a plan before we go on the attack. We're talking magic here. It takes more than muscle to navigate."

But her panic was in full swing now and like a pack of stampeding wild horses, that panic trampled her. "Fuck plans!"

She knew she had to go this instant. Right now. It was already dark, they'd already be gearing up for the demo in another hour, and then Rick would be harder to locate. She'd tried texting him, but she'd gotten no response. She'd left him five back-to-back voicemails, and he hadn't returned a single call.

"Explain to me this vision or whatever it was again," Wanda insisted, pulling Poppy's sweater tighter over her chest. "Stay focused and talk this out with me."

Again, Poppy tried to shake off the horror. "I can't speak the words, Wanda. It was horrible. I'm almost one hundred percent sure Yash was trying to tell me something with that crystal. Who else's crystal could that be but Yash's? He was pretty into the metaphysical, right? It's not a stretch to think he used crystals for more than just decoration. It had to be his. And tell me this, why did he look so upset in that picture with Rick and Avis? Then the voice, yelling at me to go to Littleton, yelling Rick's name. This all leads back to Littleton!"

Wanda's lips thinned as she gripped Poppy's shaking fingers, her eyes full of worry. "Okay, and what *if*—what if it wasn't Yash? What if it was all a trick, honey? What if it was the aura so hell-bent on seeing you dead who's calling out?"

Tears began to slip from her eyes, her heart bashing so hard against her ribs, she thought it would explode. Her panic was no longer on the rise, it was everything—all consuming.

"No! You all have to listen to me! That crystal belonged to

Yash! He was trying to tell me something. I have—to—go!" she roared, the words shooting from her mouth like bullets.

"Miss Wanda? What can I do to soothe Mistress Poppy?" Arch asked, his eyes darting and as frantic as Poppy felt. "Tell me. I'll do anything to ease your suffering until Miss January arrives."

Poppy backed away, holding up her hands. She knew she looked like she'd lost her mind, but the pressure of the urgency, this need to get to Littleton, flooded her, overwhelmed her to the point of leaving her head a jumbled mess.

"Nothing! I don't need anything—I have to leave!"

"Poppy-Seed, my boo, I'm beggin' ya—listen! Listen to me!" Calamity ordered from the island counter, jamming her round face into Poppy's shoulder.

Poppy's eyes darted toward the feline, searching for a focus, a way to rein in this horrible, despicable fear, but she couldn't. There was no stopping this. So she shook her head again until her eyeballs rolled and the pound in her temples grew.

"Nononono!"

"Miss Nina! What's going on?" a gruff, gentle voice called from the doorway.

"Jesus Christ, thank fuck you're here, D! Somethin' ain't right with our girl. Help us!" Nina called out.

An enormous man, the size of two linebackers, was suddenly in her line of vision, his round face and soothing eyes seeking Poppy's. "Gimme your hand, Poppy. Give it here now," he demanded, but it wasn't with impatience or upset urgency. He said it with a calm that somehow pierced her anxiety.

She gave him her hand, his large palm enveloping her fingers. "I'mma need you to listen to my voice, Poppy." He paused, making sure he had her attention before he said,

"Name's Darnell and I'm a demon. Thass right, you heard correct. Demon. But I ain't a bad one. So you listen up. I'm here to help, but you gotta let me."

Holding Darnell's hand was like floating in a protective bubble of soothing bath water. Suddenly, everything stilled, and she nodded as though in a trance.

He bobbed his head of shortly cropped hair in approval, his smile kind. "Nice. Good girl. Now you just listen. We're gonna fix this, but you cain't go runnin' off. You got to stay close, okay? Bad stuff happens tonight if you ain't careful. You're too new to be off on your own with all this other nonsense floatin' about to boot. Now, promise ol' Darnell you'll stay close."

"Pro...mise," she stuttered, weak as relief eased her tension, massaged her muscles until they began to quiver.

It was then Darnell pulled her close to his barrel chest, rocking her in a light sway to ease her shakes. "I got ya now. You just breathe. Just close your eyes and breathe, Poppy. Fo' this is through, we gonna be good friends. Promise you that."

Friends. She liked friends, especially ones like this, who smelled like the woods and a warm, crackling fire. Mercifully, her face began to relax, the throb in her head eased.

Someone stroked her back. "That's it, sweetie. Just relax. January will text soon."

Marty. That was Marty being Marty. A mom.

As she drifted further, someone else draped a blanket over her, warming her to a pleasantly toasty state.

"Thank goodness for you, Master Darnell. She was growing quite frantic. Where would we be without you, fine fellow?"

Darnell's chuckle rumbled in her ear, lulling her, and as her eyes closed and her body became calm, she drifted away.

She only vaguely heard the call of her name...a frenzied cry, if she were to label it. But she was too focused on how peaceful being tucked into Darnell's embrace, a perfect stranger's embrace, was probably the best thing since landing a gig in the chorus of *The Lion King.*

* * *

HER BACK HIT the ground with a thwack, stealing the breath from her lungs. The ground beneath her soggy and cold. No longer was she drifting in calm waters.

Instead, that damn panic was back, gnawing her from the inside out. Her eyes flew open, adjusting to the enveloping darkness greeting and whooshing about her ears. Loud voices, rough and harsh, swelled around her then faded, and then she realized where she was.

Littleton.

In the garden by the front door, surrounded by the bonsai trees. The building was dark, clearly, everyone gone for the demolition. How the hell had she ended up here? Where was everyone? Darnell, the strangest dichotomy of a demon ever? Nina, Wanda, Marty, Carl, Calamity? How had she been zapped here?

What was happening and why? What was she looking for?

Get up, Poppy! Get up! Get Rick! some unknown force screamed in her brain. So, she did as it told her, using her arms to piston her upward. A wince of pain jabbed her just below her breasts, making the effort to sit up straight a painful one.

Get Rick!

But where is he? She wanted to scream, rising to her haunches and using the bench in the garden as leverage to pull herself up. All sorts of words from the space around her assaulted her then.

Death. Evil. Agony.

Throwing her hands up in the air, Poppy clenched her fists in frustration as her eyes surveyed the landscape of the building. She heard someone yell "twenty minutes" from what sounded like just outside the gates, reminding her this building was scheduled to blow.

The diner. Maybe Rick was at the diner with the rest of the tenants, waiting to watch the big demo? Hadn't Arnie said they were going to make a party of it?

Running toward the gates, her hand had just reached out to open them when the voice screamed again, "*Get Rick!*"

Fighting that disturbing panic, Poppy stopped in the middle of everything. Simply stopped and looked up to the sky for guidance, attempting to sort her panic from reason.

"Okay, listen. I'm freaked out here. You keep yelling at me to get Rick, but I don't know where Rick is or why I have to get him. Can I have a noun, please? Like a location? I'm happy to get Rick if you'll just tell me how!"

She listened again for the voice, but there was nothing. Absolutely nothing but the sound of her heartbeat crashing in her ears.

Raising her face to the sky, Poppy grimaced, still fighting a full-on panic attack. "Huge batch of help that was. Thanks for nothing," she mumbled—and then she heard someone calling her name.

"*Poppy! Up here!*"

Cocking her head, she turned to look toward Littleton. Was that Rick? Had he suddenly found his voice? Squinting, she looked into the darkness of the building, desolation swarming her and landing square in her chest.

"Poppy!"

Frowning, she realized that was definitely Rick. Why would he be in a building they were preparing to demolish in now less than twenty minutes?

That was when it hit her. The words death, evil, agony.

Did someone have him in the building? Maybe the aura? Could the aura detach itself from her and harm Rick?

If it can lob you across the woods, of course, it can attach itself to Rick, moron.

Maybe that was why she'd felt the pressing need to get to Littleton? Because Rick was being held captive by the aura?

Scraping her hand over her back pocket, Poppy discovered she didn't have her phone. She couldn't call January or Nina or anyone, and she was the dreaded A word.

Alone. Something she wasn't supposed to be no matter what.

Her hands went clammy and shaky. If she left and went to find a way to contact the girls, and Rick really was in the building, he could end up dead. January had said the aura wanted death.

"Poppy!"

Looking up, she pinpointed where his voice was coming from and decided there was no other way. She had to go look. Whipping around, Poppy's eyes scanned the surrounding area for any signs of help, but the place was deserted.

"Get Rick!"

As another tidal wave of fear coursed through her, she knew he was in the building. She felt it in her bones, and there was nothing left to do but go in and find him.

Without another thought, and with the small consolation that she was pretty quick on her feet, Poppy took off for the interior of the building, pushing her way through the front doors.

* * *

"*SHE WHAT?*" Rick asked just before he realized his voice had returned.

"Well, look who can fucking talk, would ya? Thought you had laryngitis? Or was that pussy-itis?" Nina crowed, jamming her face in his.

Clenching his jaw, he forced himself to respond rationally. Nina was only looking out for Poppy, and for that he was grateful. If it meant he had to suffer her threats, he'd do it gladly.

"I'm as surprised as you. Forget my voice for now and tell me what happened to Poppy."

Nina snapped her fingers. "Dis-a-fucking-ppeared, dude! One minute Darnell was rocking her like a damn baby, the next she was just gone."

Fear flooded his gut, making him lean against the door of his house for support. The cold, clear night above appeared harmless but had somehow become chock full of danger.

He hadn't even stuck the key in his door before the women, Carl, and a new man he hadn't identified yet swarmed him, all talking at once about Poppy's disappearance as they prepared to go find her.

His plan had been to ask Poppy to come to the diner with him to be with the seniors and watch the demo. He didn't want to leave them alone in case there were any concerns, but he couldn't stand to leave this thing between them for another second.

And now she was gone. Vanished into thin air. Which meant he had to take action now. Turning to Nina, he asked, "What was happening before she disappeared? Why was Darnell rocking her?"

Nina poked him in the chest, her anger with him apparent as she used aggressive hands to straighten her jacket's hood. "That damn building of yours! She hasn't said much because *you* just can't seem to communicate and digest without clamming up, but she's been having some pretty shitty feelings about not only your BFF, Pip-Pip-Cheerio, but about that damn building and everyone's willingness to skip off to fucking Great Neck. She felt like it was her job to advise you, not dump on you about something she didn't damn well understand. Also, when she *did* try to tell you how she felt about your buddy, you walked out, Ricky baby."

"Nina!" Marty scolded, knocking Nina in the shoulder. "That's not true! He asked her to allow him to wrap his head around the fact that she thinks Avis is a misogynistic ass! Not the same thing, Vampire."

But Nina wasn't having any of Marty's guff. "Well, I'm here to tell you, we don't play like that. We fucking duke it out until it's a GD dead issue. We don't walk the fuck away because this is what happens!"

Shit. Shit. Shit. Yash had always been on him about expressing himself better, and he'd been right. He did suck at sharing, but he'd been so blindsided by the look on Poppy's face and her conviction Avis was a scumbag, he'd needed to process.

So he shook his head at Marty, his eyes apologetic. "No. It's true. I didn't *walk away*-walk away, but I did need some time to process what she was saying about Avis. It surprised me, in truth. But she never said a damn thing about Littleton."

"All I can tell you is she was off on a tangent, Rickster," Calamity called from his feet. "She went on and on about how she had to go to Littleton after she saw a picture of your old familiar Yash and found one of his crystals. January said she has the gift of intuition—"

"And if you'd stuck this shit out instead of goin' all stiff upper lip, you'd know that, wouldn't you, *Rick*?" Nina accused, driving a knuckle into his shoulder hard enough to make him wince.

But he deserved her scorn, her disgust. He had asked for a reprieve because Poppy's dislike of Avis cut so deep. He'd needed time to parse how he was going to make both rela-tionships work. He wanted his relationship with Poppy to work on more levels than just her assignment.

Wanda grabbed Nina by the arm so quickly, Rick almost couldn't believe what he was seeing. "Stop condemning a man for gathering his thoughts instead of spewing a bunch of crap and potty language to fill up space, Nina! Not everyone operates like you, Mistress of The Night. We don't all just lash out. Now shut up and let's figure this out. She was going on and on about getting to Littleton. Maybe that's where she is?"

As he continued to process, something else cropped up. The word *intuition*. "Wait, what's this about Poppy being intuitive?"

Wanda smoothed her gloves over her hands, fiddling with them in a nervous gesture. "January said she had the gift of intuition, but Poppy wasn't sure if her intuition was muddied by this aura, or if she really was experiencing bad mojo about Littleton. So she kept it to herself because she had no proof to back up her claim other than a 'feeling.'"

Same thing she'd said about Avis. Looking out into the dark of night, his street silent, he was once more reminded of the coming blood moon. His eyes scanned the sky; the swollen moon, still a buttery yellow, hadn't begun the change yet, but the vibe was there. The ever-present warning about the things that could happen on the night of a blood moon.

Maybe that somehow tied into Poppy's intuition? It wasn't uncommon for the blood moon to create havoc and play tricks with your mind if you were emotionally sensitive and didn't know how to handle the sensory overload. Poppy was new to this, maybe this was just a case of systems overload?

But then why was he having this sudden urge to find her at all costs? As though if he didn't, something bad was going to happen? It didn't matter, all that mattered was this time he wasn't going to ignore his gut.

"Let's forget everything else and find Poppy. We need to get there fast if I'm going to stop the demo."

"Wait!" Darnell, one of the biggest men Rick had ever laid eyes on, ordered. "Man, don't rush. We gotta fan out a little. You ladies go to Littleton, I'll keep Carl close. If she's there, y'all text me and I'll come runnin', but if she comes back here, I don't want her to come back to nothin'. The blood moon makes for the crazy if you don't know how to keep your head on straight. If that's what's doin' this to her, I can help. Y'all good with that?"

Rick slapped him on the back, grateful to this stranger for jumping into the fray. "You're right, Darnell. Thank you for keeping a level head." Turning to the women, he asked, "Are we all in agreement?"

"Let's find our Tiny Dancer," Nina said, her mouth a determined slash of crimson on her face.

"All in!" Wanda shouted, looping her arm through Marty's.

As Rick prepared to chant a transportation spell, first, he prayed he could actually pull it off. His magic was peanuts compared to most, but it was *really* peanuts because he hadn't used it in so long.

Second, he prayed to the Goddess that they'd find their Tiny Dancer.

CHAPTER 18

The voice swirled around the empty halls of Littleton, all but deserted and dark with only the light from the streetlamps shining into the windows to illuminate the desolation.

The moon had risen, beautiful and soft, making her wonder when this blood moon thing happened. But the pull of it, the thread of connection Poppy felt to it, called to her in a way that left her distracted, and she reminded herself she had to stay focused and find Rick.

All the doors to each apartment had been removed, leaving each entryway she peeked into a stark reminder her days here were a closing chapter.

Sadness permeated the air as she fought her way up the stairs, calling out Rick's name.

"Poppy!"

Now he sounded as though he was downstairs, maybe in the lobby? She'd just been there, and he was nowhere in sight. What was going on?

Stopping in the stairwell, she forced herself to gather her

senses and listen. Really listen. "Rick, where are you?" she called out.

But there was no answer, so she followed the unmerciful wail of her name back down to the lobby, skidding out of the stairwell that dumped her to the left of the elevators.

It was all she could do to keep her feet under her when she heard someone say, "There you are!" Startling her almost to the point of making her cringe.

More panic swept over her. Surely they were going to demo Littleton at any minute? Who was left in the building? Oh my God. Was one of the seniors still here?

Poppy poked her head around the corner, careful to stay pressed flat to the wall, but she couldn't see well enough to distinguish who the figure was.

There was a heavy scrape of something against the floor and a grunt, but still, she couldn't make out any definitive features. Yet, her skin crawled and goose bumps rose on her arms when a dark shadow moved, with only a thread of light from the front doors to help her see.

But she didn't really need to see the shadow for identification. All she needed was to hear the shadow speak. "I've waited a long time for this, you bloody beauties! A long, long time."

Avis.

Fuck, fuck and fuckity-fuck. This intuition thing obviously had its downside, and finding out she was right about Avis was definitely one of them. Whatever he was up to, it was no good. Her bones said as much.

As the picture became clearer, and Poppy watched Avis flit about the lobby, she didn't know what the hell he was doing, but she knew it was something really bad. Super bad. But what? What did Littleton have to do with this bad feeling?

Yeah, they were knocking the building down, but no one

but her seemed to care. Rick had been honest with Mr. Rush during the sale, so what was Avis doing milling about here, talking to some pillars? She'd bet her bobbleheads it had something to do with magic.

By hell, when all was said and done, she was going to insist someone give her a history lesson in magic and familiars. Like from the beginning of the beginning so she knew all the ins and outs.

And then that damn persistent voice called to her again. *"Poppy!"*

"Goddammit, knock it off!" she muttered under her breath while Avis used his weight to shift one of the pillars holding those stones matching the spire on the roof.

With sudden clarity, something hit her.

Now, more than ever, she was convinced Rick wasn't in the building at all—but *she* was, and that was probably right where Avis wanted her to be. She didn't know why, but she knew she was right.

Foiled again, McGuillicuddy.

* * *

"WHERE THE FUCK ARE WE?" Nina yelled to Rick over the strong wind.

"The roof of Littleton!" Rick yelled back, tucking his face to his chest to block out the torrent of leaves slapping at him.

"Are you insane? Dude, they're gonna blow this thing the fuck up!" Nina bellowed her anger in his face.

Marty and Wanda clung to one another, fighting the sheer force of the wind, Marty's face chock full of worry. "Why are we here? Where the hell is Poppy in all this?"

A spell. Someone had cast a spell on Littleton.

He'd done a transporting spell a million times as a warlock. He'd pictured in his mind exactly where he wanted them to end up—in the garden of Littleton—but somehow, they'd landed on the roof? It had to be a spell blocking him out of the interior of the building. But why?

"Follow me!" he yelled over the howl of cold air as he fought his way to the staircase leading to the top floor. Lightning cracked above their heads, illuminating the spire in front of them, casting an ominous, almost evil glow upon it.

Reaching for the door, he wrapped his frozen fingers around the handle and instantly jumped back. "Fuck!" he yelled, the burn of his flesh a sharp jolt.

"Shit!" Calamity cried. "Is it a spell? Jesus and hellfire, what's going on?"

Gripping his hand to his chest, Rick's eyes wildly sought another way to get off the roof.

"January!" Wanda called out. "Thank God you're here!"

The doctor raced across the rooftop, her eyes wide, her clothes flapping in the gusts of wind as she reached for his injured hand. "What happened?"

Rick grit his teeth, the hot ache of his burned hand throbbing. "Forget my hand, I can't get the damn door open! We think Poppy's down there. We need to get there now!"

January's nostrils flared as her eyes flitted across the landscape of the roof. "A spell. Someone cast a spell here. Can you smell it? Who's preventing you from getting down these stairs?"

As the wind battered Nina's slender body, she drove herself into it with determination. "Fuck this! If the kid's downstairs, I'll just jump over the side. I can fly, remember?"

Rick didn't even have time to think about the fact the vampire could fly, but if he got Poppy out and was still alive after doing it, he was going to re-subscribe to *Paranormal World News*, because he was severely out of the loop about his own kind, let alone vampires.

"No!" January howled, grabbing Nina's arm and spinning

her around. "This doesn't call for brawn, Nina. It calls for magic. I don't know what's happening or why, but if you walk into something with bad magic meant to harm, your fists won't save you! Now I need you all to listen to me. Everyone hold hands. Calamity, Rick, we need a revocation spell. I can't do it alone, Rick. So wind up, buddy, and use that magic!"

As they all held hands, bowing their heads into the raging wind, Calamity on Rick's shoulder, he closed his eyes and began to chant the spell with January with only one thought in mind.

Get to Poppy.

* * *

THERE WAS NO SLIPPING past Avis through the front doors, but as she turned to run back up the stairs and bust a window in order to possibly jump to safety, Avis called out to her. "Don't bother, darling. There's no way out."

No way out?

"Yes, you heard me right, Poppet. I've put a spell on you," he sang, his giggle ringing in her ears. "You can't get out, and no one else can get in. You can try of course, but your efforts will be wasted."

So she was either going to blow up with him—which was ludicrous because why did someone as bloated with ego like Avis have a death wish—or actually have to find the balls to confront him and try and stop him.

Which meant it was go big or go home.

And as she watched him push three of the pillars together to form an almost square, knowing this meant something dreadful, at least if she was judging by the screaming protest of her belly, Poppy made her move.

"Avis?"

His blond head whipped upward, and he squinted into the dark, but then he smiled that brilliantly perfect smile, the one with subtext evil written all over it. "Did I mention how glad I am you've joined me? Not that you had actually had a choice."

"A choice?" He'd zapped her here? What happened to the warlocks had weak magic rule?

"How do you suppose you got here? Me, of course! I've been practicing my spells like a good chap for a very long time," he said on a sadistic chuckle. "You'll want to stick around anyway. This should really be something for a first-timer like you."

Licking her lips, she stayed in the shadows, waiting for the right moment. Maybe he was just bluffing about this spell? "Where's Rick, Avis?"

Scratching his head, he sighed forlornly. "I don't know if *you* don't know, darling. But he doesn't really matter tonight."

Her skin crawled at his use of the endearment, but she needed to know what was happening—what he was doing here. "Shouldn't you be hitting the road? Isn't this place going to blow soon?"

His laughter filled the entryway, bouncing off the marble tile. "Oh, indeed, it's assuredly going to blow. Just not in quite the way you think, sweet girl."

Okay. He was stark raving banana pants, and she wanted out. Turning to make a break for the stairs again, she rammed right into an invisible wall, cracking her head. Ignoring the sting, Poppy reached out and attempted to penetrate the darkness of the stairwell only to find her hand smacking against something hard and cold.

"I did tell you there was no way out, didn't I, Poppet?"

The moment Avis said the words was the moment she felt as though she'd been punched in the gut. Something seared her from the inside out, hot and plodding its merry way to another one of those demonic pukes.

Gripping the corner of the wall, she waited until the pain passed and managed to grit out, "Why are you here, Avis?"

Straightening his spine, he squared his shoulders and leaned an elbow on one of the pillars. "Because I have to be here, pretty lady. Tonight's the night."

"For?" she croaked.

"For the main event, of course. It's the blood moon, Poppy. Even though you're new to this, surely someone's told you the power tonight has. It isn't just Samhain, it's Samhain plus."

Right, right, right. The blood moon lifted some veil, bad things could happen. Sometimes it opened portals. Call ghostbusters.

Oh.

Oh, oh, oh. Without knowing how or why Poppy made a connection. Avis was a bad dude. A bad warlock dude. Bad warlock dudes probably liked to do bad things—maybe they even liked to do them with bad spirits. Bad spirits wanted into this world. Tonight, with it not only being Samhain but the blood moon, it was like bad spirit spring break, and she'd bet her eyeballs Avis had bought a ticket.

As the realization hit her, so did the agonizing return of the pain in her belly, a sure sign she was on to something. She was right. She didn't know the details, but she knew she was right.

Gritting her teeth and fighting the urge to double over, Poppy asked, "What's the main event, Avis?"

He clucked his tongue. "First, why not come out of there, Poppy. You're too pretty to let anyone put Baby in the corner," he teased, motioning she should join him. "Second, the main event is your death. Among other things."

Yeah. She got it now. Well, mostly. The details remained

fuzzy. For instance, why he wanted her dead was a mystery. "So you were the one who brought me here? You were the one who was calling my name? You made the vision I had. You made me think it was Yash. *You're* the aura!"

Moving a step closer in her direction, Avis cocked his ear. "Well, duh, Sugarlumps. I know, I know. You're thinking, 'Well, golly. I knew I didn't like him, but I never thought he was this big of a prick.' Am I right?"

A scream bubbled in the back of her throat at the pain searing through her belly, but she refused to give in.

Sweat pooled between her breasts, her hair soaked, but she clung to the wall, pressing her forehead into it, seeking the cool surface to soothe her.

"Winner-winner-chicken-dinner," she spat. "I'm not surprised, mind you. I knew I hated your stinkin' fancy-pants guts, but I just couldn't connect the dots. I haven't been doing this long enough to fully comprehend all the reasons these things are happening to me. So why don't you fill me in? What the hell are you doing, why is my death on your plate, and why isn't this building falling to dusty bits of rubble by now?"

He flapped a hand in the air and winked. "Oh, that. Because it never *was* going to fall to dusty bits of rubble, Goose. As we speak, those utter buffoons from the demolition crew are having some sort of technical difficulties. They can't figure it out because there's nothing to figure out. It's just a simple spell that, in the end, won't matter one ding-dang bit. In fact, right now they're trying to call our man Rick for instruction on what to do next. But they won't reach him."

A spike of fear, insidious and hateful, threaded its way through her veins. "Why won't they reach him? Did you hurt him?"

"Bah! I would never hurt Rick. I'm sure he's safe somewhere nursing his spell-driven laryngitis. But I *would* hurt everyone around him in order to get what I want, and that, I'm afraid, includes you. I am, indeed, the aura. Or the person responsible for the insidious aura attached to you."

"But why?" she squeaked, swallowing hard. "Why would you do that?"

He sighed, exaggerated and long with a roll of his eyes. "Because you're trouble, Poppy McGuillicuddy. It wouldn't have been long before you found out about me, and I couldn't have Rick's familiar interfering with what's mine. When I found out you lived in this building, I knew Yash's spirit had something to do with all this. It's too much of a coincidence."

"Yash's spirit?"

How the hell did he know Yash's spirit had anything to do with this? Oh, God. *His spirit*. That meant he was dead. *Nonononono!*

"Well, of course! You do realize warlocks do all sorts of magical things like summon spirits, don't you, ninny? So I summoned his—and I have to tell you, he fought it like a caged tiger. Rick would be proud. But in the end, I discovered what I knew anyway. He created that little accident you had with that feline familiar. Yash sent you to Rick to stop me from getting to Littleton. That's what all those ugly feelings you've been having are about, by the way."

The impact of his statement wasn't lost on her, but the focus of his words was Littleton. What was so important about Littleton? Still, she clung to the notion, if she could just get one small break in this pain, she could make a run for him.

And then what, Poppy?

So she kept talking. "But why do I have to die?"

"At first, I just wanted to rid myself of you. Like you, I, too, am intuitive. I sensed your dislike of me from the moment we met. That could bring nothing but heartache, you being Rick's familiar and all. So you had to go. But when I realized Yash was in the mix, it wasn't long before I knew he'd find some afterlife way to tell you what happened, and it would be curtains for me before I could get to this point. I'll give you this—you're strong, Poppity-Pop. Especially strong for a newb. Alas, I decided to turn the tables. When I couldn't get rid of you, I decided to invite you to join me tonight instead."

Another white-hot knife of pain cut through her stomach, making her clench her fists so hard, she dug holes in the palms of her hands with her nails. "Join you for what? What does that mean?"

"For the sacrifice, charming girl."

A bolt of lightning streaked across the sky, illuminating Avis for the first time since she'd found him—and his face terrified her. He didn't look at all like what one would expect when they planned a diabolical deed. No. He looked quite calm and very pleased with himself.

"The sacrifice? *I'm* the sacrifice, aren't I, Avis?"

He clapped his hands, the sound sharp and jarring. "And the door prize goes to Poppy McGuillicuddy!"

CHAPTER 19

*L*anding in the garden of Littleton, Rick was the first to come to a standing position, pushing his way out of the bonsai spiral trees and latching onto Nina while scooping up Calamity.

As the women helped each other rise, Calamity whispered to him, "You see that motherfucker? He's in there. Poppy was right! He's a crazy bastard!"

"I can't see a damn thing, Calamity," he hissed back, squinting into the darkness of the building.

"I can," Nina confirmed, stroking Calamity's ears. "Vampire sight and all. That fuck's in there, and I smell Poppy. She's fucking petrified, dude. So now what? If we can't rush the motherfucker and take him out because of this magic shit, what's our next move?"

"I got this! Everyone stay put!" Calamity whisper-yelled, leaping from Rick's arms and scampering to the entryway door.

January came up behind him, putting her hand on his arm. "Who is that, Rick? And do you smell what I smell?"

Fuck, he sure did. Death. He smelled the summoning of death.

The pit of despair in his stomach grew. "That's my partner, Avis."

"*A warlock?*" January hissed her surprise. "He not only put a spell on this place to keep us out but to keep Poppy inside. How the hell did a warlock get this much power? Where is he getting it from?"

January's question was valid. Where was Avis getting the kind of power it took to cast all these spells and summon death?

Then something hit him, something that reminded him of the spell he'd done for his father when he hadn't known any better.

Avis must have some kind of item, a talisman, a crystal, something correlating with the blood moon.

"He has to have something—something that brings all the forces together tonight."

And then something else hit him—hit him like a punch to his kidneys. "I couldn't figure out why we wouldn't schedule the demo after Samhain, but Avis said it was a great way to begin again—it was symbolic. It would bring us good fortune."

January groaned with a soft emission of air. "Goddess, we need to get Darnell here fast! He's going to summon spirits from the other side in return for something, using the thinning of the veil—and I can almost guarantee you, Poppy is his sacrifice."

* * *

THE SHUDDER of her breathing was almost impossible to hide, the pain writhing through her so ungodly, she wasn't even sure she could move, let alone rush the bastard and knock him down in an effort to get away.

"You might as well come out, Poppy. Why not learn some of your rich history by letting me explain what I'm preparing to do before you die."

"I can hear you just fine from here." She all but screamed the words, driving her forehead into the wall to give her something other than the screech of her stomach to focus on.

"Suit yourself," he offered amicably then patted the stone on the pillar. "See these stones, Poppy? Simply put, when placed together at exactly the right moment, they summon those pesky little spirits wanting into our world, and I've made a deal with them."

"I hope you got free Wi-Fi," she quipped, letting her head fall back on her shoulders as sweat poured from her face.

"Hah!" he barked. "You're truly brilliant. I wish we could have been friends. Anyway, here's the deal. I came across these stones quite by chance. When we were scouting buildings, and I ran smack into your Littleton, I almost shat myself. I don't know how these stones got here, as out of place as they are with the gauche decor, but here they were. I was intrigued! So I took pictures. I Googled. Lo and behold, I discovered these stones, or cornerstones, are ancient, mystical to my people, and here they were, left to rot with scads of wrinkled tenants. I couldn't let that happen. Especially after I realized what they could do!"

Because Avis appeared to enjoy sharing his coup, likely due to the fact that he had no one else who liked him long enough to have a cocktail with him, let alone spend enough time with him to tell a story, Poppy bit the bait while she stalled.

"What can the stones do?"

He popped his lips in disappointment. "But don't you want to know how I pulled all this off? How I got here tonight? I feel like you're in such a rush, and I have a bit of time to spare until the moon is in full cycle. It's not like *you* have anywhere to go either."

Woe is the long-winded storyteller. But maybe, if she kept him talking, someone would show up. Surely by now, the girls and Calamity had made the connection? She prayed someone made the connection. *Please, God, let someone make the connection.*

Until then… "Okay, Avis. I'm all ears. Tell me the story," she encouraged, wincing as another stab at her gut stole her breath.

He paced back and forth, pinching his temples. "Where was I? Oh, yes. The stones. Anyway, this presented a problem. The stones being here. I couldn't remove them without arousing suspicion in the spirit world. They're touchy little buggers. So I contacted Mr. Rush and made him an offer I *thought* he couldn't refuse…"

The hair on the back of her neck rose, knowing he wanted her to ask why Mr. Rush had refused. "So he refused?"

"Did he ever. But that was okay because I had a plan B."

She only wished *she* had a plan B. Jamming her fist into her stomach, she fought another raging bolt of pain and asked, "What was Plan B? Kill Mr. Rush?"

She attempted to make the question come off as bored, knowing he'd find that disappointing.

"Don't be silly, Poppet. That was too risky, too obvious. I'd only been here a dozen times trying to buy the building from him. We even had a heated conversation about it. If he turned up dead, surely suspicion would be cast upon me."

"That's very cover-your-bases smart of you. So what did you do next, Avis?"

"Went to Disneyland." Then he laughed at his joke, a full-blown batch of hysterical giggles. "I'm kidding, I'm kidding," he gasped out, shaking off his laughter and sobering. "I simply found a spell to cast on him to make him agree with everything I say—it proved quite useful, actually. I used it on everyone here."

Ahhhh. All the pieces clicked into place then. The reason everyone at Littleton was so excited about moving. The reason Mr. Rush was so dead-eyed when he'd nodded yes to her question about selling. The crazy response Arnie had given about being an adult who could make his own decisions.

"So you cast a spell, attacking their free will and coercing them into giving up their homes?" The son of a bitch. If she lived to see Rick again, she was going to so rub his face in this.

"I did!" he shouted with glee. "I was sorry to see what that did to Mr. Rush. I think I got a little heavy-handed with the do-as-I-say spin I put on it, but he's still alive, right?'

"The spell was what made Mr. Rush have the stroke?" *Damn him.*

"Alas, 'twas. And I worried something fierce when you went to visit him. I thought surely he'd find a way to tap out his distress, write it on a piece of paper, but it seems I'm better than I thought."

Oh God. Avis was sick. So sick.

Sucking in a breath of air, Poppy said, "Which brings us back to this moment. Why are you doing this, Avis? What does Avis Mackland gain from all of this?"

Avis jammed his hands into the pockets of his pants. "Well, like I said, I made a deal. I give these spirits the freedom they so crave at just the right time, when the blood moon is at its peak on Samhain, and summon them by pushing all four of these pretty cornerstones together. Then I offer them your soul, and I become the most powerful wizard of all. No one will ever mock my lack of power again. *No one*."

Mock his power? So he was just power hungry? What motivated that greed? What could he prove with this power? Who did he want to impress?

Yeah, Poppy. Who do men like Avis usually want to impress with their power?

A woman.

"Who made fun of poor Avis's lack of power? *Was it your girlfriend?*" she antagonized as a surge of relief flowed through her. She didn't know where it came from or why, but it was like someone had injected life back into her.

And now, she wanted his balls.

"Don't speak of things you don't know, Poppet. They'll only bring you grief," he warned.

Straightening, Poppy rolled her head on her neck, easing the tense muscles and taking another deep, pain-free breath.

"How much more grief-ish does it get if my soul's going to be sacrificed? So c'mon, Avis. Just tell me, what brought this on—this desire to be a wizard? This need for the ultimate power? What does a wizard do anyway but wear robes and pointy hats? And by the way, you didn't answer my question. Was it a woman? Someone you loved who didn't love poor little Avis back?"

As she peered around the corner, she noted he was definitely becoming angry. The lines on his face were harsh as he stepped from the shadows, the purse of his lips tight. "I said, leave it alone, Poppy. *Leave. It. Alone.*"

Fat chance. She tested her knees, bending them, flexing them for her planned steamroll—until Avis stopped her preparation in its tracks.

"You know, you didn't ask me about Yash."

"But I did ask you about Yash. At the diner, Avis." The moment she said the words was the moment her heart picked up, kicking into overdrive. Why was Yash such a big deal?

And then she remembered the picture of the three of them in front of Littleton, and how pained Yash's eyes had looked.

"But you didn't ask me why I'd seek his spirit when he betrayed Rick so callously. I mean, surely you'd ask yourself why he'd help Rick's friend if he didn't help Rick. You didn't even ask why he'd toy with fate to help Rick. That's a significant part of this story."

Closing her eyes, she already knew the answer, but she was going to ask the question as she continued to limber up with a silent ballet plie squat. "I don't want to steal your thunder, Avis. You go ahead and shine on, Superstar."

He chuckled. "You've been a peach about indulging me. Thank you for that, Poppy." Shaking his arms out, much in the way she was doing, he said, "Yash found out what I was up to. He knew what those stones meant. He intuitively sensed the spell I placed on everyone here. He was going to blow the whistle. I couldn't have that."

"And then…?"

"And then I planted evidence proving he'd stolen our money, which again, another simple spell. And then I murdered him."

It was the last straw. The last bit of filthy gleeful statement she could allow him to spew from his mouth, the last second she could stand to hear his voice.

Rage filled her and took over, and without another thought, Poppy charged him, running at him like some demented bull and crashing into his midsection.

Avis folded in half, his torso collapsing as she drove him against the wall of the lobby until she felt the satisfying crack of his frame against the wall.

She landed on him, moving quickly to straddle him as she

gathered up his shirt in her fist and laid one square on his jaw, the crack of his flesh so exhilarating, she almost cheered.

He lay immobile, his breathing shallow enough that Poppy took a deep breath of relief and began to climb off him, ready to make a break for the entryway doors and get help.

And that's when shit got real.

CHAPTER 20

"*D*id you hear him?" Calamity hissed. "He's as GD whacked-ass, certified nutter! We have to find a way to get in there!"

On Calamity's instruction, they'd crept toward the doors to listen to what was happening in order to form a plan. As Rick heard Avis go on and on about how he'd tricked the tenants of Littleton, almost killed Mr. Rush with a stroke, and murdered Yash, rage had simmered deep inside him—deep and hateful.

Poppy had been right. Her intuition had been right...and he'd been a fool. All these years, all this time.

Now, as he watched in horror while Avis used spell after spell to toss Poppy around like a ragdoll, they couldn't get inside. He'd somehow created a barrier, keeping everyone out.

The wind howled, leaves blew, and his stomach turned as his fear grew.

"Wait!" he whispered as inspiration struck. He'd once seen Yash instruct two witches in the art of attacking a spell from two different sides, using their wands. "I have an idea.

240

Nina, please tell me you have your wand."

She yanked it from her back pocket and held it up, but her eyes were confused. "And what do you want me to do with the fucking thing? Turn water into wine? That's as good as it gets with me right now."

January's eyes widened, her hand gripping his arm in her excitement. "I know what you're going to suggest. Yes! Good plan!" she cheered. "Nina, just do as I say. Rick, you and Calamity focus your minds on breaking this spell. We're going to need every bit of magic between us. Marty, Wanda, Darnell, the second I give the all clear, make a break for the door. The more people in there trying to get her out, the better. We cannot let him put those stones together, or all hell will break loose. Literally."

Nina placed a hand on Carl's shoulder. "You stay here, Buckeroo. Got it?"

He grunted his consent, patting her on the arm before she turned to January, her eerily beautiful face bathed in deter-mination. "Tell me what to do, Doc."

As January positioned them, Rick caught a glimpse of the moon, its hue beginning to change, ramping up his fear Avis would kill Poppy. But if it was the last thing he did, he'd get her the hell out, and he'd avenge Yash's death.

No matter how he had to do it.

* * *

AVIS LIFTED HIS HAND AGAIN, using his magic to slam her against the floor until she was certain she'd broken a rib.

Then something caught his attention, a flash of light from outside the building. Flashes of yellow and purple, two bright beams of light aimed at the entryway. That moment of distraction was exactly the moment she needed. If she could just get to the stones, maybe break one, would it help thwart the summoning of the spirits?

Lifting herself from the ground, Poppy catapulted toward the first stone she could get her hands on, the acute stab of pain in her ribs amplified when she attempted to knock one off the pillar.

But Avis was quicker, and with another lift of his hand, he slammed her back against the far wall.

Poppy screamed out her frustration, yelped as her head cracked against the wall and snapped back. "*Stop!*" she bellowed. Goddammit, where was all that errant magic she'd been throwing around earlier this week? Why couldn't she turn him to stone?

But she realized, as she slid down the wall, she had no idea how she'd done it to begin with.

Avis began to push the last pillar into place, using his shoulder, clenching his teeth as he hardened his jaw from the strain.

Her pulse crashed in her ears, her terror at what was to come if she couldn't stop him forcing her to push harder. Using her palms, she crawled her way up the wall, gasping for breath, each inhale an agony all its own.

"*Nooo!*" she screamed, lunging for him in an arc of air and pure determination, landing at his feet and grabbing for them, tripping him.

But it was too late. It was too damn late. Rather than hinder him from pushing the last stone into place, she helped him, knocking Avis's upper body into the pillar.

The click of that last stone falling into place, the burnt umber of the moon as it came into its own, resonated around the room, hissing a sigh of blissful satisfaction.

There was a small moment of eerie silence when the world stood still. When the horror of what had just occurred held its breath.

And that's when the screeching started. Out of every corner of the lobby, out of the stairwell, from every closed window, black, insidious shadows appeared, their snarls and cries reverberating, echoing.

They dove for her all at once, snapping at her, opening their unhinged jaws until she stared into the abyss of blackness. Long, knobby fingers grabbed at her, tearing at her sweater, ripping her skin.

Screaming, she fought them off with a screech of fear, using her fists, kicking at them as they battered her, toying with her, scratching at her face.

"Poppy!" someone yelled over the howl of freezing wind and flying entities.

Her eyes sought the voice just as one of the spirits dragged her upward by the back of her sweater.

But then Rick was there, grabbing at her feet and yanking her from the clutches of the spirit, pulling at her legs until she thought they'd detach.

She landed in his arms, wrapping her hands around his neck and falling against him in semi-relief, until she heard Calamity's voice.

"Rick! Get the fuck out of the way!"

Rick lobbed her over his shoulder, making her cry out from the pain in her ribs, and ran toward the entryway, but a spirit waited for him, one whose teeth gnashed as he sprayed drool.

A flash of Marty in werewolf form skidded across her line of vision as she attacked the spirit, sinking her teeth into it just as Darnell clapped his hands together, making the room shake, and turning the spirit to a pile of ash.

Wanda and Nina bum rushed a group of ghouls, their cackles racing around the room, whirring in her ears as they took pleasure in swatting the women down until January zapped them with her wand.

Poppy struggled to free herself from Rick's shoulder so she could help as the world fell apart around them. The air, thick with the stench of death, grew more oppressive, choking her.

In the middle of this chaos, in the height of an all-out war, Avis appeared out of nowhere, that clown-like smile on his face. As flames burned behind him and the lobby began to crumble in chunks, he pointed at Rick. "Old chap—so glad you could join the party. You work too hard, old man."

As though in slow motion, Rick set her down on the ground, his wide chest heaving, his thick thighs flexing before he said with dead calm, "I'm going to kill you, Avis. I'm going to kill you, and I'm going to enjoy the hell out of it."

Without warning, without preamble, Rick let out a rebel yell, racing at Avis until their bodies made contact and he had him on the ground. His arm swung high, preparing to slug Avis—until Avis disappeared, leaving Rick's fist to crash to the cracking marble floor.

As Rick howled his frustrated rage, Avis used it to his advantage, reappearing right in front of Poppy. There was no time for her to scream, no chance to send out a warning before he snatched her up like pulling a flower from the soft earth and ran.

Poppy clawed at his arm, using her nails to dig into the flesh, but Avis couldn't be stopped. He headed straight for the stairwell, his arm around her waist, taking the steps two at a time as though she weighed nothing more than a sack of potatoes.

Her feet dragged painfully against the stairs, the backs of them bashing into hard metal until she lost her ballet slippers and her feet were bare.

Someone screamed, "He's got Poppy, and he's headed up to the roof! Don't let him get to the roof!"

Which made her pause. What was on the roof?

Don't panic, Poppy. Use what's inside you, a voice whispered in her ear.

Debris from the falling chunks of the building hit them on their way up flight after flight of stairs, Avis's grunts resonating against the walls, but he kept hauling her upward as the voice insisted she act.

It's all there, Poppy—use it!

When they reached the top of the steps and pushed through the door, he dumped her without ceremony on the scratchy roof tiles, the glow of something far brighter than the moon forcing her eyes upward.

Poppy's mouth fell open.

The spire she'd so loved had turned into a raging inferno. Screams tore through the sky, spirits clung to it, cackling their glee while their wispy bodies blew in the cold air like flags.

The spire. The spire was the center of all this—a portal. The clarity of the answer hit her. This was what January had been talking about. The spire was a portal to the spirit world.

As she attempted to scramble backward and away from the sight before her, Avis grabbed the back of her sweater and began pulling her toward the spire.

"Let me go, you crazy bastard!" she yelled, punching up at his arms, arms much stronger than she'd ever thought possible.

Her heels were raw from digging into the roof's shingles to thwart Avis, on fire by the time he lobbed her at the base of the spire.

But Avis was determined, crazed with strength and tenacity. Gripping either side of her sweater, his eyes glazed with his victory, he yelled over the roar of the inferno. "This is it, Poppet! The time is here!"

Her eyes flew upward even though she wanted to hide

them; they were forcefully drawn to the screech of something, a screech laced with tormented rage.

Holy, holy hell. This must be what he was sacrificing her to. This mottled, horned, winged monster, clinging to the front of the spire by his clawed toes.

Poppy! Use what's inside you. Use it now!

"Use what?" she screamed out in frustration as sweat poured into her eyes, her throat raw and aching, her ribs burning with white-hot ripples of pain. *"What do you want me to use?"*

But she didn't hear the answer as Avis rose up, his eyes aglow, his hands raised to the sky. "This is my sacrifice! Take her!"

With those words, the demon swooped down, his wings flapping in graceful slashes of air, and snatched her up.

"Popppyyy!" She heard a stilted cry just as she was lifted from the ground. "No, Popp-yyy!"

Carl? Oh my God, was that Carl?

"Get out, Carl!" she heard herself scream. "Run, Carl, run!"

The moment she felt the claws of the demon sink into her arms, she caught a glimpse of yellow, a thick thread of light, zigzagging across the sky and zapping the demon.

"I will fuck you up!" Nina roared, her wand high in the air.

Marty and Wanda stood behind January, as though bracing her, and then her wand was flashing colors, shooting a cannonball of flames at the demon as she snapped backward against the women, falling against them from the force of her wand's magic.

The demon's scream ripped through the night, bellowing his anguish at the hit, but still he climbed higher, using his wings as leverage, pumping the air.

Use what's inside, Poppy! Fight your fear and use what's inside!

What was inside? For the love of fuck—why was everything so damn cryptic?

Her terror took hold, threatening to make her pass out until she saw movement from the corner of the spire.

Spears of flames and spewing embers in purple and orange fell to the ground; pieces of the stone began to fall away, and in the middle of it all?

Carl.

Climbing his way up the side of the spire.

CHAPTER 21

*H*ow had he slipped past them? How had he managed to make his way up all those stairs without any of them seeing him?

"Carl!" Poppy screamed, twisting in the demon's grip. *"No, Carl, no!"*

But Carl wasn't listening. Somehow, in his stiff-limbed, duct-taped-together determination, he was attempting to rescue her.

She knew in his mind, he was only being valiant and kind. He was Robin Hood, climbing the castle wall to save Maid Marian.

A whole new kind of panicked terror swept through her when she realized she was helpless—until she heard Rick yell, "Poppy! Use your hands, I'll recite the spell! We'll do this together! On three!"

Use her hands? Because that had worked before? This man was as crazy as a bedbug. What the hell good were…

Her hands plus his magic! They were fated. January had said so. Poppy didn't know if she was supposed to say something when she did it or even what exactly she was supposed

And then Calamity's terror-filled voice bellowed out, "Nina! Get out of the way!"

Poppy's eyes couldn't help but be drawn to whatever was the cause for so much fear in Calamity's voice. She caught a brief glimpse of the demon taking an upward climb, his wing almost clipping the back of Nina's head before Calamity leapt through the air and caught the demon's wing.

It missed Nina's head, shaking the feline off in the process and launching her over the side of the building.

Wanda took off at a run, soaring over the edge of the building, her hair flying upward behind her until she disappeared.

The devastation surrounding Poppy clutched at her gut, heightened her fear, but if she saved no one else, she was going to save Carl.

Swallowing hard, Poppy fought more panic, trying to keep her eyes on the prize, choking on the acrid smoke as she almost had her hand on Carl's sneaker. The sneakers he'd so proudly shown her just yesterday. The one's he wanted to wear trick-or-treating with his Nerd-Tech costume.

"Avis Mackland, what the hell have you done?" a voice from the heavens soared across the sky.

The rumbling of the spire, the flames, the howl of the demon—all of it came to a screeching halt at the sound of the voice.

Poppy blinked, her vision blurred by sweat, her fingertips aching from using the pads to claw her way up the spire.

"I said, what the hell have you done, you spineless, wilted piece of shit? Answer me, Avis!"

As everything stopped, as the embers from the flames drifted to the ground, as the rush of sound and motion ceased, someone or something plucked Poppy and Carl right off the spire and set them down on the roof, where a woman —a gorgeous woman with swaths of red, curly hair, a gold lamé dress acting as a second skin, and a body like a movie star—held Avis around the throat.

Wanda appeared from the corner of the roof, Calamity safely in her arms, while Darnell helped Marty up, brushing her swirly blonde hair free of ash.

Rick was the first at Poppy's side, scooping her up and holding her close. "Jesus…Jesus, you're one tough *gringa*," he whispered against the top of her head, tucking her body into his as he cradled her.

"Let me go, you hag!" Avis spat as he struggled against the woman's hand.

"The hell I will, you utter moron! Look what you've done, Avis. Look!"

"Who are you?" Poppy blurted before she could stop herself, spitting her hair from her mouth.

The woman's head turned, her gorgeous locks billowing behind her in a stream of burnished copper. "Forgive me. I was so caught up in this buffoon's buffoonery, I didn't introduce myself. I'm Drucilla, a witch, of course."

January's shoulders sagged as she let out a breath of air. "God, it's good to see you, Drew! I didn't know how much longer my wand was going to hold out."

"January!" she squealed in delight, giving Avis a good shake. "It's been ages, hasn't it? Bring it in, honey!" She held out her free arm and gave January a squeeze.

Nina eyed this new woman with the skepticism she did everyone, but she held out her hand. "Nina Statleon."

"Oh, my Goddess! I've heard all about you! You're big news all over the realm. Half vampire, right?"

Nina's eyes narrowed as she squared her shoulders. "Right."

Drucilla rolled her eyes and shook Nina's hand with a hearty pump. "Now, now. Don't get your back up. I'm a friend, not a foe, girlie."

January took a step back, pushing her long hair back under her knit cap. "Everyone, this is my good friend Drucilla. You can thank her for saving the day."

Drucilla used a hand to flap in January's direction. "Aw, stop. You'll make me blush all kinds of red, and it clashes with my hair."

Poppy couldn't believe anything clashed with this woman's anything.

Rick held out his hand now, too, and smiled a weary smile of gratitude. "Thank you."

Drucilla jabbed a finger in the smoky air before accepting Rick's handshake. "You're the infamous Rick! Goddess, after Yash's description of you, I'd know you anywhere. *Phew*, are you a dish, huh? No disrespect to you, Poppy."

Both she and Rick spoke at once. "You know Yash?"

She smiled then, a smile with a hint of sorrow to it. "I do. He's doing wonderfully, Rick. I promise you. He's very happy in the realm. At peace, joyous, surrounded by his herbs and flowers. He's the one who was sending you those messages tonight, Poppy. He's always been with you. He knew you'd take care of Rick, and he knew I was the person to stop *this* dipshit." She gazed down at a trembling Avis, her seductive blue eyes narrowing. "You do know you're in for it, right? Oh, are you in for it, *bloke*."

"How...?" Poppy began to ask but found she couldn't quite form a sentence.

Drucilla's eyebrow arched. "How do I know Avis?"

Poppy nodded, leaning against Rick for support, her feet unable to hold her up properly.

Drucilla smiled, dazzling and perfect. "He's the reason I doubted who I really was. He's the one who mocked me for one of the hardest choices I've ever made when I confessed why I was breaking up with him. He's my ex, aren't you, Simpleton?" she gave him another hard shake for emphasis.

The woman. She'd known it was about a woman. "So this was all for you, wasn't it?"

She sighed, her slender shoulders moving up and down. "Regrettably, yes. Isn't it just like a simpering idiot to want a bunch of power he wouldn't know what to do with if you slapped him in his kisser with it, just to get revenge on his ex?"

Poppy snickered a laugh, holding her ribs, but Rick frowned in confusion. "What? Revenge for what?"

Drucilla flicked a finger at Avis as her eyes surveyed the damage. "*This*—this right here is why I'm glad I'm a lesbian. This whole big show, complete with demons and screeching winged things and a play for power, was all about how I allegedly broke poor baby Avis's heart and called him a weakling warlock, just before I left him and his whiny self for my partner, Louisa. We could have ended our relationship peacefully. He could have been happy I'd finally figured out who I was and just let me go when I was honest enough to tell him I was in love with someone else. But nah. Instead, he openly ridiculed me, harassed me and when that didn't make me change my mind and come back to him, I guess he set about planning his revenge."

Avis struggled against her, his face red with rage, spittle at the corners of his mouth. "I hate you! You deserved every ugly word I spoke, you deceitful bitch!"

"And I guess you showed me, didn't you?" she asked, her gaze sweeping over Avis's face before she looked at the group. "I don't know what he planned to do with all the power once he got hold of it. Wave it in my face? Show me his big, bad wand? Make me regret leaving him for the love of my life? What were you thinking you'd do if you were actually smart enough to get all the power?"

"Make you pay, you stupid cow!" he seethed at her, his

face a mask of hatred. "You ruined me. You broke me! You humiliated me!"

Turning Avis to face everyone, Drucilla bobbed her head as she gripped the back of his neck and forced him to gaze at the havoc he'd wreaked. "Uh-huh, and just look at me pay, *mate*. Ugh! Would you look at the mess you made? Do you have any idea the spells I'll have to cast to fix this? Now say goodbye to the nice people, you homophobic moron, you're coming with me. We have a murder to address with the powers that be."

"Rick!" he pleaded, grabbing at Drucilla's wrists, twisting and arching his body to release her grip. "Don't let her take me! You know what they'll do to me! You're my best mate, Rick!"

But Rick averted his gaze, his jaw tight, his strong body rigid and tense.

Drucilla eyed them all and smiled. "I have to go now—because, you know, this jackass summoned every demon from here to eternity and ruined a perfectly lovely blood moon. But I hope we all meet again under happier circumstances. Poppy? You're one of the bravest souls I know. Welcome to the realm, sweet girl. Chat soon!" And with those words, she and Avis were gone.

Poppy blinked once more, still wrapping her head around the last hour. "Who was she again?"

January laughed at the shock on Poppy's face. "Drucilla. Her name's Drucilla, and she's one of the most powerful witches in the realm, and all I can say is, thank Goddess she showed up."

"Not a lie," Nina quipped, taking Calamity from Wanda and scratching her ears as Carl hobbled toward her. "Fuck, I'm getting too old for this shit."

"But you used the hell out of that wand, Chief! I'm so damn proud of you!"

Marty scanned the length of Poppy's body, her eyes sympathetic. "Oh, honey. You took some beating. C'mon. We'll take you home and patch you up."

But Poppy grabbed her arm and pulled her close, soaking in the vanilla scent of her hair. "Thank you for coming for me tonight. I…all of you," she whispered over Marty's shoulder, her eyes meeting Nina's.

Nina ran her knuckles over Poppy's hair. "Nah, Tiny Dancer, thank you for saving my boy here. I'd be lost without him."

Carl thumped her on the back with the hand not falling off his wrist. "Thaaank…you, Poppp-yy."

Giving him a gentle squeeze, she fought tears of relief. "*How* did you get up here, Carl?"

Nina's eyes narrowed at him then. "My boy here might still be learning to talk, but he's a damn good listener. I'm betting, while we were out there like a bunch of hens clucking in a freakin' henhouse, gearing up for that whammy of a spell, he was listening to every word and somehow, he figured out he needed to be on the roof. Somehow, he got past us in that mess downstairs. Am I right, little dude?"

His crooked grin almost faded as he gave Nina a look of pure guilt. He didn't need to explain, though. Instinctively, Poppy knew he'd made the connection between the stones and the spire. How he'd done it might always remain a mystery, but he'd valiantly thrown himself in harm's way to save her because Nina, these women, had taught him what heroism was all about.

Poppy shuddered another breath, refusing to consider all the things that could have gone wrong. "You tried to save me, Carl. You're a real-life Robin Hood. I won't ever forget that. *Ever.*" And then she hugged Nina, wrapping her arms around her waist. "I know you hate this right now, but just gimme a minute, and we'll act like this never happened."

Nina barked a laugh, looping her arm around Poppy's neck. "You're all right, kiddo. We good now?"

Poppy instantly let go with a weak grin. "We're good."

Wanda and Darnell, their eyes lined with exhaustion, gathered her up in a quick hug. "Let's get you home. You need some sleep, and maybe a Xanax. Make that two," Wanda teased.

Poppy's head fell back on her shoulders as she laughed, and she caught sight of Rick, who smiled back at her.

He held out his hand to her, and she took it, letting him pull her close. "I have to apologize, Poppy. I'm sorry I didn't know what to do with what you told me. You were right. I was wrong. I'm sorry I just couldn't hear you."

She shook her head, laying her cheek against his chest. "No. I understand. What I said was hurtful. You'd lost enough. I get it." And she did. With hindsight, she understood how hard it had to have been to hear something so ugly.

Rick's heart, steady and strong beat beneath her ear. "The thought of him hurting you scared the shit out of me, Poppy. It made me realize how much I want to start over. So what do you say to that? Starting over? Getting to know each other?"

She tipped her head back and gazed up at him with a smile. "I say, *si, si, señor*."

As the cold wind blew, and the moon shone down on them, he pressed his lips to hers, sealing the deal.

"All right, you two. Lay off the GD kissy face and let's get the fuck outta dodge. My pain-in-the-ass familiar deserves some tuna and you two need all the Band-Aids."

Poppy giggled at Nina as they began to walk toward the door of the building, stepping over the chunks of the spire and spitting piles of embers, but then something hit her.

Something she somehow couldn't bear after all this.

She stopped and said, "Wait. Does this mean it's over? I mean, because I don't need bodyguards twenty-four-seven, are you guys just gonna leave?"

Nina rolled her eyes. "Fuck no, Miss Needy. Once you're a part of the family, you're a part of it forever. No one escapes the clingy fucking claws of OOPS."

"Hear-hear!" Calamity cheered.

As they headed for the door, Poppy giggled again.

Yeah. Hear-hear.

EPILOGUE

Thanksgiving Day...

One new familiar/dancer/actress who'd found her purpose; a sexy, rediscovering-the-joys-of-being-a-warlock hottie developer; a half vampire, half witch with continually improving wand skills; a pretty blonde werewolf who doted on her little girl and did the best smoky eye on the planet; a halfsie with a secret to share; a therapist witch and her adorable family; a manservant who bastes a turkey like no other; a demon who has big plans for some Thanksgiving leftovers; a snarky cat who's reluctantly, but willingly, learning to meet her witch halfway; a gentle zombie who will never climb another tree again, so help him God; a fresh-from-the-nursing-home ex-apartment building owner; happy, healthy children galore; football-watching spouses; and more accidental victims and their families than anyone can keep track of anymore, gathered together at Rick's big warehouse to celebrate a very special day of thanks...

Poppy passed the platter of turkey to Rick, who stole a kiss from her, making her heart pound in giddy joy. "You know, after all these nights we've stayed up talking ourselves into a coma about almost everything ever in the history of ever, I don't know if you like white or dark meat. Which is it, Familiar?"

They had indeed talked themselves into a coma as they jumped into dating each other hardcore. Rick had made a real effort to not only get to know her but to really communicate—all his woes, all his fears, all his sadness about losing Yash. And nothing thrilled her more.

As their relationship developed, they learned how much they had in common. Except for Brussels sprouts. She still hated them, and he still loved them. But she counteracted her disgust of them by eating cans of sardines as they snuggled on her couch at Littleton or his big bed at his house.

Running her hand over his jaw, she giggled. "I like either-or, but you know what I *really* like?"

He lifted one eyebrow in a teasing arch. "Brussels sprouts?"

"Don't make me break out a can of sardines, Ricky baby," she teased back.

"Tell me, Poppy McGuillicuddy, what is it you really like?"

"Your bed. Wow. Where did you get that mattress?"

Wrapping his arm around her waist, he hauled her close, leaving her tingly all over as he laughed. "Know what I like?"

"My ugly dancer feet?"

"*You* in my bed. Every day, all day."

"But if I'm in your bed all day, every day, we'll never get anything done. I have classes to teach now."

"Have I mentioned how proud I am of you?"

"For actually getting a job that pays me in real money?" she joked, wrapping her arms around his neck.

"For doing what you love. For being so beautiful while you do it."

Her new job made her so incredibly happy, but more than that, it fulfilled her. Each day when she walked through the doors of Miss Mona's, she was overwhelmed with purpose. No, it wasn't a fancy school, where tutus and rhinestone-covered dance costumes were paid for by rich parents.

It was at a community center for low-cost childcare, where the children who needed somewhere to go until their parents picked them up could come and do all sorts of activities, from art to acting to dancing, and she wouldn't have any other job.

She loved teaching. It wasn't something she'd ever considered until Rick had suggested it one night, as they ate spaghetti and made googly eyes at one another. She'd taken his suggestion and run with it, landing a job just a week later. The pay wasn't big, the hours were pretty long, but the payoff was priceless—literally.

Word had gotten back to her via Miss Mona that her class was the most popular and all the kids wanted to dance with Miss Poppy.

Rick, on the other hand, had taken some time off from his company, allowing via delegation his employees to handle the current remaining jobs. He was in the process of some soul-searching about his chosen line of work, and he turned to her often to discuss the plans he had to mix more charity work, like the work he'd done in Africa, with the fancy high-rises he was known for.

He claimed it was in honor of Yash. Yash, who'd been exactly the person Rick always knew, and while he still suffered immense guilt for not believing in his long-trusted friend, he was working his way through his emotions by sharing them with Poppy.

As a result, she was falling madly in love with him. A love

so deep, so complete, she could do nothing but thank the fates for bringing them together every night before she went to bed. The best part about that was, Rick was falling in love with her, too.

He just didn't know it yet—he only suspected. But she did. In her gut, just like she knew what had happened to her was meant to be.

"You know, I saw Arnie this morning just before you picked me up. He said you owe him a game of chess."

Rick barked a laugh. "That old coot, he creams me every time I even look at a chessboard."

She loved that everyone was back where they belonged at Littleton—with one exception. *Rick* was now her landlord, not Mr. Rush.

Mr. Rush, once the spell Avis had put on him was lifted, had decided as much as he loved his tenants and the building his father had owned, he wanted to be free of entanglements and the kind of work that went into being a property owner.

So he'd sold the building to Rick with the promise he'd love it the way Mr. Rush did, and Rick had set about honoring his promise by updating the building with all sorts of amenities—one of them being a doorman named Mortimer, who'd become a favorite with the residents.

He'd given her apartment back to her with the offer of free lodging, but she'd declined and insisted he accept payment each month, knowing full well it wouldn't be much longer than a year before they were married.

But Poppy McGuillicuddy had hit adulting hard, and even though she'd let go of one dream, she'd found another in Rick, and in the new people in her life she'd come to truly love.

Even Nina, who was the crustiest of her newfound loves, made her smile when she showed up at her doorstep, sweet Carl, Calamity and Charlie—and sometimes Hollis, Marty's little girl—in hand, inviting her to take a trip to the library or the movies with them.

They all talked often. Marty and Wanda called to invite her to shop or stroll the park with a crabby Nina, and Darnell made regular appearances to have lunch and be sure she was learning how to cast out demons, should the need ever arise.

January played a huge role in helping her to learn everything there was to learn about the white witch way and being the best, most informed familiar. But mostly, she taught her to embrace her intuition with open arms as they chatted over cups of tea.

She'd gone to bat for Poppy with Familiar Central, ensuring she could remain Rick's familiar, citing all sorts of assignments that had turned romantic, and the powers that be had consented.

The words Nina had spoken that night were true. Once you were a part of the family, you were a part of it forever. No one escaped the clingy fucking claws of OOPS—ever.

And no one was more grateful that was true than Poppy. As she looked around the table, she grinned. Thanksgiving had never been filled with so much chaotic gratitude.

"So, can I have everyone's attention? We have an announcement!" Wanda chirped from the other end of the table, her hand entwined with her husband Heath's.

Poppy tapped her glass with her fork to gain everyone's attention, smiling at the abundance of food Arch had prepared for their Accidental Thanksgiving. "Hear-hear to announcements!"

As the group quieted, Wanda and Heath gave each other knowing glances, their eyes warm and bright with love. Then they grinned as though they had a secret.

"So, what's the big news?" Marty asked with a smile as she

leaned into her husband Keegan, dropping a forkful of fluffy mashed potatoes into her mouth.

Poppy gripped Rick's hand and sighed a happy sigh. She had a pretty good idea what Wanda and Heath were about to share, and she almost couldn't wait until the words were out in the universe.

"C'mon, Wanda!" Nina cheered, cutting up small pieces of turkey for Calamity and Charlie. "Do it! Do it!"

Inhaling a deep breath, Wanda gazed out over the crowd of her dearest friends and family and said, "We've decided to adopt!"

There was a small silence while everyone absorbed the news, each member of the large group grinning as realization struck.

Then a roar went up from the room, a roar of so much joy, Poppy's throat tightened. Everyone jumped up at once, rushing to congratulate them.

"Does this mean you'll be so busy with a kid, you'll quit riding my ass now?" Nina asked, hugging Carl close to her side.

"Nope. It means I'll be practicing my mothering skills on you with even more intensity," Wanda teased, letting Nina envelope her in a hug.

Marty threw her arms around both the women and squeezed. "Oh my God! If it's a girl, think about the shopping we can do. We'll be like a force of nature! Yay to girl power!"

"Yeah, yippee and skippee," Nina groaned her displeasure. "I can't wait to teach the little bugger how to buy scarves in discount fucking bulk."

Calamity skipped down the length of the table and launched herself at Wanda, landing on her chest as Wanda's hands wound around her and cuddled her close. "Does this mean you're going to forget about me, Auntie Boo? Will I be like the redheaded stepchild? Is all that delish tuna a thing of my past?"

Wanda's head fell back on her shoulders, laughter, free and easy, spilling from her throat. "It just means I'll set two places at the table from here on out."

Nina scratched Calamity's ears, a smile on her face. She and Calamity had come a long way since Poppy had met them. After Calamity saved Nina that night with Avis, knocking her out of harm's way, and Nina realized Calamity could have died, their dynamic shifted from full-time antagonistic to part-time, and it was wonderful to watch.

Poppy hovered in the background, waiting her turn to congratulate the happy couple, and when that chance came, Wanda reached for her hand and squeezed it hard, pulling her into a tight hug. "You're one smart lady, you know that?"

She grinned, so wide she thought her face would split. "Nah. You figured it all out on your own. You're going to make the best mom ever, Wanda Schwartz-Jefferson, and I'm going to smile as the universe unfolds just the way it should."

Wanda squeezed her even harder, her soft sweater brushing comfortingly against her cheek. "Thank you, Poppy," she whispered, her words laced with tears. "Thank you from the bottom of my heart."

Rick pulled her away from the crowd, his eyes warm. "She's right you know."

Snuggling up against his hard length, she asked, "Who?"

"Wanda. You're one smart lady. I think I like you. I think I like you a lot."

"Well, I should hope so. I let you use my toothbrush."

"In the interest of liking you a lot, I have a question. I just don't want to flub it."

She leaned back in his arms with a chuckle. "You? Flub something? You're the master of words. How can you even say such a thing?"

"You're mocking me."

"I totally am, but let me give you a piece of advice. It is only those who never do anything who never make mistakes."

He paused, looking down at her with his comical skepticism. "More Yash?"

She grinned and giggled. "I think so. It just hits my brain out of nowhere. I think I'm just the messenger."

Rick grinned, pressing his lips to hers. "Well, in the interest of Yash's wise words and doing something...wanna be my girlfriend?"

"As in your steady Saturday night lay?"

"As in my steady, *every* night lay—my everyday everything, too."

"Can I think about it?" she asked, threading her fingers through his silky hair.

"Nope. Now or never, McGuillicuddy."

"Then in the interest of missed opportunities, the answer is yes. I'll be your steady. I hope you brought your warlock ring to see the deal. Otherwise, it's not official," she teased, running her palms over his broad chest

"Oh really?" he asked, before capturing her lips and devouring them in a kiss that left her toes curling. "Official enough for you, *mi corazón?*"

Gazing up at Rick, cherishing his eyes so full of the love he wasn't quite ready to confess, she whispered, "*Si, si, si,*" before she planted her lips back on his and sealed their forever deal with a sigh rich with contentment and laced with forever.

Forever and ever.

The End

But wait! I hope you'll come back in 2017 and join Wanda for her journey into adoption and creating a family of her own, and along the way, a possible love interest for our sweet Carl. Also, *The Accidental Mermaid* is on the 2017 horizon, too! No matter what, my deepest wish is you'll all come back for more of the Accidentals' crazy shenanigans, but most of all, you'll share in their true love of family and friends!

PREVIEW ANOTHER BOOK BY
DAKOTA CASSIDY

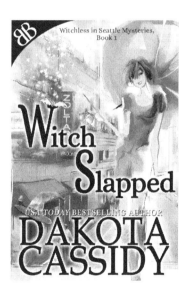

Chapter 1

"Left, Stevie! Left!" my familiar, Belfry, bellowed, flapping his teeny bat wings in a rhythmic whir against the lash of wind and rain. "No, your other left! If you don't get this right sometime soon, we're gonna end up resurrecting the entire population of hell!"

I repositioned him in the air, moving my hand to the left, my fingers and arms aching as the icy rains of Seattle in February battered my face and my last clean outfit. "Are you sure it was *here* that the voice led you? Like right in this spot? Why would a ghost choose a cliff on a hill in the middle of Ebenezer Falls as a place to strike up a conversation?"

"Stevie Cartwright, in your former witch life, did the ghosts you once spent more time with than the living always choose convenient locales to do their talking? As I recall, that loose screw Ferdinand Santos decided to make an appearance at the gynecologist. Remember? It was all stirrups and forceps and gabbing about you going to his wife to tell her where he hid the toenail clippers. That's only one example. Shall I list more?"

Sometimes, in my former life as a witch, those who'd gone to the Great Beyond contacted me to help them settle up a score, or reveal information they took to the grave but felt guilty about taking. Some scores and guilty consciences were worthier than others.

"Fine. Let's forget about convenience and settle for getting the job done because it's forty degrees and dropping, you're going to catch your death, and I can't spend all day on a rainy cliff just because you're sure someone is trying to contact me using *you* as my conduit. You aren't like rabbit ears on a TV, buddy. And let's not forget the fact that we're unemployed, if you'll recall. We need a job, Belfry. We need big, big job before my savings turns to ashes and joins the pile that was once known as my life."

"Higher!" he demanded. Then he asked, "Speaking of ashes, on a scale of one to ten, how much do you hate Baba

Yaga today? You know, now that we're a month into this witchless gig?"

Losing my witch powers was a sore subject I tried in quiet desperation to keep on the inside.

I puffed an icy breath from my lips, creating a spray from the rain splashing into my mouth. "I don't hate Baba," I replied easily.

Almost too easily.

The answer had become second nature. I responded the same way every time anyone asked when referring to the witch community's fearless, ageless leader, Baba Yaga, who'd shunned me right out of my former life in Paris, Texas, and back to my roots in a suburb of Seattle.

I won't lie. That had been the single most painful moment of my life. I didn't think anything could top being left at the altar by Warren the Wayward Warlock. Forget losing a fiancé. I had the witch literally slapped right out of me. I lost my entire being. Everything I've ever known.

Belfry made his wings flap harder and tipped his head to the right, pushing his tiny skull into the wind. "But you no likey. Baba booted you out of Paris, Stevie. Shunned you like you'd never even existed."

Paris was the place to be for a witch if living out loud was your thing. There was no hiding your magic, no fear of a human uprising or being burned at the stake out of paranoia. Everyone in the small town of Paris was paranormal, though primarily it was made up of my own kind.

Some witches are just as happy living where humans are the majority of the population. They don't mind keeping their powers a secret, but I came to love carrying around my wand in my back pocket just as naturally as I'd carry my lipstick in my purse.

I really loved the freedom to practice white magic anywhere I wanted within the confines of Paris and its rules, even if I didn't love feeling like I lived two feet from the fiery jaws of Satan.

But Belfry had taken my ousting from the witch community much harder than me—or maybe I should say he's more vocal about it than me.

So I had to ask. "Do you keep bringing up my universal shunning to poke at me, because you get a kick out of seeing my eyes at their puffiest after a good, hard cry? Or do you ask to test the waters because there's some witch event Baba's hosting that you want to go to with all your little familiar friends and you know the subject is a sore one for me this early in the 'Stevie isn't a witch anymore' game?"

Belfry's small body trembled. "You hurt my soul, Cruel One. I would never tease about something so delicate. It's neither. As your familiar, it's my job to know where your emotions rank. I can't read you like I used to because—"

"Because I'm not on the same wavelength as you. Our connection is weak and my witchy aura is fading. Yadda, yadda, yadda. I get it. Listen, Bel, I don't hate BY. She's a good leader. On the other hand, I'm not inviting her over for girls' night and braiding her hair either. She did what she had to in accordance with the white witch way. I also get that. She's the head witch in charge and it's her duty to protect the community."

"Protect-schmotect. She was over you like a champion hurdler. In a half second flat."

Belfry was bitter-schmitter.

"Things have been dicey in Paris as of late, with a lot of change going on. You know that as well as I do. I just happened to be unlucky enough to be the proverbial straw to break Baba's camel back. She made me the example to show everyone how she protects us...er, *them*. So could we not talk about her or my defunct powers or my old life anymore? Because if we don't look to the future and get me employed, we're going to have to make curtains out of your tiny wings to cover the window of our box under the bridge."

"Wait! There he is! Hold steady, Stevie!" he yelled into the wind.

We were out on this cliff in the town I'd grown up in because Belfry claimed someone from the afterlife—someone British—was trying to contact me, and as he followed the voice, it was clearest here. In the freezing rain…

Also in my former life, from time to time, I'd helped those who'd passed on solve a mystery. Now that I was unavailable for comment, they tried reaching me via Belfry.

The connection was always hazy and muddled, it came and went, broken and spotty, but Belfry wasn't ready to let go of our former life. So more often than not, over the last month since I'd been booted from the community, as the afterlife grew anxious about my vacancy, the dearly departed sought any means to connect with me.

Belfry was the most recent "any means."

"Madam *Who*?" Belfry squeaked in his munchkin voice, startling me. "Listen up, matey, when you contact a medium, you gotta turn up the volume!"

"Belfryyy!" I yelled when a strong wind picked up, lashing at my face and making my eyes tear. "This is moving toward ridiculous. Just tell whoever it is that I can't come to the phone right now due to poverty!"

He shrugged me off with an impatient flap of his wings. "Wait! Just one more sec—what's that? *Zoltar?* What in all the bloomin' afterlife is a Zoltar?" Belfry paused and, I'd bet, held his breath while he waited for an answer—and then he let out a long, exasperated squeal of frustration before his tiny body went limp.

Which panicked me. Belfry was prone to drama-ish tendencies at the best of times, but the effort he was putting into being my conduit of sorts had been taking a toll. He was all I had, my last connection to anything supernatural. I couldn't bear losing him.

So I yanked him to my chest and tucked him into my soaking-wet sweater as I made a break for the hotel we were a week from being evicted right out of.

"Belfry!" I clung to his tiny body, rubbing my thumbs over the backs of his wings.

Belfry is a cotton ball bat. He's two inches from wing to wing of pure white bigmouth and minute yellow ears and snout, with origins stemming from Honduras, Nicaragua, and Costa Rica, where it's warm and humid.

Since we'd moved here to Seattle from the blazing-hot sun of Paris, Texas, he'd struggled with the cooler weather.

I was always finding ways to keep him warm, and now that he'd taxed himself by staying too long in the crappy weather we were having, plus using all his familiar energy to figure out who was trying to contact me, his wee self had gone into overload.

I reached for the credit card key to our hotel room in my skirt pocket and swiped it, my hands shaking. Slamming the door shut with the heel of my foot, I ran to the bathroom, flipped on the lights and set Belfry on a fresh white towel. His tiny body curled inward, leaving his wings tucked under him as pinhead-sized drops of water dripped on the towel.

Grabbing the blow dryer on the wall, I turned the setting to low and began swishing it over him from a safe distance so as not to knock him off the vanity top. "Belfry! Don't you poop on me now, buddy. I need you!" Using my index and my thumb, I rubbed along his rounded back, willing warmth into him.

"To the right," he ordered.

My fingers stiffened as my eyes narrowed, but I kept rubbing just in case.

He groaned. "Ahh, yeah. Riiight there."

"Belfry?"

"Yes, Wicked One?"

"Not the time to test my devotion."

"Are you fragile?"

"I wouldn't use the word fragile. But I would use mildly agitated and maybe even raw. If you're just joking around, knock it off. I've had all I can take in the way of shocks and upset this month."

He used his wings to push upward to stare at me with his melty chocolate eyes. "I wasn't testing your devotion. I was just depleted. Whoever this guy is, trying to get you on the line, he's determined. How did you manage to keep your fresh, dewy appearance with all that squawking in your ears all the time?"

I shrugged my shoulders and avoided my reflection in the mirror over the vanity. I didn't look so fresh and dewy anymore, and I knew it. I looked tired and devoid of interest in most everything around me. The bags under my eyes announced it to the world.

"We need to find a job, Belfry. We have exactly a week before my savings account is on E."

"So no lavish spending. Does that mean I'm stuck with the very average Granny Smith for dinner versus, say, a yummy pomegranate?"

I chuckled because I couldn't help it. I knew my laughter egged him on, but he was the reason I still got up every morning. Not that I'd ever tell him as much.

I reached for another towel and dried my hair, hoping it wouldn't frizz. "You get whatever is on the discount rack, buddy. Which should be incentive enough for you to help me find a job, lest you forgot how ripe those discounted bananas from the whole foods store really were."

"Bleh. Okay. Job. Onward ho. Got any leads?"

"The pharmacy in the center of town is looking for a

cashier. It won't get us a cute house at the end of a cul-de-sac, but it'll pay for a decent enough studio. Do you want to come with or stay here and rest your weary wings?"

"Where you go, I go. I'm the tuna to your mayo."

"You have to stay in my purse, Belfry," I warned, scooping him up with two fingers to bring him to the closet with me to help me choose an outfit. "You can't wander out like you did at the farmers' market. I thought that jelly vendor was going to faint. This isn't Paris anymore. No one knows I'm a witch—" I sighed. "*Was* a witch, and no one especially knows you're a talking bat. Seattle is eclectic and all about the freedom to be you, but they haven't graduated to letting ex-witches leash their chatty bats outside of restaurants just yet."

"I got carried away. I heard 'mango chutney' and lost my teensy mind. I promise to stay in the dark hovel you call a purse—even if the British guy contacts me again."

"Forget the British guy and help me decide. Red Anne Klein skirt and matching jacket, or the less formal Blue Fly jeans and Gucci silk shirt in teal."

"You're not interviewing with Karl Lagerfeld. You're interviewing to sling sundries. Gum, potato chips, *People* magazine, maybe the occasional script for Viagra."

"It's an organic pharmacy right in that kitschy little knoll in town where all the food trucks and tattoo shops are. I'm not sure they make all-natural Viagra, but you sure sound disappointed we might have a roof over our heads."

"I'm disappointed you probably won't be wearing all those cute vintage clothes you're always buying at the thrift store if you work in a pharmacy."

"I haven't gotten the job yet, and if I do, I guess I'll just be the cutest cashier ever."

I decided on the Ann Klein. It never hurt to bring a touch of understated class, especially when the class had only cost me a total of twelve dollars.

As I laid out my wet clothes to dry on the tub and went about the business of putting on my best interview facade, I tried not to think about Belfry's broken communication with the British guy. There were times as a witch when I'd toiled over the souls who needed closure, sometimes to my detriment.

But I couldn't waste energy fretting over what I couldn't fix. And if British Guy was hoping I could help him now, he was sorely misinformed.

Maybe the next time Belfry had an otherworldly connection, I'd ask him to put everyone in the afterlife on notice that Stevie Louise Cartwright was out of order.

Grabbing my purse from the hook on the back of the bathroom door, I smoothed my hands over my skirt and squared my shoulders.

"You ready, Belfry?"

"As I'll ever be."

"Ready, set, job!"

As I grabbed my raincoat and tucked Belfry into my purse, I sent up a silent prayer to the universe that my unemployed days were numbered.

NOTE FROM DAKOTA

I do hope you enjoyed this book, I'd so appreciate it if you'd help others enjoy it, too.

Recommend it. Please help other readers find this book by recommending it.

Review it. Please tell other readers why you liked this book by reviewing it at online retailers or your blog. Reader reviews help my books continue to be valued by distributors/resellers. I adore each and every reader who takes the time to write one!

If you love the book or leave a review, please email **dakota@dakotacassidy.com** so I can thank you with a personal email. Your support means more than you'll ever know! Thank you!

ABOUT THE AUTHOR

Dakota Cassidy is a USA Today bestselling author with over thirty books. She writes laugh-out-loud cozy mysteries, romantic comedy, grab-some-ice erotic romance, hot and sexy alpha males, paranormal shifters, contemporary kick-ass women, and more.

Dakota was invited by Bravo TV to be the Bravoholic for a week, wherein she snarked the hell out of all the Bravo shows. She received a starred review from Publishers Weekly for Talk Dirty to Me, won a Romantic Times Reviewers' Choice Award for Kiss and Hell, along with many review site recommended reads and reviewer top pick awards.

Dakota lives in the gorgeous state of Oregon with her real-life hero and her dogs, and she loves hearing from readers!

OTHER BOOKS BY DAKOTA CASSIDY

Visit Dakota's website at http://www.dakotacassidy.com for
more information.

A Lemon Layne Mystery, a Contemporary Cozy Mystery Series
1. Prawn of the Dead
2. Play That Funky Music White Koi
3. Total Eclipse of the Carp

***Witchless In Seattle Mysteries, a Paranormal Cozy Mystery
series***
1. Witch Slapped
2. Quit Your Witchin'
3. Dewitched
4. The Old Witcheroo
5. How the Witch Stole Christmas
6. Ain't Love a Witch
7. Good Witch Hunting

***Nun of Your Business Mysteries, a Paranormal Cozy
Mystery series***
1. Then There Were Nun
2. Hit and Nun

Wolf Mates, a Paranormal Romantic Comedy series

1. An American Werewolf In Hoboken
2. What's New, Pussycat?
3. Gotta Have Faith
4. Moves Like Jagger
5. Bad Case of Loving You

A Paris, Texas Romance, a Paranormal Romantic Comedy series

1. Witched At Birth
2. What Not to Were
3. Witch Is the New Black
4. White Witchmas

Non-Series

Whose Bride Is She Anyway?
Polanski Brothers: Home of Eternal Rest
Sexy Lips 66

Accidentally Paranormal, a Paranormal Romantic Comedy series

Interview With an Accidental—a free introductory guide to the girls of the Accidentals!

1. The Accidental Werewolf
2. Accidentally Dead
3. The Accidental Human
4. Accidentally Demonic
5. Accidentally Catty
6. Accidentally Dead, Again
7. The Accidental Genie
8. The Accidental Werewolf 2: Something About Harry
9. The Accidental Dragon
10. Accidentally Aphrodite
11. Accidentally Ever After
12. Bearly Accidental
13. How Nina Got Her Fang Back
14. The Accidental Familiar

15. Then Came Wanda

16. The Accidental Mermaid

The Hell, a Paranormal Romantic Comedy series

1. Kiss and Hell

2. My Way to Hell

The Plum Orchard, a Contemporary Romantic Comedy series

1. Talk This Way

2. Talk Dirty to Me

3. Something to Talk About

4. Talking After Midnight

The Ex-Trophy Wives, a Contemporary Romantic Comedy series

1. You Dropped a Blonde On Me

2. Burning Down the Spouse

3. Waltz This Way

Fangs of Anarchy, a Paranormal Urban Fantasy series

1. Forbidden Alpha

2. Outlaw Alpha

20849788R00180

Made in the USA
Lexington, KY
07 December 2018